T0146865

HIDDEN VALLEY

JOHN A. W. INMAN

BALBOA.PRESS

A DIVISION OF HAY HOUSE

Balboa Press books may be ordered through booksellers or by contacting:

Balboa Press
A Division of Hay House
1663 Liberty Drive
Bloomington, IN 47403
www.balboapress.com.au
1 (877) 407-4847

Print information available on the last page.

ISBN: 978-1-5043-2136-5 (sc)
ISBN: 978-1-5043-2137-2 (e)

Balboa Press rev. date: 04/28/2020

CONTENTS

THE ESCAPEES

CHAPTER 1

LES MURPHY

Barnaby Maximum Security Prison was forty-five kilometres north of Riverbend in southern New South Wales. The prison was in a valley eight kilometres from the nearest town with only one road in and out called Barnaby Drive, but known locally as The Crims's Highway. National parks surrounded the valley, and it lay on the northern side of a range of mountains going west of the Great Dividing Range. Barnaby housed some of the most dangerous criminals in New South Wales, with murderers, rapists, hit men, paedophiles, crime bosses, and drug barons—a real cesspool of humanity. In its fourteen years of operations, no prisoner had ever escaped.

Amongst this prison population were some who did not deserve to be there. Les Murphy was one such inmate. In 1989, aged twenty-four, he was sentenced to twelve years for killing John Roe with an axe. He was six-feet-two tall and weighed 102kg. He had dark brown eyes and blondish hair. Before he went to prison, he had been; a real bushie and worked as a contract farm fencer around the Armidale, Tamworth, and Gunnedah districts. He was quoting for every fencing contract he could, as he had his eye on buying a better truck for work. Les had loved his lifestyle; often while fencing he would camp out rather than shack up in a shepherd's hut or shearing shed. He loved the outback, the bush, the native wildlife, but he had little time for foxes, feral cats, wild dogs, pigs or goats. For this reason, he always had his 22-magnum rifle with him to dispatch any non-native wildlife to the here-after.

Les's fencing routine included two to three hours of spotlight hunting every third day depending on the weather. His primary focus were foxes and their pelts, for which he received good payment although prices had been falling over the last few seasons. Rabbit and rabbit stew were often on the menu because of these forages.

Ever since his father's death in a tractor accident on 9 January 1976, when Les was eleven years of age, he'd had a fascination with the stars. It started after a family friend told him to pick out a star because that would be a dad to him, watching over him. He had chosen the Constellation of Orion, or the Hunter, as it was often called. In Australia and New Zealand, it was the Pot or the Saucepan, one of the most prominent constellations of the Aussie summer. It's two brightest stars were Beta, also known as, Rigel, and Alpha, or Betelgeuse was the seventh brightest star in the sky; it gave off as much light as forty thousand times our sun. It was a massive star — a blue supergiant. Diagonally opposite Rigel was Betelgeuse, a red supergiant with a mass five hundred times greater than our sun. Les, chose Betelgeuse because he liked the name, and over the years he talked to his dad through the star while out camping in the summer. He had moved on from the simplistic eleven-year-old mourning the loss of his dad, to a place where he received comfort from these talks.

In 1986, Les and his school sweetheart, a brunette named Gail Pritchard, lived in a small town between Armidale and Tamworth. Gail was a slim, beautiful girl with a huge smile and flashing green eyes. In April, Les was finishing a huge fencing contract for a farmer near Gunnedah. On the Monday evening, Gail's phone rang.

"Hi love, how are you?" Les asked.

"Les, it's so good to hear your voice, I've missed you heaps. How is the job going?" she asked.

"That's what I'm ringing about. I expect to be home around lunchtime on Thursday." After talking for nearly an hour, they said their goodbyes. As Gail walked into her bedroom, two strong arms grabbed her from behind and threw her onto the bed. In the dim light, she saw the outline of two men.

"Any noise from you, bitch, and you're dead," said one man.

"Do you want money? I was paid today, you can have all of it; just don't hurt me." Pleads Gail.

"Shut up, bitch," said the other man as he backhanded her across the face.

The attack started, and for forty minutes they brutally raped Gail. They were very careful in that they wore masks, gloves, and condoms. After the attack, the men told her not to say anything or they would come back and put her through such hell she would beg them to kill her. Gail sobbed on her bed for a couple of hours, then had a long shower, trying to wash the feeling of filth off her body.

It was not till five o'clock the next morning that Gail determined she would do all she could to get these men for what they had done to her. She contacted the Tamworth Police. At 6 o'clock, Detective Sergeant Luke Cross knocked on Gail's door. Luke, forty-three years of age and father of three girls, had transferred from Sydney just two years prior. A rugged six-feet-four, experienced, and very fit detective with a couple of bravery commendations and a success rate of 91 percent in solving crimes, Det. Cross was very organised and filed away every bit of information he received about the cases he worked. Det. Cross and his partner, Detective Kathy Godfrey, dealt gently with Gail. At nine o'clock, a forensic team arrived to look for clues. They found little—only one pubic hair.

3

Luke said to Gail, "We will need to compare this hair with your partner; his name is Les, isn't it?"

"Yes, Les Murphy, but why do you want to compare it with him?" Gail asked as she wiped the tears rolling down her cheeks.

"To make sure it isn't his hair."

"But why? Do you think it was Les?"

"Certainly not. We just want to make sure it belongs to one of the two men who attacked you. We don't want to waste time trying to track down a suspect if it is Les's hair."

"You're right. Sorry, I wasn't thinking." And she started crying once more.

"That's okay. I really hope it isn't Les's, as it is possibly the only thing we have to work with."

Det. Cross filed the pubic hair in the evidence file of Gail Pritchard, knowing he could not use it yet. But later it may be very important when DNA profiling was finally accepted and allowed to be used as evidence in Australia. Det. Cross had followed with great interest the development of DNA profiling in both the UK and the United States.

Det. Cross encouraged Gail to contact Les and get him home, but she decided not to as he had already said he would be home on Thursday. Det. Cross had two suspects in mind: John Roe and his brother Allan. Both stood over six feet tall and were persons of interest in another rape only four months earlier, down towards Werris Creek. Like with Gail, there was no hard evidence and no witness apart from the victim, who was uncertain the rapists were the Roe brothers.

The public prosecutor took the Roe brothers to court, even though the evidence was not compelling. At the committal hearing, the police prosecutor withdrew the charges for lack of any substantial evidence. As the jubilant Roe brothers walked out of the court, they purposely walked past Gail and Les. John Roe looked at them with sadistic eyes and grinned a grin of pure evil. In that moment, Les was 100 percent convinced that these two low lives were guilty. But without evidence, nothing could be done. He watched them leave the courthouse and drive off in a white 1986 Ford F100; the same vehicle that Les has wanted to buy.

Det. Cross apologised to Gail, "Gail, I am so sorry. I know they are the ones who attacked you, but unfortunately, I cannot prove that. The only evidence I have is anecdotal. But with God as my witness, I promise you we will get them. If there is anything you can remember or anything you need to talk about, call me."

Gail nodded, and Det. Cross noticed the tears rolling down her cheeks.

"I am so sorry we couldn't nail them," he said, "but believe me, I will get them."

Les turned back from watching the departing Roe brothers and saw Gail crying. He put his arms around her. She leaned into him and buried her face into his chest, sobbing heavily. For the next eight months, Les worked closer to home, making sure he was home each evening.

By that Christmas, there had been two more rape assaults with the same patterns, one up near Glen Innes, the other over near the coast just north of Coffs Harbour. The differences with these two latest attacks to Gail's and the one in Werris Creek was the attackers made their victim take a shower afterward and scrubbed them down. They then poured bleach over the bath, shower and bathroom floor. Before leaving, they bound the victim up with twine widely available at supermarkets, hardware stores, and many other retail outlets across the state.

Det. Cross was in no doubt who was responsible for these attacks. He was frustrated because of the lack of evidence at any of the crime scenes. He felt powerless and angry because he felt that he was letting down all the victims, not just Gail.

A week after Gail's attack, she and Les moved into Tamworth where she would not feel so isolated. Gail was slowly recovering and in June '87, a little boy, Morgan, was born. Both were excited and life was looking good for the young family.

One morning in mid-August '88, Les said to Gail, "Hun, there's a good contract on offer just south of Tenterfield; I reckon I could knock it over in eight days depending on the weather."

"That sounds good, have you already tendered for it?" Asked Gail.

"No! I wanted to talk with you before I did that. If it doesn't feel right, just say so."

"Les, I love having you home each night. And I know that if you tendered for this contract, it would cause me some grief." And as she started thinking about what she had just said, she paused, as tears rolled down her cheeks.

"Well, I won't put in for it, I'll let it go." Said Les.

"No, Les, I didn't mean that you don't put in a tender."

"But, I am concerned about you, honey. I don't want you to be scared or anything like that. You and Morgan, are the best thing that has ever happened to me."

"Oh, Les, I love you so much. It's just, I have been thinking about the control that those bastards have had over us. I just don't want them controlling what we can and can't do any more. That gives them too much power. I don't mean that we stop being careful. We have Bluey, who is an excellent watchdog. Then there are the sensor lights on the four corners of the house. We have locks on every door and window. And yes, they made us do that. But I am sure that like me, you don't want our house to become a prison, let out each morning on day release, and being locked up at night." Expresses Gail.

"No," replied Les, "that is the last thing I want. I don't want Morgan growing up in an atmosphere of fear. But I know that I will be sick with worry about both of you."

"Les, to be honest I will be worried and scared, but I will not let them control our life altogether. I want you to put in for that tender."

Les, took Gail into his arms, and hugged, and kissed her. "You and Morgan are my whole life, and I don't want this episode dictating what we do as a family."

Les, won the tender and finished the job on Monday, 17 September, a day earlier than expected. After packing his truck, the time was just after four-thirty, and he makes the decision to drive the 290 kms home. Estimating he would be home by eight o'clock, to surprise Gail, and Morgan.

Driving through a town north of Glen Innes, Les approached the town's only set of traffic lights when they changed to amber, then red. As he pulled to a stop, the vehicle on his left turned left in the same direction Les was travelling. As the vehicle, a white Ford 1986 F100 with two male occupants, made its turn, the driver looked directly into Les's headlights. Les immediately recognised the driver's face and the evil callous grin of John Roe. His blood ran cold. Everything in his body said that they had just committed another rape. He decided he would follow them at a distance.

Fifteen kilometres south of Armidale, the Roe brothers turned off down a dirt road. Les didn't know what to do! *Where does this dirt road go? Could the Roes be setting a trap for whoever was following them?* he asked himself.

As he sat stopped at the dirt road, a highway patrol officer pulled up behind him and the patrol officer walked up to Les's driver's side door and said, "Good evening, sir, I'm Senior Constable Rick Knowles. Do you have a problem I can help you with? May I see your driver's license?"

Les's brain was racing, trying to work out how he should answer Senior Constable Knowles. *Evening officer, I just followed the Roe brothers who just drove down this dirt road, and I suspect them of committing another rape. I have no proof that they have raped someone, just a gut feeling.* Instead, Les replied, "Hi, Officer, I am a fencing contractor and looking for Doctor Yates property. I thought it was around here, but I am not sure in the dark. Is it this dirt road?"

Fourteen months earlier, a month after Morgan's birth, Les had done a fencing job for Dr Yates in this area.

"No, this track goes down to the river approximately two kilometres away, there is a great fishing spot called Billy's Hole," said Senior Constable Knowles. "But you are near the Yates property, and it is hard to find in the dark. It's called Cargill's Lane, follow me and I will indicate the road for you."

"That is very kind of you," Les replied, "but haven't you got other things to do?"

"Actually, I need to head back to Tamworth. I finish early tonight as I am taking my family for a three-week holiday to New Zealand tomorrow, and we fly out at eight o'clock in the morning."

"Good on you," said Les, "have a great holiday."

Les, followed the patrol car and when Senior Constable Knowles indicated Cargill's Lane, Les flashed his lights, and turned down the road. He drove 100 metres, stopped and turned off his lights, waited another ten minutes, then drove back to the dirt road the Roe brothers had turned down. Not using the accelerator, he let his truck's motor slowly propel him down the road. He turned off the lights and relied on the moonlight to negotiate the track. Through the trees he glimpsed a fire some 200 metres further on. Not wanting to announce his presence, he slowly pulled on the handbrake, bringing the vehicle to a halt without the brake lights glowing. Turning off the cabin's interior light, he alighted from the vehicle on the passenger side. Slowly and quietly, Les crept through the bush towards the campsite at Billy's Hole.

Billy's Hole was part of the river which here was thirty metres wide and just on 300 metres long, and eight metres deep. The hole had resulted from a limestone cavern which collapsed, a sink hole hundreds if not thousands of years ago.

Les thought, *If I can get close enough, I may hear what they are talking about, and they might say something I can tell the police.* Les's hunting skills of moving silently through the thick Australian bush enabled him to move so close that he could hear the Roe brother's conversation as they sat on the bank of the fishing hole drinking beer. From the moonlight it looked like they and others had been camping here for a couple of days, if not longer.

This was the way they had alibied themselves in Gail's attack; they claimed that they were out fishing for a couple of days, befriending other weekend campers also staying at Billy's Hole. They made sure the campers knew they intended to stay another couple day's fishing.

As he stood hidden in the bushes listening, Allan Roe, turned towards his brother and said, "Did you see how scared she looked when she walked into her bedroom and saw us standing there?"

"Shit yeah, she was so scared she couldn't scream, she tried but nothing came out, the dumb bitch," replied John.

"She certainly had a great body, great boobs, but she didn't like you scrubbing her down in the shower." Said a grinning Allan.

"You are right, she was really hot, and that's the reason I picked her out. But how pathetic was she in pleading for her life? We haven't killed any of our seven targets," replied John.

Les thought, *The police only know of four, and the one tonight makes five. That means there are two other women out there, so scared, shattered, and embarrassed that they have never come forward.* By this time, Les could not think of anything but stopping these two animals. He knew if he did not do it, they would keep on getting away with it and destroying more lives.

Without thinking, he stepped out from the bushes and said, "Hi, guys, remember me?"

"Shit, where did you fucking well come from?" asked a startled Allan.

Both John and Allan looked at him with no recognition.

"No! Where in the fucking hell are we supposed to know you from?" asked John.

Les said two words, "Gail Pritchard."

"Shit," said John, as both brothers instantly put two and two together and recognised the intruder.

Allan, went white as a ghost with fear, but John, just grinned that evil grin of his. It was the same grin as that outside the court.

John said, "So what are you going to do now? You're unarmed, and there's two of us. When we kill you, we will fucking bury your body up the mountain where no-one will ever find your sorry arse." Looking at Allan, he shouted, "Let's kill him, Allan."

As they rushed at him, Les knew John, would be the one he would have to stop as he was bigger and stronger in the body than Allan. Summing up the situation, Les stepped forward to his right and crashed a huge hardened fist into Allan's face, breaking his nose and knocking him out. At the same instant, John Roe tackled him, driving him sideways and thumping him into the ground. Rising to his feet, John kicked and kneed Les as he lay on the ground, as he struggled to get to his feet John's onslaught continued. Jumping onto Les, he repeatedly punched him around his head. Les, knew he had to stop John's attack, or he would be killed and never see Gail and Morgan again. With fear driving him, he dived at John's legs, knocking him off balance and causing him to fall to the ground. As Les struggled to get to his feet, John Roe's fist caught him in his kidneys, and then he landed a couple of punches to Les's head. Once more he slumped to the ground. With his head beginning to swirl, Les, could feel himself on the verge of blacking out. Then for no reason, other than sheer cockiness, John Roe stopped his attack and stood in front of Les.

"After I kill you, you fucking prick, I'm going to that little dead-end street in Tamworth, with the green weatherboard house third on the right, and this time I will not only rape that bitch Gail Pritchard, I will brag how I killed you before I strangle the life out of her." Proclaims a grinning menacing John.

The realisation the Roes knew where he and Gail lived, so infuriated Les that with all the strength he could muster he punched John's groin and hit him flush on his testicles. As John doubled up and fell to the ground groaning and holding his groin. Les, staggered to his feet only to be knocked to the ground in a tackle

10

by Allan, who still had blood freely flowing from his shattered nose. As they wrestled, they rolled towards some tea tree shrubs on the edge of the cleared camp area. Allan was not a fighter, swinging wildly at Les's head. He delivered two glancing blows. Les saw an opportunity and crashed his fist once more into Allan's broken nose and face. The lights went out once more for Allan.

Trying to get to his feet, Les glimpsed John swinging an axe at him, but it never hit him. In the dark John did not notice that Allan, and Les, while wrestling on the ground had rolled under two taunt eight-gauge wire clotheslines, that some thoughtful camper had set up with two strainer posts and stays. As the axe arched down towards him, its handle, just below the head, hit the nearest of the two wires and the springing action of the strained wires threw him flat onto his back. Les, made most of the opportunity to jump to his feet, grab the axe and sink it deep into John Roe's forehead.

Limping, staggering, falling, and crawling, Les made his way back to his vehicle, but collapsed from exhaustion at its side. An hour later he came to, looked around, remembered what had happened and what he had done and vomited. Getting into his vehicle, Les drove home to Gail and Morgan. To explain his injuries, Les, lied to Gail for the first time in their relationship.

"I got caught up in a brawl in the pub in Glen Innes, but you should see the other guy." Les, reasoned if he told Gail a lie, she would know nothing, and would not have to lie for him and get herself into trouble. Gail, suggested she take photos of Les's facial injuries and bruising. This was something she did not do when she was attacked and may have lost some evidence for the forensic tests.

The morning after the killing of John Roe, a couple of guys arrived at Billy's Hole at six-ten for some early fishing. They found John Roe dead, with an axe sunk deep into his skull. Finding Allan, under the bush groaning, they helped him up and rushed him off to hospital. Later, they notified the police of their gruesome discovery at Billy's Hole.

By noon, the fishing hole was swarming with police looking for clues about what had happened; their first thoughts were that it was a fight between the two brothers that got out of hand. The investigating detectives waited until doctors gave the all clear to interview Allan. He had a broken nose, and a compressed fracture to the left cheek, resulting in a concussion. The hospital organised a team to operate on Allan's cheek and nose at two-forty-five.

It was eight-twenty p.m. when doctors allowed the police ten minutes to question Allan, who had a fair bit of time to get his story worked out. He had asked the doctors about John, but all they would say was that he was the only one brought into the hospital. Allan, assumed that John was alright, but wondered why he had not visited him.

"Hi, Allan, I am Detective Ted Freeman, and this is Detective Jim Roberts. We would like to talk to you about what happened at the fishing hole known as Billy's Hole."

"What has my brother told you?" Allan asked.

"Absolutely nothing," replied Det. Freeman.

"Well, when can I see him?" asked Allan.

"Allan, I am sorry to have to tell you, but your brother is dead, that is why we need to talk to you. How did this happen? Did the two of you have a disagreement? Did John do that to your face?" asked Det. Freeman.

"John's dead? Oh no, fuck no, we never had a fight, it was this other bastard." Allan grimaced in pain.

"Which other guy?" asked Det. Freeman, as Detective Cross entered the room and nodded to both detectives.

"Mind if I stand in and listen?" Det. Cross asked.

"Be our guest, Luke," replied Det. Roberts. "Do you know the patient?"

Allan looked at Det. Cross but didn't recognise him.

Det. Cross smiled and said, "Yes, I know him."

Allan's memory flashed, and he screamed, "All those fucking charges were dropped. We are innocent."

"Yeah," said Det Cross, "see you two later."

He walked out of the room, followed by Det. Freeman, Det Cross turns and said,

"Do I know Allan Roe? Sure do. I am just pissed off that whoever killed John Roe didn't finish by killing Allan as well. They are, were, a pair of scumbags."

After Det. Cross departed, Det. Freeman asked Allan, "How do you know Det. Cross?"

"That bastard tried fitting John and me up with a rape charge, but it got thrown out of fucking court."

"Okay, let's get back to Billie's Hole." Said Det. Freeman.

"Like I was saying, John, and me were having a beer after a big day of fishing, when suddenly this fellow charged out of the bush and attacked us. We just defended ourselves against the bastard. The fucking bastard did this to me." Allan felt his face.

Det. Freeman asked, "Is this person known to you and your brother?'

"No, I couldn't see in the dark who the prick was, we'd never laid eyes on him in our lives," lied Allan.

"Do you know why he attacked you?" asked Det. Freeman.

"No, he was just some looney tune bastard, some nutter," replied Allan.

"So, you have never seen him before?" asked Det. Roberts.

"No, not really, I don't think so; it was dark, and we were out in the bush. It all happened so fast," said Allan.

"And you don't have any idea why he picked you two out and attacked you?" asked Det. Freeman.

"No, he was some fucking idiot. Look, I am not feeling too good right now. Call the doctors. I don't want to talk anymore. My face is killing me."

Det. Freeman said, "We will let you sleep, but we will be back to talk to you and get a statement."

Back at Billy's Hole, the police were gathering as much evidence as they could. At the morgue, they removed the axe from John's skull and sent it away to dust for prints. As many of the campers had used this axe over the weekend, Les's fingerprints were only one of several fingerprints found on the axe.

Four days later, Det. Freeman and Det. Roberts re-interviewed Allan as he waits to be discharged. A mumbling Allen Roe tells them they had not left the fishing hole since Saturday morning, and the eleven other campers at the hole could confirm that. Tracking down all those at the fishing hole wasn't easy, as most were not locals, but fishermen from several inland fishing clubs who had maps marked with the location of good fishing holes.

Allen, only supplied some first names and couldn't or wouldn't say where they came from. After checking with the three other locals who were there that weekend, no-one could say for sure where the other fishermen came from: one said Sydney, another mentioned Newcastle, and the third said down round Canberra. The police investigation into the murder stalled as tracking down those present at the fishing hole got nowhere and none of the fingerprints matched any in police records.

It was not till Senior Constable Knowles, returned from his family holiday, and read of the events that happened in his patrol district. He read the report about the attack and murder at Billy's Hole the night before he flew out. The date prompted his memory of his conversation with Les. He could not remember his name, and no report was made because at the time it was just a simple direction inquiry. Senior Constable Knowles thought, *Could, it just be a coincidence Les stopped at the track that leads to Billy's Hole?* Senior Constable Knowles remembered Les was looking for Dr. Yates's property. He talked to his boss about the incident and got permission to check with Dr Yates about the fencer, his name and his address.

In the initial phone call, Dr Yates said that his farm foreman Dean Foster would be the best one to talk to. Setting an appointment time, Senior Constable Knowles met Dean Foster, a massively built man standing just a shade under two metres tall with very broad shoulders.

"Hi Dean, I'm Senior Constable Knowles. I want some information about a fencing contractor who I think may have done some work for you?"

"That would be Les Murphy, a darn good fencer and a great guy. What has he done?" Asked Dean Foster.

"I don't know if he's done anything, I just need to know when he last worked for you, that is for Dr Yates."

"From memory it must be at least a year ago, maybe longer," replied Dean.

"So, he hasn't worked on the property in the last month?" asked Senior Constable Knowles.

"That's right, the last time Les worked for us was 12 months ago at least. Come over to the office and I will look it up in the books."

In the office, Dean Foster opened the large red ledger book on the desk. He found the fencing section and said, "Yes, here it is, July '87, seven day's work from the ninth to the sixteenth. Nothing since then."

"Thanks, Dean, that's all I need to know. See you later. By the way, what is the address you have for Les?"

Dean gives Les's Tamworth address to Senior Constable Knowles and said, "If I can help give me a burl."

"Thanks, I will. See you later," replied Senior Constable Knowles as he headed for his patrol car.

Knowles, talked to his boss, and Det. Freeman and Roberts interviewed him. The two detectives talked to Det. Cross about the Roe brothers and the thrown-out charges Les Murphy's name was mentioned again. Detectives Freeman and Roberts drove out to Les and Gail's home, but Les, was away fencing and Gail told them he wouldn't be home till tomorrow.

"What's wrong? Is Les in trouble?" an anxious Gail asked.

"We think he can help us in an ongoing investigation into a minor incident. Get him to pop into the police station the day after tomorrow, that's Thursday, around ten-thirty, thank you." Det. Freeman and Roberts turned and walked away.

At ten-thirty Thursday morning, Les arrived at the police station for his appointment with Det. Freeman.

Sitting down in an interview room, Det. Freeman asked Les, "Have you ever been to Billy's Hole?"

"No, why do you ask?"

"Well, there was a murder down there the same night you told Senior Constable Knowles, that you were looking for Dr Yates's property because you had a fencing contract to fulfil. But we know you already knew where the property was located as you had completed a contract in July '87, fourteen months earlier. And we also know you have done no work for the Yates farm since then. Les, did you kill John Roe?" Det. Freeman asked, not expecting a reply.

"Yes, yes, I did. I killed him with an axe," confessed Les.

"Are you confessing to John Roe's murder?" a surprised Det. Roberts asked.

"Yes, I killed that scumbag. I have no regrets. He needed killing. He and his brother are the rapists you guys have been looking for."

Les, told them of his suspicions that earlier that evening the Roes had committed a rape up north, but he had no evidence. And no reports of a rape had ever surfaced. Allan Roe, admitted to being up north of Glen Innes, but fishing at a well-known water hole. The two spent half the afternoon fishing and making themselves known to a couple of local lads as a pre-arranged alibi. The police concluded Les's attack was an act of revenge for the Roe brothers' suspected rape of his partner, Gail. As Les had admitted his guilt at his arraignment, there was no trial, just a sentencing date, and in February '89, Les was sentenced to 12 years' prison.

Det. Cross, visited Les immediately after court, to assure him he had not given up on a conviction for Gail's rape. Luke continued to follow the development of DNA testing and evidence overseas. The same year Les went to prison, the first conviction based on DNA testing in the USA saw Gary Dotson sent to prison for twenty-five to fifty-years for rape.

In the Australian Capital Territory, Desmond Applebee was the first person in Australia convicted using DNA testing, which had been extracted from blood and semen on a rape victim's clothes and was a perfect match to Applebee's DNA. In Victoria, police confronted George Kaufman with DNA evidence, and he confessed to the rape of sixteen women over a four-year period in the south-eastern suburbs of Melbourne.

Les Murphy, escaped from Barnaby Maximum Security Prison on 25 November 1993.

CHAPTER 2

BOB WALKER

Bob Walker was born on 7 April 1955. He stands five-feet-ten tall, has thinning dark brown hair with a light mixture of grey, hazel coloured eyes, weighs in at ninety kilograms. Immigrated to Australia from England in 1978. A jack-of-all-trades, he worked mainly in the western bush-free parts of NSW, the flat country plains where mixed farming existed of crops, and stocks. Bob's ability was working with beef cattle. He was a man of weak character, holding grudges for years, and always thinking and planning how to get revenge on those he thought had done him wrong. Any action he took was well planned and executed; he had a very cruel and brutal streak, but he never had the strength of character to confront a person face-to-face. In England, he was a person of interest in the torching of a house which left the sole occupant in hospital with third-degree burns to 65 percent of his body. The occupant of the house was instrumental in Bob being sacked from his job at a timber mill.

Those who knew him in various outback pubs of New South Wales, had the feeling that he was hiding out from something or someone, maybe a wife in England. Bob would just laugh the suggestion off with an offhand remark, "You are all crazy."

In 1982, Bob, felt the need to relocate after being suspected of criminal behaviour, in the disappearance of farm machinery, but police could not prove his involvement in the thefts. He applied for a position as a farm manager for the beef property of a Macquarie Street surgeon, Dr. Paul Burman, in Marulan, twenty-five kilometres north of Goulburn. At his interview, he told Dr. Burman that he has never worked on a farm in the mountains and bush of New South Wales. Some excellent references from farmers won him the position. His living quarters were the smaller two-bedroom cottage between the main house and machinery sheds. The whole arrangement suited Bob down to the ground, with the doctor and his family visiting two weekends each month, he had a lot of time to himself. Dr. Burman, was a hard man to work for. Each time the he came, Bob went over the books and showed him what work he'd completed since the last meeting. Then Dr. Burman would make a list of things to be done around the farm, and what cattle to send to the sale yards over the coming weeks.

Bob, had a good relationship with the family, apart from the doctor. Sandi, the doctor's wife and their two daughters, Shaye, and Rachel, and two sons, Matt and Adam, seemed to enjoy Bob's friendship and the help he gave them while they were at the farm. But his relationship with the doctor was a very clinical business arrangement. The doctor wanted his pound of flesh for every dollar he paid Bob. Dr. Burman was not one for small talk and he never, apart from the initial interview, inquired about Bob's personal life and family. For five years, Bob put up with the doctor's dollar-pinching ways. He put up with it because it suited his never expressed desire to be out of circulation. On top of this, Bob took pride in seeing the improvement on the farm each year, and each year he waited for the doctor to put up his wages, as he'd agreed to do when he was hired. But no rise ever came, and he never received the promised bonus for five years work in 1987.

Bob's character never let him confront the doctor over the non-payment of promised pay rises, and five-year bonus. His dislike for the doctor grew more intense each year. Inwardly he believed that a pay-day would come, even if he had to make it happen. Over the six years Bob worked for the doctor, he gleaned a lot of information about the family's movements when at home in Sydney, such as the route the kids took to get to school. He learnt about Sandi's social tennis twice per week, her weekly appointment at her hairdressers, and her Friday out with her girlfriends.

Bob, took special note of the eldest daughter, Shaye. He watched her grow through her early teens, and her bodily development, till her peers at school considered her the most beautiful girl in the whole school. Not only was she beautiful, she was an excellent all-round sports person. Bob, told Shaye, she reminded him of a lass back home in England. Shaye, took it as a compliment, and being so trustful she did not see the evil in his eyes.

He learnt that when Shaye had finished all lessons at school, she had time off to study at home to prepare for her upcoming High School Certificate exams. The weekend of 12 and 13 September 1988, Bob, was surprised to see the latest model Holden Commodore Sedan, red in colour follow the doctor's BMW into the farm instead of Sandi's Mercedes. In the car was Shaye, Rachel, young Matt, and the driver who was a clean cut, well-built young man of around twenty-years of age.

Bob, met the family at the gate of their homestead, and Shaye grabbing the young man's hand, brought him over to Bob and said, "Bob, I would like you to meet my boyfriend, Nate."

Bob, shook Nate's hand in greeting and replied, "You are a lucky fellow, this girl is a real gem."

"Yes, I know," said Nate, as he looked at Shaye and gave her a kiss and a bear hug. Neither Nate, nor Shaye, noticed the look of hatred in Bob's eyes towards Nate.

21

Through contacts in Melbourne, Bob, bought a false Victorian driver's licence (before photo ID's were required) for a Peter Ford, from Carlton. A week later, on 1 October, Bob contacted a car rental yard in Liverpool, Sydney, and arranged the hire of the latest model red Holden Commodore sedan.

"I'm coming up to meet a friend on his way home to Newcastle, I will be there around eight-thirty a.m. on Tuesday, 6 October. I will return it by seven o'clock Wednesday evening, October 7." Stated Bob.

"About payment, Mr. Ford, could you send a cheque as a deposit?" asked John Malouf, the rental car company's owner.

"Look, I can't do that as I had my home burgled last week and my cheque book was stolen. By the time I get a replacement cheque book from the bank and post it, I will beat it to Sydney. Anyway, I will pay cash. Do you give a discount for cash, Mr. Malouf?" Asked Bob.

"No, sorry, our prices are very low as they are. We look forward to seeing you on Tuesday. Thanks for your business."

Driving up to Liverpool early on the Tuesday, Bob, ran through his plan in his mind. *Sandi starts her tennis at nine-thirty every Tuesday, so she will leave home just before nine o'clock. Shaye, will be home by herself from nine a.m. to one-thirty, the time Sandi returns from her tennis, and lunch.* He picked up the red Commodore right on time, as soon as the gates opened. He identified himself as Peter Ford by showing the fake licence, signed the relevant papers, and took the keys and headed off to the Burman residence. He was strangely excited as his adrenaline rose, but there were some self-doubts and what-ifs racing through his mind.

At nine-thirty, on that fateful Tuesday morning in October, Bob drove the red Commodore into the doctor's large Baukham Hills property, with its high front fence and a huge tree lined U-shaped driveway. A smile crossed his face as he realised, he couldn't be seen from the road. If anyone else but Shaye, was home and answered the door, Bob's plan was to say that he wanted to talk to the doctor about finishing work on the farm.

As he pulled up to the front entrance, Shaye, saw the car from her upstairs bedroom window, and assumed it was an unexpected visit from Nate. She raced down to open the front door for him. As she swung open the door, she was surprised to see Bob standing there on the other side of their security door. Bob, was equally surprised when the door flew open before he had rung the bell.

"Bob, what are you doing here?" she asked. "I see you're growing a beard as well." Says Shaye.

Thinking quickly, Bob replied, "Is the doctor by any chance at home? It is urgent that I speak to him."

"No, dad's, at the hospital, he has a very big operating schedule today."

"What about your mother, Sandi, is she home?"

"No, she is at her tennis. I'm here by myself studying for my High School Certificate."

Not having anticipated being confronted by Shaye, before he was ready, Bob was taken back a bit as he tried to work out what he should do next.

As his mind searched for an answer, Shaye said, "Bob, are you all right? You look pale. Is anything wrong?" Asked a concerned Shaye.

Out of concern for him, Shaye, forgot everything her parents had taught her about home, and personal security. Unlocking the security door, she stepped outside, and did not see Bob's hardened fist smash into her face. The back of her head was driven into the sharp corner of the brickwork around the door frame, and she slumped, dying to the tiled veranda floor. Not realising that he had killed her, Bob, took a roll of black electrical tape from his pocket and bound her hands, feet, and covered her mouth. Then he placed her gently into the boot. He sped out of the driveway, causing an oncoming vehicle to swerve violently into the gutter on the other side of the road. The other driver blasted his car horn, as a neighbour diagonally across the road, working in his garden looked up and saw the red Commodore speeding down the road, with the other car up on the gutter. Running over he checked on the driver who was shaken up but otherwise okay. He looked at his watch, noted the time was nine-thirty-seven, and that he had better finish up as he and his wife were meeting their newly married daughter at ten-forty-five in Parramatta.

As things turned out, the only part of the house Bob touched was low down on the security screen door, as he moved it to bind Shaye's hands with the electrical tape.

When Sandi, arrived home just a little past one-thirty, she parked her car in one of the four garages. With tennis gear in her arms, she walked towards the front entrance, looking at and smelling the beautiful fragrant flowers in the gardens between the garages and the house. Stepping up the front two steps, Sandi, immediately saw the pool of blood at the front door. Her anxiety increased as she opened the unlocked security screen door. She hurried inside, calling out to Shaye. But no answer came, only the noise of Shaye's music system playing in her room. Sandi, ran from room to room shouting out Shaye's name.

Hysterical, she rang her husband, "Paul, I think something terrible has happened to Shaye; she is missing, and there is a pool of blood at the front door. I'm terrified and don't know what to do."

"Touch nothing. Just ring the police, and I will come home straight away." Replies a very concerned Paul.

In response to Sandi's frantic phone call, two uniformed police officers arrived at the house at one-fifty-eight. They talked with Sandi, and try their best to calm her. One went to the squad car and radioed back to their supervisor, that this was a job for the detectives. The police officers secured the crime scene and continued to support a distraught Sandi, who was crying and visibly devastated.

At two-twenty-seven, Paul's BMW screamed to a halt at the front steps. Sandi, runs out to him and collapsed into his arms sobbing, "Something terrible has happened, I can feel it. Why, why? Who would have done this to us."

Paul, suggest they go inside and get themselves something to drink. As they approached their front door, the senior constable told them their home was now a crime scene, and they could not enter.

"You are right, sorry," said Paul. and takes Sandi back to where she had been sitting on a patio lounge.

Twenty minutes later, two detectives, Det. Luke Ryan, and Det. Short, arrived to take charge of the investigation. Det. Ryan, the 39-year-old senior detective, talked to Paul and Sandi, who were seated on the large patio lounge. Detective Short, spoke to the two uniformed police and took notes of what they said. He then instructed them to go door-to-door, to ask neighbours for any information they might have. He then, radioed for a forensic crew to be sent as-soon-as-possible. The two uniformed officers, plus two others called in, conducted the door-to-door knocking and one officer came across the gardening neighbour, who told them of the red Commodore.

"Do you know what time this red Commodore left the doctor's residence?" asked one officer.

"I sure do, it was nine-thirty-seven as I had to get ready to go with my wife to meet our daughter for lunch, in Parramatta."

"Was there anything else you can tell me about the vehicle and its driver? Was the driver male or female?" Asked the officer.

"I am pretty sure the driver was a man, but I didn't really get a good look at him, everything happened so quickly."

"Was he a young person or was he older?"

"I am sorry, but like I said before I didn't get that good a look at him."

"Thank you very much, the detectives may want to talk to you later," replied the uniformed officer.

The forensic team located strands of blond hair and blood on the corner of the bricks, where Shaye's head had hit it. The next day, forensic tests confirmed the hair and blood belonged to Shaye.

Meanwhile, the uniformed officers reported back to detectives Ryan and Short, about the red Commodore with a possible male driver, was seen speeding away from Dr. Burman's residence.

As the two detectives go to the patio lounge to talk to Paul and Sandi, their other daughter, Rachel, and sons, Matt and Adam, arrived home from school to see the police looking around their property. Racing up to their parents, the doctor told them of their sister's disappearance.

Det. Ryan asked, "Do you know anyone who drives a red Commodore?"

"Yes, Shaye's boyfriend, Nate, but what has he got to do with all this?" asked Paul.

"A red Commodore was seen speeding out of your driveway earlier today. We need to know Nate's surname, and where to locate him." Said Det. Short.

"That is ridiculous," blurts out Sandi, "Nate. would never hurt Shaye. He loves her. He is not that type of person. He wouldn't hurt anyone, or anything,"

"That may be so, but we will need to talk to him to eliminate him as a suspect," replied Det. Short.

"You're wrong about him," yelled Rachel, "he would never harm Shaye."

"We don't know if he is involved or not, but we still have to talk to him," Det. Ryan said.

"They are right," said Paul, "they must check everything out. His surname is Campbell, and he lives in a flat in Parramatta; I will get the address for you."

The forensic team asked them, "Where in the house is this information kept?"

"In my office," replied Paul, "we will go in the back through the kitchen door, down a short hallway to the office."

"OK, but don't go anywhere else," said the forensic chief and sent one of his men with Paul.

Later that afternoon, detectives Ryan and Short drive over to Nate's flat, which he shared with two other young guys. Before walking up the stairs to the first floor flat, they check out the rear exits, and any windows from the flat. There was only one rear garage in which Nate's red Commodore was parked. They checked all the exits that came out through the common laundry. All windows in the complex had security screens. There was no possibility of a fast rear exit. It was four-twenty-five when they knocked on the door. Det. Ryan heard a male voice inside say, "Who's that? Aye, have we paid the rent this week?"

Another voice said, "How in the bloody hell are we supposed to know who's knocking? Just open the door and find out."

"Hello, how can I help you?" said Nate's flat mate, Ray.

"Are you Nate Campbell?" asked Det. Ryan.

"No, Nate's in his room, whom will I say wants him?" Ray asked.

"Detective Ryan and Detective Short," replied Det. Ryan.

"Shit! What has he done?"

"Just get him will you, young fellow?" said a stern Det. Ryan.

Peering into the flat, the detectives noted it was a typical young guys' pad. The sink was stacked high with dirty plates, cups, pots and pans. Empty beer cans, and pizza boxes lay on the floor of the lounge room, with clothes spread around. The music inside loud.

"You want to talk to me? What's it all about?" Inquired, Nate, dressed in just a pair of shorts.

"You keep company with a Miss Shaye Burman?" Asked Det. Ryan.

"Yes, she's my girlfriend, what's this all about?"

"Shaye is missing, and I was wondering when you were last at her home?"

"Missing! What do you mean? What's happened?" asked Nate with concern.

"Just answer the question, please. When were you last at the Burman residence?" asked Det Ryan in a very authoritative manner.

"Um, Sunday night, we watched a DVD in the family room. Tell me, what do you mean she is missing? And why are you questioning me in this manner?"

Ignoring Nate's question, Det. Ryan continued, "You drive a red Commodore sedan?"

"Yes, but why?"

"Where were you between nine-fifteen and ten o'clock this morning?" Asked Det. Short.

"What, you think I had something to do with Shaye's disappearance, you are a crazy man!" screamed Nate. "I was at work from seven-thirty this morning. Surely you don't think I had anything to do with it, do you?"

"We have a reliable witness who saw a red Commodore sedan speeding out of Dr Burman's residence, around the time we believe Shaye went missing," said Det Ryan.

"Well, it wasn't my car; I have been at work all day, and my car was parked in the company's carpark all day," replied Nate as tears welled up in his eyes.

"Can anyone back up what you just told us?"

"Yes, my boss and about twenty other workers; they will tell you my car never left the carpark till I left for home at four o'clock."

"We will check this out." Replied Det. Short.

"That's fine, I haven't lied to you, what I told you is the bloody truth," said a distraught Nate. "Can you tell me anything else? Is she alright?"

"We don't know, Nate, there was a pool of blood found at the front door."

"Blood? Shit, what's going on, where is she?" asked Nate as tears ran freely down his cheeks.

"We don't know, but believe me we will find her, you can bet your bottom dollar on that," said a softer Det. Ryan as his instincts told him Nate, knew nothing and was not involved. "Have you got a number we can contact you on?"

"Yes, yes, my mobile number is, shit I can't think of it. Aye, Pete," Nate, called his other flat mate, "can you remember my mobile number?"

Pete answered, "Sure can," and quoted it.

"Thanks for your help, Nate, we will keep you informed," says Det. Ryan.

"Right, I hope you catch the bastard who's done this."

Nate's story checked out, and he was removed from the possible suspect list.

Back at the crime scene, the forensic team had dusted and taken a number of fingerprints from the front door area, and just inside the foyer. One set of a thumb and index finger of a left hand were of most interest near the bottom of the security door, which seemed an odd place for prints. They asked the Burman's for a list of all the people they remember had used the front entrance in the past week, such as friends, workmen, and delivery drivers. They also asked the Burman's if they could take the family's fingerprints to eliminate any on the doors.

The next day Alex, the forensic team leader, rang Det. Ryan. "Aye Luke, we have come up with a big fat zero; there is no match in our database to any of the prints we took."

"Bloody hell, that's not what I wanted to hear. I feel this guy has form somewhere, so how about sending them overseas and see if we can get lucky?"

"Already done that, detective, will get back to you as soon as we hear anything."

"Thanks, Alex, we really need to identify him as quick as we can."

So far, the red Commodore sedan was their major clue, and the police prepare a media release to be sent that night to all radio and tv stations, for broadcasting on Wednesday morning, pleading with the public for help.

A little after eleven p.m., Bob Walker, walked down the road from his motel to a payphone, using a voice scrambler to make a call to the Burman's home. He puts in a $1 coin and dialled. The phone in the Burman's house rang once more. All evening family, and friends, had been ringing to offer any help and comfort they could.

When the phone rang, Sandi looked at Paul and said, "I can't answer that, I don't want to talk to another person again tonight. Would you please answer it?"

"Hello, Paul Burman speaking."

"Just shut up and listen, I will only say this once if you want to see your daughter again. Get $100,000 dollars in unmarked used bank notes, and no bloody running numbers, fifties and one hundred dollar notes only. I will ring you tomorrow at lunch, just have the money ready. And do not involve the police, or you will never see her again." He hung up the receiver before Paul could say anything else.

"Don't go, wait, who are you? Don't hang up. He's gone," said a very pale looking Paul.

Sandi, was straight to her feet sensing something was amiss. "Who was that?"

"I don't know. He did not tell me who he was. I didn't recognise the voice. The bastard claims to have Shaye, and he wants $100,000 by tomorrow."

"We had better tell the police," said Sandi.

"No! He said if we involve the police, we will never see her again."

"Well, what are we going to do?" asked a desperate and crying Sandi.

"We have to get the money, it's our only hope," replied Paul as he flopped down into an armchair, his face empty of any colour as the tears flowed. The only sound was the sobbing of two frightened parents facing any parent's ghastliest nightmare.

Suddenly, Paul said in a resigned voice, "We have to tell the police, they are the experts in these sorts of things. They will give us some advice on what the best course of action is."

"But you said the caller told you not to involve the police." Said a crying Sandi.

"Kidnappers always say that, so the experts say. Sandi, we have to involve them. Let's ring that detective; what was his name again?"

"Um, Luke someone; that's right, Detective Luke Ryan. I will get his card."

She left the room and returned shortly with Det. Ryan's card. "Look, he wrote his mobile number on the back and told me to ring him no matter what time it is."

Paul rang the number, and it was answered immediately.

"Det. Ryan, whom am I speaking to?"

"Detective, it's Paul Burman. We just had a phone call from a person claiming to have Shaye. He wants $100,000 tomorrow if we want to see her alive."

After talking together for fifteen minutes, Det. Ryan said, "I will be at your home at eight-thirty tomorrow morning, as there is nothing we can do tonight. Tomorrow we will set up equipment that will give us a chance to trace his call when he rings back. Try to get some sleep, as you will need all your strength in the days to come. See you in the morning."

In a small, out-of-the-way motel one street back from the Hume Highway, and three kilometres south of the Liverpool railway station. Bob Walker, returned to unit 6 at the far end of the small six-unit complex. He checks on Shaye, wanting to transfer her to his own car and to take her back to the farm, where he had planned to kill her after having fun with her. When he opened the boot, he tried to rouse her but couldn't, and for the first time realised she was dead.

"Shit, not again," exclaims Bob.

Killing her was always in his plan, yet he was disappointed to find her dead. He quickly changed his plan and drives down south to the Royal National Park, just south of Sutherland. Driving two kilometres past the park's unmanned toll booth, he turned left at a

31

huge gum tree onto a fire trail. Driving approximately 200 metres, he stopped and looked around. He carries Shaye's body 100 metres left into the bush. With the light from a full moon, he threw her lifeless body into a small hollow and quickly covered her with stones, leaves and some branches and then headed back to his motel room. It was two a.m. Wednesday.

At twelve-twenty-seven that day, Bob, looked at his watched and decided it was time to ring the Burman's. When the phone rang, Det. Ryan reminded Paul to hold off answering the phone until the technician gave the nod.

As soon as he received the nod, he answered the phone, "Hello, Paul Burman speaking, how can—"

It was all he said before being told, "Shut up and listen." The scrambled voice said, "Do you have—" he is interrupted when a hotel maid opened the door. Bob, quickly swung around, his hand holding the voice scrambler dropping from the phone.

"Oh sorry, Mr. Ford, I thought you had already left," said the startled maid.

Realising he was still holding the phone, he slammed it down, which left Paul Burman frantic.

"Are you still there, hello, hello? He's hung up on me." Paul looks utterly helpless as he stands with the phone in one hand, looking around at those in the room.

"What happened, what made him hang up?" asked Det. Stone.

"I don't know. I think I heard another person's voice; I think it was a woman's voice, yes, it was a woman, and she seemed to have surprised the guy."

Det. Ryan, looks at the technician and asked him to replay the call. The technician using headphones replays the tape and nodded. "Yes, it definitely is a woman's voice. I think our guy separated the scrambler from the handset, when she startled him as her voice becomes clearer, but I will have to wait till I get it back to the lab to filter out all the background noise."

Meanwhile, Bob, put on a pair of latex gloves, took a cleaning cloth and a bottle of Methylated Spirits and wiped off the boot lid, the front seat, steering wheel, and the inside of the driver's door, especially the handles, and around the radio, and dashboard. In the boot, he tried to scrub and wash away a dry pool of blood. When he finished, he put on a pair of leather gloves, placed his overnight bag on the front passenger seat and returned the car to the rental yard, received his cash deposit, and said goodbye. With overnight bag in hand, he calmly walked out and around the corner to where he had parked his own vehicle. With a sigh of relief, he started his car and began the ninety-minute drive back home to Marulan.

While Bob was driving back to Marulan, the technician in the police forensic laboratory filtered out all the background noise. He contacted detectives Ryan and Stone and arranged for them to hear the tape. At the same time that Bob, arrived home in Marulan, Detectives Ryan and Stone walked into the police lab and were directed to Ken, the technician, who was waiting for them.

"G'day, guys, I have something very interesting for you to listen to," he said and pressed the start button on his machine.

"Oh sorry, Mr. Ford, I thought you had already left."

"That's all there is, as the scrambler this guy used is pretty good. I doubt if I will get anywhere near the guy's real voice."

Det. Ryan said, "You can bet his name isn't Ford unless he is really dumb. I wonder where this Mr. Ford was leaving; was it his office, maybe his home, his workplace, his club? Where was this mongrel leaving?"

"You didn't pick up anything else on the tape that could help to locate where he was?" asked Det. Stone.

"No, nothing, it is pretty sterile apart from what you have already heard."

"Well, it's more than what we had an hour ago. We just need a couple more clues. Someone will have seen something or heard something, it's just the bloody waiting that is the pain in the arse.

Thanks once more, Ken, we will keep you in the loop," said Det. Ryan as he and Det. Stone left the lab.

Arriving home just on four p.m., he noticed that there was no red light flashing on his phone answer machine. *Good! No-one has tried to contact me, so no-one can say I was not at the farm working.*

That evening, the Win 9 National News told the story of the missing doctor's daughter, but nothing about the ransom call. Shaye's parents make an emotional plea to the kidnapper, pleading he release their daughter unharmed. Det. Ryan also asked for help to track down the red Commodore sedan.

The next morning on Thursday, Remi, a young employee of the car rental yard, cleaned the red Commodore. Starting inside, his cloth came up clean with not even a bit of dust, but he thought nothing about it. He moved to the boot and as he looked inside; he noticed a mark on the carpet where someone had tried to clean up a spill. This started his mind racing after hearing the police on the radio yesterday, and seeing the story on the National 9 News.

So, the young detailer went to his boss and said, "Boss, did you hear about that missing doctor's daughter yesterday?"

"Yes, why?"

"Well, remember they were looking for a red Commodore. I think it is the one we rented out on Tuesday. When I was cleaning it, I found a stain in the boot that could be blood."

"Really, you are kidding," said John Malouf.

"No, come and have a bow-peep."

John Malouf, a sceptical guy at the best of times, looked at the stain and said, "That's not blood, you are letting your imagination run away with you."

After the young guy finished work, he went home. Later, while eating dinner with his family and watching the National Nine News, the police plea for help in locating a red Commodore is aired again. He told his family that he thought the car in the rental yard was the red Commodore the police were looking for.

"Did you say anything to your boss?" asked his dad.

"He thinks I'm stupid and that my imagination is too active, but I still think it's blood in the boot. Another thing, the car was spotlessly clean inside, with not a speck of dust anywhere. I have never seen that with any other rental that I've cleaned."

"If you think that, call the cops and let them decide if it is the car they are looking for." Replies his father.

The young detailer rang a radio station and asked, "Could you give me the phone number to ring about that kidnapping, and the red Commodore?"

"Sure can, do you have something to tell?" asked the radio presenter.

"Yes, I think I do."

"Do you want to share it with me?"

"No, I really want to talk to the copper in charge."

When he rang the number, and told them he had news about the red Commodore and wanted to speak to someone about it.

The answering officer said, "It's Detective Ryan that is heading up that investigation. Can I have your name and number and I will get him to ring you immediately."

"When will he ring?" Asked Remi.

"Well, he is actually finished for the day, but I can still contact him. What is the nature of your information?"

"I know where that red Commodore is!"

"You do, are you sure?"

"Pretty sure."

"Have you told anybody else and if you have, what do they think?"

"Well, my boss thinks I am stupid, and it's just my wild imagination at work."

"What makes you so sure?"

"I work at a car rental yard and part of my job is to clean the cars when they are returned. This red Commodore came back in yesterday, and when I was cleaning it this morning, it was already wiped clean inside. However, the wheels and the body were covered in dust, so the renter had driven it along a dirt road. And I think in the boot there is a bloodstain."

"Give me your phone number and Detective Ryan will ring you back within ten-minutes. And thank you."

Waiting for that return call seemed to take forever, but it was only six minutes later. Det. Ryan, listens to Remi who tells his story once more, and gives the home phone number of John Malouf.

"Hello, is that Mr. Malouf, Mr. John Malouf who owns the Liverpool car rental yard?" Asks det. Ryan.

"Who wants to know?"

Detective Ryan. I am investigating the kidnapping of Shaye Burman and I believe you might have the red Commodore we are looking for."

"What, who have you been talking to? Don't tell me, it's that crazy kid Remi who has rung you! He is a bit of a drama-queen who saw the sensational in everything."

"Maybe so, but he has me interested and I would like to see that car tonight."

"Why tonight? Can't it wait till tomorrow?" replies a testy John Malouf.

"Listen, John, a young lady is missing, and we are trying to find her before something bad happens to her, so I would appreciate your help tonight."

"OK, I will be down at the yard in ten-minutes."

"Hang on, I'm not that quick, let's say thirty-minutes from now."

"Alright, see ya around eight-fifteen, right?" Replies a disgruntled John Malouf.

"That's it, oh, and thanks for your co-operation." Said a sarcastic Det. Ryan.

Arriving at the rental yard at eight-twenty, Det. Ryan, looked at the red Commodore and the stain on the carpet.

"Now, let me see your hiring agreement, and who it was that rented this car."

When he looked at the rental agreement and saw the name, Peter Ford, a smile crossed Det. Ryan's face. *I'm coming after you, you bastard, and I will get you. And I bet you are not that dumb to use your own name. I will not rest till I find you and arrest you.* "Mr. Malouf, did this Peter Ford show you any identification, like his driver's licence?"

"Yeah, we never let anyone rent a car without providing their ID, it's against the law not to see ID." Said a more co-operative, John Malouf.

"Look, we will impound this car. I believe it may be the car that the kidnapper of Shaye Burman used. I will get the forensic squad take this car tonight." Declares Det. Ryan.

"How long will you have it?"

"It will be awhile, and if it turns out to be the kidnap car, it will be tied up till after there is a conviction by the courts. And by-the-way, that young guy who rang us has been the best help we have had from the public so far. Give him a fair go."

"What am I supposed to do without one of my cars for hire? Lose money?"

"We will give you a receipt and you can put in a claim for reimbursement for any loss," said Det. Ryan. "Is there anything else that you can remember about our Mr. Peter Ford?"

"That bloody Pommy, no, I can't remember anything." Replies an annoyed John Malouf.

"Is he English?" Asks an excited Det.Ryan.

"As English as cricket, as they say."

As he waited for the forensic car-carrier, Det. Ryan, rang the Victorian Police Licence verification unit's twenty-four-hour number. He gave the details, and after checking their computer files, Det. Ryan was told that Peter Ford died in 1985, from a drug overdose.

The forensic squad checked out the car. The blood stain in the boot was human and tests matched it to blood at the front door of the Burman's home. The only print apart from those of the young detailer were the thumb and index finger of a man's left hand when he adjusted the rear vision mirror. It came as no surprise the prints were a perfect match to those on the Burman's security screen door—they belonged to Mr. Peter Ford.

Over the weekend, all leads, no matter how credible they seemed, were checked out, but little came from them. The Monday, after the kidnapping, there had still been no contact made between the kidnapper and the Burman family. Sandi was an emotional wreck, hardly sleeping, and cried at any mention of Shaye. Paul had taken time off work to be with his wife and family. That same morning, Det. Ryan, received a call from the fingerprint division.

"Det. Ryan, we have got some good, and bad news for you regarding those fingerprints we sent to Interpol. The good news is that these match the prints found on the sheet of plastic used to wrap the body of a young lady kidnapped from outside her front door on August 10, 1977, just outside of London. When we sent those prints out, they went to this unsolved kidnapping murder, so your kidnapper and the British kidnapper murderer are the same person. The bad news is that they don't have a clue who they belong to. And before you ask, I have already sent you a full printout of the report; you should have it within the hour."

"Thanks, this will help, I hope. I wonder if he has been a naughty boy elsewhere apart from London, and here?" Says Det. Ryan.

"There is no finger proof evidence that he has been, but you never know. All the best in the hunt, will catch you later."

"Thanks again, I owe you one. Next time we meet, it's my shout."

As he waited for Det. Short to show up, Det. Ryan, ran over what he knew about the kidnapper, jotting down the main points in his official police notebook:

1) You are not Peter Ford.

2) You have killed before.

3) You may be a Pommy, or you have lived in England.

4) The Burmans know you, as this was a planned kidnapping.

   a) The red Commodore used is the same as Shaye's boyfriend Nate.

   b) You knew where they lived.

   c) You were aware of their movements; you knew Shaye was home, cramming for the HSC.

   d) You used the voice scrambler because they knew your voice.

Det. Ryan, rang the Burman's and made an appointment for the next day, at nine-thirty. When they met, Det. Ryan, told them he believed they knew the kidnapper. Sandi, and Paul, are horrified at the suggestion, and Sandi, said the suggestion shocked her.

"He might only be an acquaintance, not a close friend, he might just be someone you say hi to around the neighbourhood. He may be a neighbour, or he might be a colleague. But he knows you, and he knows things about you and your family. We believe the use of the red Commodore was planned, and not just a coincidence; it seems he knew Shaye was home alone, otherwise it would have been too dangerous. And why did Shaye open the security door if she didn't know the guy?"

"That doesn't make it easy, as that could be any one of 100-plus people. That is some list," said Paul.

"It's a lot less than the number of adult males in NSW," replied Det. Ryan. "Another thing, this person is English, or has lived in England back in the 1970s. Does that narrow it down any for you?"

"Some of our best friends are English, but they wouldn't do anything like this," said Sandi.

"Just hang on," said Paul as he rushed out of the room. "I will be back in a flash." A minute later he returned with a letter in his hand.

"This arrived yesterday morning; it's our Marulan Farm manager's resignation. He said he is resigning because I did not pay him the wage rises I promised him at the interview. His name is Bob Walker, and he came out from England in the late seventies; I think from memory it was around '78/79."

Paul handed Det. Ryan the letter.

"Can I take this and see if we can lift any fingerprints off it?' Asked Det. Ryan.

"Sure," said Paul.

Det. Ryan placed the envelope and letter into a plastic bag.

"Did Bob do this to us?" asked Sandi.

"I don't know, but checking out the fingerprints on this letter will help to confirm it."

Det. Ryan, gave the envelope to his partner, Det. Short, and told him to get it to the fingerprint guys straight away. "Stay while they check and ring my pager the minute, they tell you anything. I will stay here a while and talk to the Burman's."

Dr. Burman, writes out the address, and name of the property, and gives it to Det. Ryan, Manin House in Bungonia Road, Marulan. While waiting for word from the fingerprint boys, Sandi, showed Det. Ryan photos she had, and school reports and a lot of achievement awards Shaye had received through her schooling and weekend sports.

Out of the blue, Sandi said to Det. Ryan, "Luke, tell me straight, you think Shaye is dead, don't you? Please be truthful."

"I am not 100 percent certain, but it doesn't look or feel good, especially since there has been no more contact from our Mr. Ford, or whoever he is."

"Thank you for that, Paul and I have come to that conclusion that we have lost her. But I feel I am betraying, or abandoning Shaye, and giving up trying to find her, if I admit this." Tears streamed down her cheeks. "Oh, I so wish that she would walk through the front door, I miss her so much. One part of my heart says don't give up, but my head keeps telling me she's gone. It's so hard."

If Paul or Sandi, had looked at Det. Luke Ryan at that moment, they would have seen the tears in the corner of his eyes. This hard-nosed cop, who had so often seen the evil side of human nature, and the devastation that evil inflicted on other humans, still had his soft side. The pain, and suffering, of other people still touched him.

"Would you like another coffee, Detective?" asked Paul.

"No, I really must go; it's eleven-thirty and I have a few things to check, but I will keep you informed. Just one thing more, do you have a recent photo of Bob Walker?"

"No, I don't think so," said Paul, "he was just our farm manager, it is not like he was one of the family, and he was not even a close friend so why would—"

Sandi, cut in and said, "I am sure Shaye had me take a photo of herself along with Nate, and Bob, standing in front of Nate's red car. She had them printed a day or two after we returned home. I will look in her room." She jumped to her feet and hurried off, returning in a few minutes.

"I had a little trouble locating them, but here it is. It is a good one of Bob, and she is so beautiful." Tears started running like a torrent down her face. Paul moved quickly to his wife's side to comfort her and put his arms around her.

She looked at Paul saying, "I'm fine, Paul, it just a thought that came to me, Shaye had me take that photo which is now helping us to catch Bob."

"I am sure that is the case," said a smiling Det. Ryan. "I will return the photo as soon as I can."

Together Sandi and Paul, say, "No, we don't want it." They looked at each other, smiled and hugged each other in an embrace of love.

While driving back to his office, Det. Ryan's pager rang. His partner Det. Short wanted to talk to him.

Det. Ryan, waited till he got to his office, which was less than ten-minutes away. As he pulled into the carpark, Det. Short came out the door and hurried over to him.

"Luke, some prints on that letter confirm they belong to a Bob Walker, also known as Peter Ford. I have contacted the Goulburn Police who have an unmarked car just up from the doctor's farm. They will detain Walker if he tries to leave. Do you feel like a drive to Marulan? I have already got the arrest warrant."

"What are you waiting for? Jump in."

On their way they passed through Liverpool and called into the car rental yard to show John Malouf the photo of Bob Walker.

"I am not sure if that is Mr Ford as he has a beard, but those eyes are his and they gave me a chill when I first met him. They were so cold and lifeless. Yes, that is Mr Ford, the fucking prick," said John Malouf.

The two detectives turned off the Hume Highway onto the Bungonia Road just 1.5 kilometres south of the Marulan township. They drive the four kilometres to the farm and asked the officers in the unmarked car to back them up. The two vehicles turn into the driveway and drive the 200 metres up to the smaller of the two houses; the one between the main house and the machinery shed, was where Dr. Burman said Bob Walker lived. Detectives Ryan and Short go to the front door, while directing the two Goulburn Officers to go around the back. Det. Ryan, knocked loudly on the door, but there was no response from inside.

Bob, had been in the machinery shed getting what tools were his, and a couple of extra items that belonged to the farm, as he was planning to leave the next day. From his hiding place in the machinery shed, Bob, watched the goings on around his cottage intently. He never thought the police would track him so quickly, after all the English police failed to catch him, and he thought he had been just as careful this time.

"Maybe he is not here. He could have already left. Remember, he resigned his position. Maybe he has been too quick for us," said Det. Short.

"Yes, I was just thinking that myself," replied Det. Ryan.

"But, let's have a look in the garages; remember he drives a blue Toyota four-wheel-drive plate number ADJ 496."

The four lock-up garages were on the other side of the main house and they looked inside each one, but the Toyota wasn't there. "We will check those other two sheds," Det. Ryan said, as he pointed straight at the machinery shed.

Watching the police from his hiding place in the shed, Bob, decided he would go out the back door of the shed, and run to the copse of trees in the paddock just seventy metres away. The two Goulburn Officers were heading for the hay shed when they saw Bob racing for the trees.

Both yelled out, "Stop, police," but Bob kept running as fast as he could towards the safety of the trees.

The four police officers fanned out and start chasing after him. The two Goulburn Officers were in their mid-twenties and fit and fast and were soon around the back of the thicket of trees. They were too quick for Bob, who tried to hide amongst some tea tree shrubs. Detectives Ryan and Short stayed at the front.

Det. Ryan yelled out, "Bob Walker, we are police officers and we have a warrant for your arrest for the kidnapping of Shaye Burman. There is no way out, you may as well give up and come out with your hands above your head."

Walker didn't reply, or move to give away his hiding place.

"Right we are coming in."

All four officers drew their service weapons and moved into the trees.

Realising he was trapped, Bob, stood up and shouted, "OK, I'm coming out, just don't shoot."

In March 1989, Walker was tried and found guilty of the kidnapping and murder of Shaye Burman, even though her body was never found. Walker rejected all the pleas from the Burman's and police to tell them what he did with Shaye's body. He was sentenced to 19 years' prison, and on release would be deported to England to stand trial for the kidnap murder allegedly committed in August 1977. Walker escaped from Barnaby Maximum Security Prison on 25 November 1993.

CHAPTER 3

THE BETTINI TWINS

Vince and Angelo were known as the Bettini twins. Angelo was six-foot-two inches of mean lean muscle and the younger of the twins by 12 minutes. He had the brains and looks. He was also the most dangerous one, cold and calculating, just like his dark brown eyes. There was nothing Angelo would not do to get what he wanted. He was obsessed with being number one, wherever he was, and whatever he did.

Vince was the muscle. He was a well-built, powerful man standing six-foot-four. He did whatever Angelo wanted, or needed to be done. He was a cold-blooded killer and his favourite weapon was a flick knife, which his victims rarely saw before it cut their throat, or was stuck into their body.

In '79, on their twentieth birthday, their father sent them to an uncle in Sicily to live and learn the ways of the Family, for five years. Both were excellent students, but Angelo disliked the fact that he had to start at the bottom, and prove himself, when every day there were others higher up the food chain that did not possess his abilities, nor his leadership qualities. During those five years, three of his fellow Mafia students disappeared, and each disappearance elevated Angelo up the ladder of potential Mafia leadership.

In '84, the long five years were over, and the twins returned to Sydney, more dangerous than when they left in '79. Immediately, they established their standing within Sydney's underworld. They concentrated on drugs, prostitution, loan sharking, and business protection schemes. In the next four years, their rise in the Sydney underworld scene was in direct relation to the demise of a number of former leading figures. The Sydney Crime Squad had one or both of them listed as POI's (persons of interest), in half a dozen unsolved gangland slayings and five major fires.

In '88, the Australian Federal Police worked with Interpol to receive confirmation of a large quantity of ephedrine, used in the production of speed, and methamphetamine. It was said to be about 1,000 kilograms and coming from an Indian chemical factory. Initial undercover police investigations in Sydney, suggested the Bettini twins would make a huge move to become number one in the drug business in Sydney, and elsewhere in Australia. The shipment was estimated to have a street value upwards of $100 million.

Different drug enforcement agencies from several nations, have tracked the freighter on its long voyage from India. Its route was to go down the Australian east coast bound for New Zealand, and Auckland's west coast Mangere Harbour. Through their undercover agents from both the Australian Federal Police, and the New South Wales Drug Division, the tip-off was that two big, fast, and long-distance game fishing boats had moved down the New South Wales south coast four months ago. These two boats would meet the freighter out in the Tasman Sea. One vessel would come out of Batemans Bay, the other out of Ulladulla harbour.

Both had been under surveillance since they relocated down the south coast. The boats have gone out fishing a lot in the last two months, often staying out all night to create the impression they were just wealthy guys who enjoyed their fishing. Sometimes, when they returned from their fishing trips, they would donate some of their catch to charities to raffle off the fish at the local pubs and clubs. Every week, a refrigerated one tonne truck owned and driven by cousins of the Bettini twins, took a load of fish back to the Sydney Fish Markets so other relatives, who were legitimate fish mongers, could sell them.

Each day the freighter would contact a Sydney number confirming where they were, and the expected time of arrival at a location. This information was then forwarded to the skippers of both fishing boats. The Australian Federal Police and the New South Wales Drug Enforcement listened to all the phone calls. The fishing boats and the freighter met as planned; the ephedrine was transferred to the fishing boats who then returned to their respective ports. Surveillance of both boats had been stepped up tighter now that the meeting with the freighter was eminent. In Ulladulla, three officers had been working on different boats within the small harbour. And they took any opportunity to talk to and befriend those on the suspected fishing boat.

This day the routine of the two boats changed; the refrigerated trucks appeared within minutes of the boats docking. In Ulladulla harbour, two-thirds of the large crates of fish were covered—this had never been observed before. The number of crates had also increased from the usual 15 to 17 crates to 25. In Batemans Bay, they unloaded on the "T" shaped wharf adjacent to the southern end of the bridge, and across the road from Raymond's Chinese Restaurant. New South Wales Police and Australian Federal Police had them under surveillance from upstairs of Harry's Bait and Tackle, a couple of doors away from Raymond's. Night cameras and night vision glasses were being used. Like in Ulladulla, the number of crates loaded were 25, far more than what had come off the boat over the months. Many crates were covered.

The surveillance in Batemans Bay, was nearly blown when the local fisheries inspector turned up to inspect the catch before it was unloaded. He had done this four times in the last couple of months, usually in the first or second week of the month. He had already inspected the boat just two weeks earlier, but this visit was a random inspection. A very dangerous inspection for the Fisheries Inspector.

All those on the wharf spotted the inspector the moment he exited his vehicle and start walking down towards the docking area. Those unloading the boat froze. They started talking excitedly in Italian. Suddenly, an elderly-looking man, who had been regularly fishing off the wharf, jumped to his feet and started yelling at the fisheries inspector.

"So, you finally came, I have been ringing you for days reporting illegal activity on the river. I suppose being bloody late is better than never. You, government bastards give me the shits." He walked over quickly to intercept the inspector, who did not look too pleased with the fisherman.

As the fisherman approached the inspector, the inspector said, "What in hell are you talking about? I know nothing about any phone calls about illegal activity on the river,"

The fisherman reached the inspector and held up his Australian Federal Police badge and told him in a lowered voice, you have walked into an undercover operation, and was not allowed to inspect the fishing boat. He was told to play along to avoid them both being shot.

"My name is Ben," said the officer, "so use it in conversation now."

The inspector's face started losing colour, but he agreed to play along.

In a loud and angry voice, Ben said, "Well, I would sack that office worker. She can't even get a message clear. I rang three times and left my message and my name. She deserves to lose her job over this fuck up."

"I apologise for the mix-up; I was told to talk to a guy named Ben. When I pulled up and saw the fishing boat, I thought it was someone on the boat who wanted to talk to me."

"Well, I am Ben, so just get your sorry arse over here," replied Ben, as he walked to the end of the "T" away from the fishing boat.

Those on the fishing boat had stopped unloading, and were talking in hushed voices, and watching the inspector. When Ben and the inspector reached the end of the wharf, Ben, started pointing under the bridge towards the northern bank of the Clyde River, and to the lights around the Boat Hire Business.

"The last week while fishing, I watched two small boats doing something at low tide over in those oyster leases."

"Well, there is nothing strange about that, it is just the owner of the lease or his workers doing work. If that is all, then you have wasted my time."

"Just hang on, sonny, and put your fucking listening ears on. They are not lease workers; they are fucking stealing oysters."

"How can you be so sure they are stealing oysters?"

"For starters, I have lived my whole bloody life down around this river, and I have seen workers working the low tide at night, but I have never seen nor heard of those harvesting oysters who finish and head up the river towards Nelligren. All their processing sheds are on this side of the river. And another thing, sonny, these guys are not working from a flat-bottom oyster barge."

"Well! Have you seen them tonight?" Inquired the inspector.

"Haven't you listened to what I am telling you? You really are one dumb fisheries inspector; it isn't low tide yet. And it won't be for at least another three hours. You come back in three hours and see for yourself"

Quietly, Ben, suggested to the inspector he should say something friendly to those on the fishing boat before he left.

The inspector left and walked over towards the fishing boat and said, "Hi, guys, how's the fishing been?"

"Not bad, rather good, just like most other days, do you want to check our catch?"

Ben's heartbeat increased. *What the fuck are they doing?* he wondered.

"I can't tonight, that old guy has put me onto some possible illegal activity around some oyster leases, so I better check it out. How much longer are you guys down here? You originally told me, you were possible staying for three to four months and it must be nearly four months now?"

"You have a good memory, inspector. We are staying while the fishing is good, but yes, we have been here four months last week. But I guess another week or two will see us out of here."

"You may see me again before you go, if not all the best."

As the inspector turned to go, he called out to Ben, "Aye, Ben, I will need you to give me your contact details so I can contact you later. I will go to my truck and grab my book and be back in a jiffy."

"Just wait a minute, sonny, I haven't had a decent bite for the last hour. Wait till I pack-up and I will come to your truck."

As Ben packed up, a guy from the fishing boat walked over to him with two large flatheads and gave them to Ben saying, "I remember you telling me not long ago that if you go home with nothing you cop it from your missus, so maybe these may silence her."

"Your blood's worth bottling," replied Ben, "these will keep the old girl happy; it is mighty kind of you." Ben picked up his gear and walked to the inspector's truck.

Under one of the parking area's lights, the inspector started pretending to write in a book while asking Ben, "Were you fair dinkum about possibly getting shot?"

"You better believe it; these guys are violent men and will stop at nothing to protect their crimes. Look, I can't tell you much at this time, but I will write down my office phone number so you can contact me in about a month's time. I will fill you in on what has and is going down here tonight. Also, I must warn you not to mention anything to anyone about tonight. This hasn't happened, you were never here, and you never met me. Do you understand what I am saying?"

The inspector nodded.

"Look, I am not saying this to scare you, but if these people and their bosses hear anything about tonight, they may come looking for you, and they won't be handing you any flatheads. It will more than likely be a bullet to the back of your head."

The inspector's eyes widened, and once again his face lost all its colour. "Ben, I won't ring you; I am just going to forget about everything that has happened here tonight."

"That would be the best thing to do, but if it started weighing on your mind, give me a ring and we can arrange for you to talk to a counsellor."

The two men shook hands and went their separate ways.

The two refrigerated one tonner headed off as soon as they were loaded, heading to the Sydney Fish Markets. A team of twenty-two surveillance vehicles in a slick-as-silk interchanging procedure followed them. Five kilometres north of Gerrigong, the two trucks pull into the truck lay-by area, halfway through the Kiama bends on the Princes Highway. Secluded behind the bushes, the four men quickly transferred the ephedrine to one truck, and the fish to the other truck, then they continue their journey to Sydney Fish Markets.

At the Sydney Fish Markets, the ephedrine was loaded into another refrigerated one-tonner with magnetic signs along both sides advertising, Nick's Fish and Chips at Fairfield. The Bettini twin's Uncle Nick owned Nick's Fish and Chips. He was as straight as an arrow and a respected member of the local community around Fairfield. The same could not be said about his two sons, who had seen their cousins Angelo and Vince living a different lifestyle with an endless supply of money, and lots of beautiful women. The promise of quick and easy money was too much temptation for them to resist.

This new one-tonner left the Fish Markets and drove around for ten minutes before turning into George Street and heading downtown. Four different surveillance vehicles followed in a rotating switching procedure, where one would follow no more

than two vehicles behind. Surveillance was for any distance from
200 metres to two kilometres, then they would turn left or right,
maybe cruise past the one tonner or pull over and let another
vehicle take over.

Turning left into Druitt Street, then right into Kent Street, the
one-tonner turned into a multi-deck carpark. A surveillance vehicle
also turned into the carpark. The one-tonner drove up to the fourth
level and parked. The driver, the twin's cousin, exited the vehicle
and walked over to the lift and descended to the entrance. There
he spoke to the attendant before heading down Kent Street towards
Wynyard.

The surveillance vehicle observes where the one-tonner
was parked descended to the third level and parked. Exiting the
surveillance vehicle, a young undercover police constable used
the lift. He exited at the fifth level, and then walked down the
stairs whistling. The passenger of the one-tonner had taken up a
position to the front of the carpark overlooking Kent Street. He
was standing two metres away from the stairs. Hearing the young
police officer coming down the stairs whistling, he turned, and
they both nodded to each other.

The passenger said, "There's a bloody lift here, why walk?"

The young constable stopped and answered, "I use it for fitness
for footy; whenever I use a car park, I park as close to the top as
possible, walk down and when I come back, I run up the stairs. It's
great for your fitness, you ought to try it."

"Shit no, fuck the stairs."

"See you later," said the young constable, as he disappeared
down the stairs. He walked down and exited out the front of the car
park, crossed the road, turned a corner, and was out of sight. After
five minutes, another car pulled into the carpark with a couple
in the front, and the young constable lying flat on the back seat
covered by a blanket. He quickly left the car and took the lift back
to the third level, where he joined his partner in the surveillance

vehicle. The couple walked out of the carpark hand in hand and disappeared up the side road.

Safely out of sight behind their tinted glass windows, the young constable and his senior partner still had a visual on the passenger up the ramp who was still standing next to the lift. What they did not observe was an identical one-tonner coming down from the fifth level that stopped in front of the loaded one-tonner. Two men quickly jumped out and switched the number plates of the two vehicles and the magnetic signs. At the same time, the passenger waved to his brother returning along Kent Street. The passenger walked back to the two one-tonners, got in the identical vehicle and drove down to the entrance where he paid his parking fee. His brother got in and they turned left into Kent Street.

"Attention all surveillance units, targeted vehicle is about to exit the car park," reported the surveillance team on level three.

The first surveillance vehicle to follow the one-tonner out of the Fish Markets fell in behind the switched one-tonner. Inside the surveillance car were two Australian Federal Police officers, Bill Norton, a 25-year veteran, and Neil Peters, a 32-year-old car fanatic. As they approached the Erskine and Kent Street intersection, Neil suddenly said,

"Bloody hell, they're switched vehicles."

"What are you going on about?" replied Bill. "That is the same vehicle, same plates."

"Yes, they are the same plates, but that's a different vehicle to the one that entered the carpark; they're switched them, I'm telling you."

"What makes you think that?" asked Bill, with a bit of concern in his voice and a bewildered look on his face.

"Just look at the springs, how high the back is off the ground; if they haven't switched vehicles, they've just unloaded a tonne of ephedrine in the car park."

"Are you certain?" said Bill. "We will look pretty stupid if you are wrong."

"Trust me, that is not the same vehicle." Said a very confident Neil Peters.

Bill immediately grabbed the two-way, "Attention Ron, and partner in the car park, come in quickly."

"Ron here, Bill, what's up?"

"They have done a switch of vehicles, stay where you are. Confirm your position."

"We have just re-entered Kent Street."

"Pull over and keep a lookout, and report any identical vehicle leaving the car park. We will continue our surveillance until we hear you have a visual. Our suspect's vehicle is just about to cross the Harbour Bridge."

Bill and Neil, were almost in North Sydney when Ron's voice came over the two-way, "Affirmative, a second one-tonner has just left the Kent Street Carpark. Their smart buggers, aren't they? What tipped you off?"

"My partner, Neil, noticed the vehicle we are following is sitting too high in the back so it must be empty."

Three new surveillance cars are called into the operation to follow the original one-tonner, while two of the original surveillance cars followed the empty one-tonner to cover all bases.

The loaded one-tonner went to a factory in Sydenham. A check revealed that the Bettini twins owned the factory, and leased it out to a cousin who imported furniture. This was a suspected money laundering business. The factory was placed under twenty-hour surveillance from the top of other factories, and a command centre was set up inside a disused building across the road, only thirty metres from the front door of the factory. Information gained by undercover officers from their informants indicated that something would go down either Thursday, or Friday night.

Friday evening, a little after nine-fifteen, the Bettini twins arrived with a second vehicle with five rugged looking men. The surveillance team, using night field glasses, quickly identified the five as soldiers of the Bettini twins. Two went into the building, the other two crossed the road, one going to the left, the other to the right to take up hidden positions. Officer Matt Newton, whispered to the team leader Bill Norton, "Looks like they have done this before."

Angelo, entered the building, while his brother Vince and the fifth soldier waited at the front door. The soldier going to the right headed straight towards the building which housed the command centre. As he walked towards them, Inspector Bill Norton quickly radioed a message for everyone to maintain radio silence till he told them it was all clear. The soldier, came to the front of the building and pushed the front door ajar, whistled and waved to Vince, and then backed inside, slowly closing the door.

Neil Peters, stuck his pistol to the back of his head and said, "Police Officer, you are under arrest. Raise your hands, keep quiet and slowly turn around."

Doing what Neil Peters told him, he turned and, in the light coming into the building from the streetlights, he saw six officers all with drawn guns pointing at him. "Fucking hell," he said.

The soldier was handcuffed and moved to an internal back room—an old freezer room whose door faced the rear of the building. Inside the freezer room there were a couple of gas lights glowing, a table and six chairs. He was searched and questioned, but remained silent, then marched out through the back entrance of the building, where several unmarked police cars were parked. Two of the back-up New South Wales police officers put him into a car, and delivered him to Central Police Station, to be held in the cells.

Right on ten o'clock, three cars pulled up, and seven men got out in front of the furniture factory. They were quickly identified as major dealers in the drug trade in Sydney. Vince, and the fifth soldier met them and checked them for weapons, finding a handgun only on each of the three drivers.

"Follow me," said Vince as he turned and entered the building.

"Attention guys," said Inspector Bill Norton, "it's going down; there are now twelve men we know about in the factory. We have one in custody, and there is one more on the outside. We will have to get him before we can go in."

"Unit Four calling, we have a person in view in the doorway of Bell's Smash Repairs. We have no cover to get to him as we are on the other side of the road."

"We must neutralise him before we can go into the factory," replied Inspector Norton.

Those in the command centre discussed what they could do to neutralise the soldier at Bell's Smash Repairs without drawing attention to ourselves.

Officer Matt Newton, a New South Wales Drug undercover operative for five years, suggested he could get this guy with no fuss thanks to his facial beard, and a bottle.

"Attention, Unit Two, do you have the marksman with you?"

"Affirmative."

"Can you get a clear shot on the guy at Bell's?"

"Affirmative."

"Good, we are sending out an officer acting as a drunk to get this guy silently. Just don't let him get hurt; take the soldier out if need be," said a serious Inspector Norton.

"Okay, will do, only as a last option."

Eight minutes later, Matt rounded the corner sixty-five metres away from Bell's, staggering, and swearing, as he moved slowly towards Bell's. Thirty metres away from the soldier, Matt, stumbled over a garbage can, swearing as he kicked at the can, missed it, and fell to the ground, letting go of his bottle which flew up in a slow arc and came crashing down on the edge of the gutter. Everyone, including the soldier, watched as it exploded, and its contents sprayed over the gutter. Getting to his feet, and continuing to swear, Matt, stood up the garbage can, and then kicked it out onto the road. Swearing, and calling the bin every name he could think of, he stopped ten metres from Bell's entrance, and the soldier. Moving in close to the wall, he urinated against it.

Feigning difficulty in getting his fly done up, he stumbled around moving ever so close to the soldier.

"Norton, to Unit Two, do we have our man covered?"

"Affirmative," came the reply.

Matt, was now at Bell's doorway and pretended not to see the soldier standing there. He turned his back and sat down on the second step.

"Aye, pop," said the soldier, not wanting some drunk as a witness, "you better get your arse out of here right now."

"Who said so?" asked an indignant Matt.

"I am telling you, you drunken piss-head, move on."

"Who are you?" asked Matt.

Bending down to say it loud and in Matt's ear, "I'm the fucking night watchman, am I'm telling you to piss off."

Instantly, Matt's pistol was in the soldier's face, pointing it right between his eyes. "And I am a New South Wales police officer, and you, you son-of-a-bitch, are under arrest. Back up and reach for the sky."

Within seconds, a member of Unit Four arrives to assist Matt.

"Target is in custody," relayed Unit Two.

"Thanks," said Inspector Norton. "Unit Two, stand down your marksman. Everyone get ready we are going in, in five minutes. You all know what to do. Remember, when we enter the building, there are twelve men that we know are in there. If they start shooting, shoot to kill. Good luck to all, let us all go home tonight."

At a given signal, two heavily armed forces simultaneously smashed in the front and rear doors, and stormed the building, spreading out as they go.

"Federal and New South Wales police," shouted Inspector Norton. "Don't move, you are all under arrest."

Being caught out in the open in the cleared loading area, the three soldiers and three drivers immediately raised their hands.

"Get down on the ground," shouted the officers as they moved in to secure the six men.

Rushing out of the first-floor office area, the four drug dealers come to a sudden stop as pistols and rifle barrels confronted them.

"Where are the Bettini Twins?" asked Neil Peters.

"Who? We don't know any Bettini Twins," replied one drug dealer. "There is no-one else here but us."

"Yeah right," said Neil.

"Angelo and Vince Bettini, it's Inspector Bill Norton of the Australian Federal Police; we know you are in here we have the place surrounded, and there is no way out. So, just come out."

Nothing but silence, come from the factory and office area.

Moving swiftly, two heavily armed tactical response team members swept into the office, but the office was empty.

Inspector Norton and Matt Newton entered the office and the inspector said, "Where in the hell did, they go?"

Matt, walked around the back of the desk and started thumping the walls with the edge of his closed fist, looking for a secret door, but found nothing. He got down on his hands and knees and started looking under the office desk. Inspector Norton heard him say, "What do we have here?" He backed out from under the desk and then reached back under the desk and flicked a toggle switch from left to right. Immediately, the floor below the desk dropped away on two hydraulic pistons, revealing a space large enough to hold four men. But no-one was in the hole. He motioned to Inspector Norton that he would drop into the hold; with his gun drawn, he dropped down the two metres and a quick glance around revealed another hinged door. This one was smaller, roughly one metre by one metre square. Matt, moved to the right of the door, and slowly pushed the door open with his left foot, bending down, only to find a two-metre-high and five-metre-long tunnel. Reaching the end of the tunnel, there was no hinged door, so he pushed against the wall in front, but it was solid. Next, he pushed against the right-hand side, and the side opened into a clearing amongst packing crates of imported knock-down furniture. Exiting the tunnel, the door closed automatically behind him. He looked around at the tunnel door that looked just like a stack of ply-wood packing crates. Looking around, he realised he had come out at the back of the office. He walked around to the front and said, "They have disappeared, but I bet my bottom dollar they are hiding in some crate."

Inspector Norton said. "Bring the dogs in."

Two New South Wales police dog handlers entered the factory, and send their dogs out, who both went in the same direction towards the back of the storage area. Within minutes, one dog began barking. "He has found someone," said the handler. In the dim light of the factory area, illuminated only by security lights, the police dog handler and other officers moved in with guns drawn. Rounding one stack of piled, knocked down imported furniture, they saw that police dog Rusty had Vince cornered. Vince had his flick knife out, and was trying to cut the dog.

Rusty's handler, aimed his pistol at Vince and yelled, "Drop the knife and get down on the floor, face down."

With a murderous look in his eyes, Vince weighed up the situation.

Once again, the handler yelled, "I won't say it again, drop the knife and get face down on the floor."

Vince dropped the knife and raised his hands.

"On the ground, face first," screamed the handler and Vince reluctantly obeyed.

Two police officers rushed past the handler and take Vince into custody.

"Where is your brother?" asked Inspector Norton.

"He ain't here," snarled Vince.

"That is a load of bullshit, we saw him enter the building." Said the Inspector.

"Well, find him if you think you are so smart," retorted Vince.

Just then the other dog handler called out, "We have something here."

JOHN A. W. INMAN

Moving another twenty metres towards the rear door, they see police dog Satan sitting quietly alongside a large packing crate. They talked to the handler, who told them that someone was in the crate.

"How come your dog isn't barking?" asked Neil Peters.

"There is no danger to him, but there is someone in that crate," said the handler.

Four officers surrounded the crate as Inspector Norton knocked on the side and said, "Angelo Bettini, we know you are in there so just come out."

Slowly the top of the crate lifted, and Angelo Bettini, stood glaring at the officers. The twins and drugs were taken back to the Joint Task Force office inside Central Police Station.

The Bettini twins, were charged with conspiracy to import a prohibited import, and the supply of a large commercial quantity of a prohibited drug. In October 1989 they were sentenced to prison for fifteen years' to be served at Barnaby Maximum Security Prison. They escaped on 25 November 1993.

CHAPTER 4

JAMES (BULL) MALONEY

James (Bull) Maloney was born 17 July 1963. He stood just a tad under six-feet-five, he was the number one enforcer of the Apache Outlaw Motorbike Gang. The Apaches goal, was to control the drug trade up and down the Australian east coast, just like they controlled most of the brothels, and were heavily involved in the club and pub bouncer/security business.

Bull's, dream, was to one day run the Apaches, and to make them the most feared bikies in the land, to control not only the sale, but the manufacture, and distribution of drugs throughout Australia. Bull's philosophy was: "With fear you can control everything, with fear you can gain silence, and loyalty, with fear you can be successful, you can be number one, the Man."

Bull's, make-up was a strange mix; on the one hand he loved children, and would never himself hurt them, nor would he let others hurt them. He hated the treatment of women within Outlaw Motorcycle Gangs, but, was not yet in the position to do anything about it. The other side of Bull was brutal. In December 1978 at fifteen, he brought home two male saltwater crocodiles, each nearing the two-metre mark in length. He had already arranged with his dad to fence in the small tidal lake on their deer farm property. The entrance to their lake was also fenced off with heavy gauge meshing. Over the years, Bull would capture kangaroos, wild pigs and goats. He would then throw them into the fenced off lake and watch his crocodiles stalk and catch them, then drag them into the water before doing the death roll. He got a fix from seeing the utter fear in the animals' eyes as well as their frantic efforts in trying to beat the inevitable end. They knew they were being stalked, and there was no way out.

Bull, was well educated and had completed his law Degree at Sydney University, but taken it no further. A career in law was not where he was heading. Money and everything else he wanted in life came quicker and easier through the bikie world and crime. He used a no-nonsense approach to problem solving, and if he thought violence was needed to solve a problem, then violence it was on a scale that terrorised all those involved. Bull's problem-solving methods impressed those in the Apache leadership, and soon he was mingling with the top-notch Apaches.

At one Campfire Council, often held out in the open with a blazing fire and surrounded by bikers, the leadership spoke about a problem in Brisbane with an associated bikies group, the Hell Riders, who were being re-badged as Brisbane's chapter of the Apaches. The Hell Riders had an over inflated opinion of who they were, and where and how they fitted in with the Apache's plans. The Apache leadership suspected the Hell Riders wanted to compete with them in Brisbane, down the track. Reports coming in indicated they were already stealing customers, and contacts in Brisbane, and throughout Queensland.

At the Campfire Council, Bull asked that he be tasked to sort it out. The leadership agreed and said they would send four others with him. Bull said that he did not need any help and that he would have the Hell Riders toeing the line within two weeks.

"If I fail, you can then send in your four-man enforcer team."

Bull rode all the next day to Brisbane, making stops along the way. One particular stop was a petrol service station on the Pacific Highway in Woodburn. Parking his bike in the shade, Bull walked over to a van which had painted on both sides Little River Deer Farm, Evans Head, approximately ten kilometres from Woodburn. The two male occupants of the van exited the van and all three men embraced. Bull and the two men entered the eating area of the service station and ordered toasted sandwiches, conversed for twenty minutes, then stood and embraced each other before they departed. Bull rode his bike, and the other two headed north with an agreed time and place to meet in Brisbane. On arrival in Brisbane, Bull contacted the Hell Riders' leaders and demanded a meeting the next evening at a location the Hell Riders chose.

At the meeting, Bull came straight to the point. "You guys have to pull your bloody heads in and toe the line. If you don't the leadership will be systematically eliminated until we get you doing what we want you to fucking do."

"Who in hell do you think you are coming in here and threatening us? We could put a gun to your head and pull the trigger and no-one would give a shit."

"It is obvious you guys don't have the balls to do that. If you had the balls, I would already be dead," replied a sarcastic Bull.

"Just wait till Leon gets here. He will kick your arse back to Sydney."

"That's right, you guys cannot even wipe your own arse without Leon's permission," taunted Bull.

"We work as a team, and we can make decisions without Leon."

"That is bullshit, and you know it. Anyway, you will have to make all your decisions without Leon from now on."

"What do you mean, without Leon?"

"Boy, you guys are dumb, you just don't get it, do you? Leon's gone, and he won't be coming back."

"Leon wouldn't leave as this is his life; he will be here soon, and he will fucking take care of you," one Hell Rider said, trying to claw back the initiative.

"No, he won't be fucking back, when I spoke to him earlier today, I convinced him to retire and leave," said a smiling Bull.

"You are full of shit; Leon would never leave. He would eat you in a fight."

Bull reached into his jacket pocket and then threw a cloth package onto the table. "Open it," he said. Inside was Leon's ring finger with his big gold ring still on it. All eyes were now firmly fixed on Bull.

"Why shouldn't we just kill you? An eye for an eye."

"You could do that, but before I came here, I gave a lawyer friend two envelopes with names, plus the locations of your drug labs and your bank account numbers. If I am not back by ten o'clock tonight, my friend will turn those envelopes over to the drug squad and vice squad. All your names and address are in there. So, the spin you put onto Leon's disappearance is that he has left the country. And you four and the rest of your rabble must toe the fucking line. If you don't and I have to come back to Brisbane, at least one of you will join Leon. And we will continue to eliminate leaders until the Apaches get what they want from you. Oh yes, Leon's enforcer, what was his name? Ox, that's it; he said to tell you guys goodbye as he has joined Leon."

It would be many years before the authorities found out what had happened to Leon and Ox. The only evidence of any foul play was that Leon's and Ox's bikes were found abandoned and lying in the middle of a suburban street with their motors running. The Hell Riders fell into line and profited by doing so.

In the bikie world, it was said Bull was responsible for twelve bikers "going away," but in truth it was fourteen goodbyes. When

Bull spoke, everyone listened. His standing in the Apaches increased, and he became one of the top three leaders of the Campfire Council.

The mistake Bull made that got him sent to prison, was the attempted murder of two undercover cops. One had infiltrated the Apaches, rising to just outside the leadership of the Campfire Council. Bull, had suspicions about the undercover cop, but his suspicion was not about him being a cop, more a traitor—he had seen him twice meeting with a member of the Apaches' biggest rival bikie gang in Sydney. He never realised that they were both undercover cops, and when he attacked the two with a baseball bat, it was just a coincidence that a local police patrol car came upon the brawl. Drawing their service pistols, they arrested Bull and called an ambulance to convey the two undercover cops to Royal Prince Albert Hospital with broken bones and facial injuries. One undercover cop was placed on life support for three days. Neither men returned to active duty.

At his trial, Bull was loyal to the Apaches all the way, never connecting them to the attempted murder of the two cops. He was a bit surprised that the cops had him down as number one suspect in the murders of nine others. But all Bull would say to the questions was, "Yes, I have also heard the same rumours. But that is all they are, rumours. Just rumours with no truth in them whatsoever."

Investigating police always thought Bull was guilty of the disappearance of a number of bikies, and other criminals. They could never place him near the last place the missing people were known to have been. One investigator believed he wasn't working alone, that he had one or more killers working with him. But there was no hard evidence one way or the other.

In May 1991, Bull was sentenced to 13 years' prison with hard labour. And in prison he was the number one suspect in the murder of two other prisoners, both bikies. He escaped from Barnaby on 26 November 1993.

CHAPTER 5

HU (JIMMY TAN) MING CHAN

In '87, the Chinese Communist Party sent Chinese national Hu (Jimmy) Ming Chan to undertake an architectural degree at Sydney University. He was also a Chinese National and Junior Provincial Martial Arts champion, of Wushu (Kung Fu) from the Shaolin Temple System that masters barehanded fighting. Hu was a loyal supporter of the Communist Party, and he was willing to do whatever the Party asked him to do.

While in Sydney, friends told him about the student unrest back home. He thought the Party would quickly quell the unrest. He had also heard the Party had instigated a 'Re-education Program' for those who spoke out against them.

In '89, Hu went home for the university's Christmas and New Year break, and caught up with a lot of student friends, in particular two he had known all his life growing up in the same area of

Beijing. Soon, Hu became aware of strong anti-Party sentiments within the students. He had never really understood the depth of anti-government feeling amongst his fellow students. This feeling had its genesis back in '86, the year before Hu had left for Sydney. He himself supported the Party, but some said his support bordered on the fanatical. He believed all should fall in line with the Party.

He returned to Sydney and his studies in February of '89. In June, he heard the news of the killing of students involved in demonstrations in Tiananmen Square on 4 June '89. The Western World reported anywhere from 500 to 1000 students had been killed by tanks. Hu found it hard to concentrate on his studies. He borrowed money from friends in Sydney, to make a rush trip back home to Beijing.

On arriving home, he learnt many of the students he had known and met with just four months earlier had perished in Tiananmen Square. Going to the Party offices, where he was known by name, he found that the official Party report about Tiananmen Square differed from what his friends told him, and what he had read in the Western press and seen on Western TV. Hu chose to believe the official Party Report.

Believing in the Party and its philosophy, Hu set out to convince his two closet friends they were wrong about the Party and its policies. After much talking night after night that often went into the early hours of the morning, Hu concluded his friends would benefit from the Party's 'Re-education Program,' for those who opposed it and its policies. With this strong conviction in his head, Hu gave their names and addresses to the Party Office. They assured him he had done the right thing and the program would work.

After three weeks had passed, Hu approached the Party Office to inquire about his friends, and how the 'Re-education Program' was going. Those at the office told Hu there was no record of his friends ever entering the program.

Hu was stunned. "But I told you about them. I saw your guys arresting them. What have you done with them?"

Two weeks later, Hu was visited at his home and warned that he was under investigation, and that he must stop this questioning of the Party about the alleged disappearance of his friends, or he would be arrested. Hu's friends were never seen again.

Back in Sydney, Hu was disillusioned and found it hard to put his mind to his studies. He started missing lectures, failing to submit assignments, and started spending more time down around China Town, where he got in with the wrong crowd. Hu walked away from his uni studies toward the dark and dangerous road of the Sydney underworld, the dark side of human nature. He got involved in dealing drugs, protection, and stand over rackets, bashings, and the spiral down this road started to spin out of control.

In early August, the Communist Party in Beijing were informed Hu had dropped out of uni and had not reported where he was staying. Officials from the Chinese Embassy Office in Sydney eventually tracked Hu down, they had orders to bring him back to Beijing. If he was not willing to return voluntarily, they were told to do whatever they needed, even kidnap him, to get him back. However, under no circumstance were they to arouse the interest of the Australian Federal Police, or state law enforcement agencies, as the operation must be done in secret. The two special agents assigned to the task were very experienced in this type of operation, having already returned home to China a number of antagonists of the Party. These two were hard-nosed, brutal agents responsible for the murders of several Chinese citizens who had opposed the Party.

The agents tracked Hu down in China Town, and for two days waited patiently for the opportune time to make their arrest. One Tuesday evening, their chance came on a back lane in China Town. As Hu walked down the lane, he was aware of people scattering out of his way, grabbing their children and rushing inside. Entering a lane, Hu saw a man slouched against the wall twenty metres away, he was also aware someone had entered the lane behind him. The agent straightened off the wall and confronted Hu. He said to him in Mandarin, "You need to go back to Beijing immediately, we will arrange your travel tomorrow. You are under arrest, you must come with us, now."

As one agent spoke, the other moved in close behind him. In a split-second Hu exploded with blinding speed, strength and agility, and used a swinging drop kick to the side of the agent's head. He dropped him cold to the cobblestones, and in the same movement turned a full 180 degrees to face the agent behind him. This other agent reached for and drew his weapon when Hu hit him with a flying drop-kick, which knocked him backwards and caused him to drop his weapon. Quickly regaining his composure, he was now in his martial arts' defensive stance. But this agent had never come up against an opponent as skilled as Hu, and not one who, at that moment, was a cold-blooded assassin. In less than thirty seconds it was all over and the agent lay there dead with a broken neck.

Hu calmly walked over to the other unconscious agent and dispatched him to the afterlife with a broken neck. He left the agents' bodies where they lay as a warning to others. The Chinese Embassy kept everything to itself, and awaited further instructions from China, as they tried to deflect the police investigation away from the two dead agents, whom they claimed were only pen pushes in the embassy workforce, and were out for a good time in China Town. The official line was they were simply in the wrong place at the wrong time. The locals heard and saw nothing; they claimed it must be some of the "bad Aussie boys" who often caused trouble in the area, which was true. The embassy tried to keep tabs on Hu just in case they were ordered to do something, but he disappeared into the Chinese underworld.

The transformation of Hu was just about finished. The killing of the two agents had tipped him over into the Chinese criminal underworld, and to complete the transformation he changed his name to Jimmy Tan.

Soon, the very mention of the name Jimmy Tan struck fear into those living in and around China Town. He banked on this fear to keep the Chinese community from talking to any authority. For fourteen months, Jimmy's standing in the Chinese underworld grew as everyone knew that to cross Jimmy Tan, was to end up with a broken neck. The New South Wales Asian Crime Taskforce had their own man, Fue, working in the restaurants of China Town for two years, and he had been watching the rise of Jimmy and making reports directly to the superintendent in charge of the Asian Crime Taskforce. Fue, reported that Jimmy was planning a large importation of heroin within the next month, but he was having trouble finding out where, and when.

One week later, the superintendent received a visit from a highly ranked Chinese Embassy official, who informed the superintendent of the time, and place of the heroin delivery, and that Jimmy Tan, formerly known as Hu Ming Chan, was the organiser, and owner of the shipment. The superintendent smiled to himself as he was given the information, because it confirmed his suspicions that Jimmy was responsible for the killing of the two agents just fifteen months previously. He also realised that the Chinese were now using him and his taskforce to do what their embassy could not do—get rid of Jimmy Tan.

With a combined force of Australian Federal Police, the Asian Crime Taskforce, and the New South Wales Tactical Support Unit, they surrounded and stormed the small warehouse in China Town, confiscating the heroin, arresting Jimmy and four other Chinese nationals. In June '91, Jimmy Tan was sentenced to seventeen years and sent to Barnaby Maximum Security Prison. On release, he would be deported back to China to face their brutal punishment.

He escaped Barnaby on 25 November 1993.

New South Wale's biggest manhunt began on 26 November 1993.

CHAPTER 6

THE MANNS, HIDDEN VALLEY, AND THE LATHAMS

The highway north to Riverbend ran between a river on one side and a rail line on the other. A blue Toyota Tarago People Mover was cruising at 103 kilometres on the road and slowly gaining on the freight train. The occupants could see the guard's van, and fourteen freight wagons that had not gone out of sight around the bend.

As they rounded the bend, Nick, the oldest of four children, yelled out, "Wow! Look how long this train is."

"It's the biggest train in the world," shouted five-year-old Mitch.

The children were excited and counted every wagon they passed: . . . 34, 35, 36, 37. John and his wife Mary looked at each other and smiled. When Mary smiled, John always said her face sparkled brightly; it was one of the things that attracted him to her. Today was a special and happy day for the Mann family.

"How far do you think it is to Riverbend from here?" asked Mary.

"Maybe 10-15 kilometres," replied John.

"I love you, John," said Mary.

"You better," replied John with a huge smile on his face. "Because I love you with every fibre of my being; you are everything to me."

Ten minutes later they approached the outskirts of Riverbend, with a posted sign that read, "Welcome to Riverbend, Population 9870." This small country town was situated in southern NSW on the western side of the Great Dividing Range. Two highways and two rail lines met at Riverbend, and the accompanying railway freight yards provided the bulk of employment opportunities for the locals.

Riverbend, was a typical country town with five pubs and four churches. The Catholic Church, and the Anglican Church each had a full-time priest. A Uniting Church had a monthly visiting preacher, and the fourth was independent. It was to this small independent church congregation of 87 members, that John Mann accepted a two-day plus Sunday morning preaching appointment for five years, starting February 1991.

The Mann family consisted of John, 39, his wife Mary, 35, four children, Nick, 11, Melita, 9, Katie, 8, and the youngest five-year-old Mitch, along with Tuffy a black and tan 18-month-old male German Shepherd. They pulled up outside the church manse, next door to the church buildings. A welcoming group awaited their arrival; some women had spent the last half hour dusting and cleaning the manse that had stood vacant for six years. The women had stocked the small pantry and refrigerator with all sorts of breakfast cereal, fruit, bread, milk and other staple food lines. One farmer had slaughtered and dressed a lamb, which his wife had packed into freezer bags and placed in the freezer.

This group had prepared a beautiful afternoon tea with hot drinks for the adults, and soft drink for the four children. The friendliness of the welcoming committee overwhelmed John and

Mary. John told the group that the truck bringing their belongings was about one hour away. Most of the welcoming group stayed and helped to unload the truck.

John had been a church minister for the past thirteen years, working in two city churches in Melbourne, and one regional country Victorian church. Some said John went through a faith crisis at the time of his appointment to Riverbend. To a degree John concurred with that assessment, but the crisis was more a shifting from a fundamentalist theology that did not help to answer some big questions and issues he had faced over the years of ministry.

Everything that happened in your life was planned by God, as His perfect will for you. For years John had held this belief that God had a wonderful plan for his life, and that whatever happened, happened because it was in that plan. John found that this fundamental theology could never bear the weight of reason, nor the experiences of other people, and the Scriptures were not as clear as those pushing this view believed. He found that thinking through the theological implications of events in his life, his families, friends, church members and the public, giving glib one-liners answers of fundamentalism just didn't cut it at the grassroots level. The same things happened to both believers and non-believers that were tragic, good, exciting, scary, and heart-rendering regardless of what you did or did not believe. For example, there had been a violent home invasion and rape of a beautiful young lady from one of his church congregations. Not only did the young lady have ongoing psychological problems, but the parents felt a devastating sense of guilt. "If only we'd had better locks, or we'd installed that security system." The day after the attack, the father spent $2900 on new locks on all doors and windows and installing an expensive security system inside and outside the home. Such was his misplaced guilt, he blamed himself: "If only, I had done this before!" he would say to those who enquired about the family.

Twice in three years, John had buried baby girls who both died from the same genetic problems of spinal muscular atrophy where their muscles just wasted away. Both parents carried the recessive genes and passed them on; "autosomal recessive genetic transmission" was the term used to describe the disease. After the death of their second baby, they were told they should not have any more children together.

"What do we do? If we had married different partners, this would never have been a problem. We both want children, so what are we going to do now?" they asked John, as tears rolled down their cheeks. Their hearts were broken.

John knew at this time that the standard fundamental answer of, *"This is all in God's perfect plan for your life, you may not see that now, but sometime in the future you will understand. Remember 'everything works together for good,"* just did not ring true. His mind went back to when, as a 13-year-old, his own father had died after two years of illness. An Anglican priest told him at his father's funeral, "You might not believe this now, but you will come to see that this is the best thing to happen to you. The Scriptures say in Romans 8.28: 'Everything works together for good to those who love God.'"

What? The best thing for a thirteen-year-old boy was to lose his dad. John found it hard to accept, but it took many years to work it through. One thing he was certain about, he could not give this same hollow fundamentalist advice to this couple, whose hearts and lives were shattered. The tears rolled down John's face as he hugged the young couple, joining them in their grief.

Then there was the young Christian couple that John married in the February, only to bury the young twenty-one-year-old husband in May, after cancer caused him to drown in his own body fluids as his lungs filled. Where was God? Was he involved in these events? Was he responsible for the baby's muscular disease and the young husband's cancer? If yes, then who wanted a God who planned for such devastation?

Evil does exist, and can invade anyone's life in a moment, in the twinkling of an eye, John thought. *Believing in God does not shield us from evil. History is littered with evil things and horrible events happening to good people. We all ask the question, why? Maybe the only answer we can honestly give is, 'That's life.'*

John, remembered that Jesus himself said something very similar. In Luke 13:1-5, Jesus was told about some Galileans, whom Pilate had slaughtered while they were offering sacrifices to God. Jesus asked,

> Do you think that those Galileans were worse sinners than all other Galileans because this had thing happened to them? I tell you, no. And remember those eighteen people who died, when that tower in Silo'am fell on them and killed them, were they worse than all other people in Jerusalem? I tell you, no.

They were simply in the wrong place, at the wrong time, that's life. Bad things happen to people, sometimes by accident, sometimes at the hands of other people, sometimes by disease, and sickness. That is life.

At Riverbend, John felt he would have a more normal family life where his wife and children were more of his life and where he was there for them. In the larger churches he felt owned by the church, and there was an implied expectation the minister should be available to the members and community 24-seven.

The first six months living in the church manse proved that the problems and issues were the same in Riverbend, as in any other congregation or denomination. It was just the names and faces that changed.

John, and Mary, decided that they should move out of the manse and purchase their own place. Throughout August, and September '91, they went house hunting in Riverbend. At the beginning of their search, they came to the realisation that in such a small town it would not take long for the public to know where they lived.

Because of this, they decided not to purchase in town, but to look for a small rural farming property out of town.

One Monday, with a freezing southerly wind blowing, they walked into the local Elders Real Estate, located inside Elders Rural Supplies warehouse. Cedric Walters, the licensee, was born in Riverbend sixty-one-years ago during the depression. His hard-working parents had to walk off their farm to find work just to survive. Cedric started working at fourteen with the local Bushes Produce Supply, and twenty-five years later brought the business, and joined the Elders Group, and introduced the first real estate agency to Riverbend.

John and Mary discussed with Cedric what they were after.

"Somewhere nearby, with around 10 to 20 acres and a house. We would love our children to each have a horse. I know John would love to have a couple of cows, and I would love both a vegie and flower garden," said an excited Mary.

"I can show you two properties not far out of town. If you are not doing anything right now, I can take you and show you around both properties, as I have the keys. The owners don't spend much time there these days for various reasons."

"Well, what are we waiting for? Let's go," said John.

After inspecting the two properties, Cedric, realised blind Freddie would know neither place impressed them. On the way back to the office, Cedric tried to point out the good points, and the possible capital growth down the track. But John and Mary thought with no electricity, only tank water, no dams or creeks and fences that were in a bad state of disrepair that they were not a good buy.

Returning to Cedric's office, Mary asked, "Have you got other properties on your books that would meet our requirements?"

"Well, no, I don't. And I don't know of any property with the other real estate agents. But, having said that, there is one place that is far bigger than twenty acres. It is a private sale as it was a large farm that was divided into four. I think there are still one or two portions for sale."

John sat a bit more upright, and said, "What's the asking price?"

"That is a good question. It is up to Josh Latham, the owner. If he takes a dislike to you, he will just say he changed his mind and he will keep it."

"What if he likes you, what are we looking at?" asked John.

Cedric turned towards John and said, "That is why I said it is a good question as it really depends upon old Josh taking a liking to you. He really doesn't need the money; it's more about the buyer fitting in. It is a close-knit little community, and it is a great place to live if Josh likes you."

"Where is it?" asked Mary, "And when can we look at it?"

"It's about twenty-five kilometres north east of Riverbend, up in the ranges on a very good sealed road. It runs right past the valley they named Hidden Valley. Josh and Sally have owned the whole valley for forty-five to fifty years. But ill health, and their age, has forced them to divide and sell as they don't want to live anywhere else but in their valley. And I don't blame them for that, it really is a lovely place to live," said Cedric. "If you want to, I will give him a ring and arrange a time for you to go out there."

"Start dialling. Thursday this week will be good," John replied.

Hidden Valley, was the remains of an enormous volcanic crater. Approximately 80 percent of its walls collapsed thousands, if not millions, of years ago, forming the crater's floor in an S-shape, and sheer rock walls for most of the rim. This S-shape was almost flat with small undulations. Outside the S and on top of the crater ridge, the land was rugged and mostly inaccessible to all but the native animals. The only opening to the valley was through a massive fissure at the southern end of the valley that went clean through the crater wall. It was almost like giant hands held the crater and had broken it apart, as you would a bread roll. Running the entire length of the valley and out through the gap was a beautiful spring fed fresh-water stream that Sally, named the 'Peaceful River.' This fissure was just under 1.5 kms long, and Josh had done a mountain of work using dynamite to clear and build a road through it.

Josh, and Sally, had first laid eyes on this valley in 1942, a couple of months prior to Josh's departure to New Guinea with the 116th AIF to stop the Japanese advance on Australia. With a love of the bush, and a great love for each other, Josh and Sally spent five days together doing what they both enjoyed, trekking through the Australian bush.

During those five days, they walked to the edge of a giant crater and saw a heavily bushed valley with a sparkling stream meandering its entire length. They knew there and then this was the place for them to spend the rest of their lives and raise a family.

Not long after, Sally waved goodbye to Josh as his troop ship left the dock in Sydney bound for Port Moresby. Sally, decided to remain positive and Josh would come back to her once the war was over. The best way she could think of to remain positive was to find out how she could purchase that valley. With the help of her's and Josh's parents, Sally purchased their valley in June 1945, and come 15 August 1945, the war ended with the surrender of Japan.

Josh, came home with malaria and spent just on two months recuperating. After the two months, he secured a job at the freight yards in Riverbend. As soon as his savings allowed, he purchased a 34 Chevy tabletop truck, which he used for carting road base (railway ballast) which he purchased from the rail yard, to build his road into their valley. Next, he carted the timber and building materials he needed to build a hut, that he and Sally could call home. In early April '47, Josh, and Sally, were married and moved into their modest little timber hut in Hidden Valley, and the story began.

From 1947 to '54, they toiled away tirelessly on their farm, turning it into a profitable beef cattle enterprise. During these years they were blessed with the birth of two sons, John, and Robert. But, as fate would have it, John was listed as MIA (missing in action) in Vietnam in '73. Sally refused to accept John was not coming home. Then in '80, Josh, and Sally, again tasted the heartbreaking pain of losing another child, when twenty-nine-year-old Robert, and his young wife were killed in a horror car crash on a trip to Melbourne. Josh, and Sally, retreated to their Hidden Valley with broken hearts. The sparkle, and the drive, especially in Sally, was all but gone. In July '87, with health problems and no more energy for living, they decided to sell Hidden Valley.

Not long after listing their valley for sale, a keen Pitt Street farmer came and started negotiations and sharing his ideas of what he would do with their valley. A dark and deep sense of loss came over them. They had already lost their two boys, and now the other love of their lives, Hidden Valley, would be lost to them forever. And while this uptown Sydney solicitor was sharing his plans, Josh, cut him off and apologised for wasting his time and said,

"No sir, Hidden Valley is not for sale while there is breath in Sally or me."

At sixty-two-years-of-age and with a heart problem, Josh, knew the farm was more than he could handle. And there was no one to leave it to. For this reason, and with Sally's loss of purpose in her life, Josh, knew to lose Hidden Valley would mean the end for Sally. And the thought of living without Sally by his side was something he just could not entertain.

After consultation with their accountant and solicitor, they decided to divide and sell the farm. But to keep the 260 acres (later known as Lot 3 Hidden Valley) surrounding the homestead and enclosing the close memories of days gone by. Agisting portions no longer required for their stock meant they could gain a good passive income. And the buyers of the other lots might appreciate an income in the early years.

CHAPTER 7

THE RESIDENTS OF HIDDEN VALLEY

Retired builders Tom, and Shirley Green, from Legge Street, Lakemba, in Sydney, purchased the 225-acre Lot 2 in mid-January 1988. They built a large, four-bedroom house, with a sleep-out that slept eight to ten. Enough room for visits by their son, daughter, grandchildren, and other family friends. The 225 acres they divided into 15 paddocks with an average of 15 acres each.

Shirley's, hobby was wool spinning, and in 1989, while touring England, by chance they came across an English breeder of Jacob sheep. This breed was claimed to have links back to Abraham's son Jacob, recorded in the Old Testament. These black and white sheep produced excellent spinning wool. Hidden Valley soon became the home of forty Jacob Sheep, thirty seven ewes of five different bloodlines, each bloodline had a different coloured ear-tag, and three rams, again of different bloodlines, all from England.

In Christmas '88, Lot 1, 210 acres were sold to a horse-loving family from Wagga Wagga. Morris Cooper, his wife Anne, along with twin daughters, Lisa and Jenny, and sons, David and Joshua. They moved into their newly built house in September of '89 and became part of the Hidden Valley community. Most weekends would see the whole Cooper clan riding their horses to explore Hidden Valley, often camping out the Friday, and Saturday nights. In February '92, the twins will move to Sydney for university.

The coming of the friendly Coopers, with their four teenage children, helped change the atmosphere of the Valley. The laughing teenagers often went visiting Josh, and Sally, and their visits had a very positive effect on Sally, who found a reason to bake again. Each day she would put on a fresh batch of cookies and scones, in readiness for these loud and full-of-life teenagers. And if they did not turn up, after eating their evening meal, Sally, would make Josh, deliver what she had baked. Josh saw the old sparkle coming back to Sally's voice, and there was a spring in her step.

One afternoon, when the kids came calling, Josh was working on the pressure pump just outside the laundry when suddenly there was a piercing scream, and not long after Sally's laughter could be heard, something Josh had not heard since Robert's death in '80, something he feared he would never hear again. He cried tears of joy.

After composing himself, he investigated the screaming and the laughter. Sally, along with three of the Cooper children, Lisa, David and Joshua, were all having a great belly laugh. However, Jenny, had tears running down her face and kept saying, "It is not funny, you would not want people to laugh at you if it happened to you, would you? Stop laughing, stop it, please?" But as she saw the funny side of the incident, she began laughing too.

"What is all the screaming and laughter about?" Josh asked.

David replied, "Jenny sat on the old lounge on the front porch," and everyone burst out into laughter once more.

"Poor Jenny, she didn't see the big python sleeping on the lounge, and she sat right on it, and it started moving and Jenny screamed. Her drink and scones went flying, and she nearly jumped over the veranda railing from a sitting start. It was the funniest thing that I have ever seen," said Lisa.

"It scared me to death," said Jenny, as she broke out into laughter once more.

Josh told them, "That old snake took up ownership of that lounge about three years ago, and each summer he claims it."

The Lathams, and Greens, became close friends, and Sally started knitting with the yarn Shirley had spun. Late one afternoon as she returned home from the Cooper's house, Sally was excited as she hurried into her kitchen where Josh was reading the paper. "Josh, Josh, I have been learning how to spin wool. Look at what I have spun. Shirley, said I did excellent for the first time. She will teach me everything she knows about wool spinning."

Josh, looked up over his glasses and replied, "That's bloody good news." He had not seen Sally as happy as this for such a long time, and tears started forming in his eyes.

"I'm so happy for you, love, and I will look forward to wearing a jumper made from wool that you spin."

The friendship with the Greens, made Sally, into a new woman, and it was like a rebirth to Josh. Josh never realised it, but their new neighbours stopped him from becoming a tired old man. Josh rented out his farm equipment to those in the Valley for a modest fee, and he trained them in the safe usage of farm machinery. He also became a consultant/teacher in most aspects of farm work.

Lot 4 (115 acres) was approximately half the size of the other three lots and the last to be sold. It was at the far end of the Valley, and adjacent to the quarry where Josh extracted all the road base for roads within the Valley. This lot had seen several prospective buyers, but Josh and Sally would not sell it to just anyone. The buyers would need to fit in with the others in the Valley.

When John, and Mary, turned up that Thursday to look at the land, and then on the following Saturday brought their children, who ran here, there, and every which way excited and laughing, it seemed to Josh and Sally that they belonged here.

"How much are you asking for all this?" asked John.

Josh, became vague and evasive about the price. "Do you want to live here?" he asked. He knew he and Sally wanted them.

"That was not my question. I asked how much you want for it. If we don't know the price, we don't know if we can afford it. So how much are you asking?"

Finally, Josh told them a figure just over $100,000 more than they could afford, even though it was downright cheap, a real steal.

Sadly, John said, "Josh, and Sally, it looks like we have been wasting your time as we cannot raise that amount even though it is the buy of the century."

Josh, looked at them and said, "You still haven't answered my question. Do you want to live here in Hidden Valley?"

"Yes!" Mary blurted out, "it's the loveliest place we have seen, and the kids (who were still running around outside and enjoying themselves) just love it, but we can't afford it."

"Well, what would you say if Sally and I carried what you can't raise as vendor finance, with no interest or repayment for ten years?"

"Why would you want to do that for us?" asked John.

"You fit in, and your children's laughter, noise and presence, is what we always wanted for the Valley; we thought it would be with our own grandchildren, but that can never happen. John and Mary, the Valley needs you and your family."

So, a deal was struck for the Manns to buy Lot 4 of Hidden Valley.

What Josh, and Sally, didn't tell the Manns, was that they had decided to rewrite their wills which said: "Upon the death of Josh, and Sally, or their inability to make their own decisions, we hereby forgive the whole debt of the purchasers of Lots 1, 2 and 4 as long as they are still living in Hidden Valley."

Both, their accountant and solicitor, tried to talk them out of this generous act, but Sally told them straight, "We lost our two boys and the chance to have grandchildren, and we have no family left as both of us are the only child of our parents. So, to whom can we leave anything? What we have written stands as is, and that is the end of it."

In November 1991, Lot 4 became the property of John and Mary Mann. Working 2.5 days with the church gave John, and Mary, the opportunity to start preparations to build their home in Hidden Valley. Josh, gave them all the help he could, even using his farm equipment, and Tom Green, volunteered his building expertise. Morris Cooper, also threw in hours most Saturdays to help their new neighbours build their home. And Sally, kept up the food, scones, cookies and drinks. She insisted that at the end of each day when they did not have to return to the Church manse, the whole family had to come for dinner. In all his life, John, had met no one as good-hearted, helpful and generous as Josh and Sally.

At the party, Shirley Green said, "Look we have a large sleep-out at the back of our place, so, if any of you have visitors and you don't have the room you are welcome to use it, if it's not already being used."

The Manns, claimed one of his four negotiated church-free weekends for their housewarming party on 6 and 7 June 1992. The party was a great success as both Mary's and John's parents attended, as did their respective siblings and families joined with their new friends from Hidden Valley. John, and Mary, took up Shirley's generous offer of housing relatives.

Sally, John's sister, at the party said, "God, is really blessing you two. It's all part of his perfect will for your lives, he must have something special for you to do here."

John, made no verbal response to these statements. He just wondered in his heart, *how can I honestly answer this?* He just smiled and turned the conversation to Shirley's wool spinning, and Sally's knitting.

Over the next twelve months, the small community became very close and supportive of each another. Every second weekend a BBQ, or party, would be held somewhere in the Valley. The Cooper teenagers, taught the Mann kids to horse ride, so too the Green grandchildren. And when the twins were home from uni, they would all go out horse riding, and camping, most Friday evenings, often in a different location in this beautiful Valley.

Nick, John and Mary's eldest, developed a love for camping, and when the Coopers were not going camping, Nick, pleaded with his parents to let him and Tuffy go out alone. John, was keen for Nick to do this, but Mary, was not as sure, but agreed if Nick would go no more than 300 metres from the house. The first night, Mary, spent most of the night peering out the kitchen window into the darkness toward a tree-lined hollow, until the warm glow of the campfire was no longer visible.

CHAPTER 8

WILD DOGS

In February '93, Nick, became more adventurous and wanted to go further away from the house to camp. Mary, was not keen for this, but John, assured her Nick would be all right, provided he stayed on their property, and Tuffy was with him.

One Friday, towards the end of February, Nick, got off the school bus, collected Tuffy, and set off for the northern end of their property where the stream from the national park entered the farming land of Hidden Valley. With Tuffy by his side, Nick felt invincible. Tuffy was a magnificent, fearless, three-year-old German Shepherd who was a 52kg ball of muscle. Selecting a campsite next to the stream near where it entered their property, Nick, looked at the national park's rugged and heavily bushed terrain, and compared it with the green paddocks of the farming land. He decided it would be more exciting in the rugged crumpled walls of the Valley, which was the edge of the national park. This could be the adventure of his and Tuffy's life.

Putting on a small backpack, he said to Tuffy, "Let's go exploring, but don't tell Mum, or Dad."

The duo set out on this great adventure. Tuffy, was excited and as they walked, he was busy smelling all different things, but at no time did he let Nick out of his sight. Nick, followed the stream as far as he could. The going was hard, trying this way and that way over, or around huge rocks, and dense bush. One hundred metres away from their boundary fence, they came across a crystal-clear mountain pool, about 20 metres long and at its widest, maybe eight metres. The pool was alive with water insects. Boatman were on top of the water, frogs they startled jumped into the pool, and Nick saw some tadpoles. As they walked up one side, Nick, noticed a two-metre-long Eastern Brown snake sunning itself on a flat rock. At the same time that Nick, saw the snake, the snake heard Nick and quickly slithered off the rock and disappeared amongst the boulders.

Trekking another 100 metres from the mountain pool, the stream disappeared under a bushy knoll. As they climbed up over the rocks, some bush wallabies bounded off into the scrub. Looking back towards their farm, Nick, realised they had been slowly but surely getting higher. On top of the rocky knoll, he could not see where the stream had gone. *Maybe there was an underground spring, and this was the start of the stream?* Then he heard the unmistakable sound of water falling into a pool. Picking their way through the dense bush, mostly tea tree and black wattle, they came across a small waterfall, dropping about four metres onto rocks, and into a pool. This pool was about half the size of the first mountain pool. As there was no visible outlet, Nick thought the water from this pool was draining out underground into the larger pool.

They were now over 300 metres from their boundary fence, and a good 30 metres higher than the valley floor. Finding a way up the cliff face that the water had fallen over was not easy. They went first to their right, but it was far too steep and dangerous. Going back across the waterfall pool, they pushed through the thick bush for 15 to 20 metres before they came across a well-worn animal track that disappeared behind some very big rocks. The track climb steadily to the top of the cliff. Relocating the stream once more, they came to a massive rock slope some fifty to sixty metres long and rising some four metres to its highest point. Down this slope the stream had spread out to well over twelve metres wide, with its water sparkling in the sun as it cascaded down over ledges and rifts in the rock. It looked fantastic.

Above this rise, there was a flattish, lightly bushed plateau that stretched for 25 metres, with the stream running on its western side. Four small black wallabies heard Nick, and Tuffy, and raced away, startling a mob of grey kangaroos, and within seconds all had disappeared into the dense growth.

At the end of the plateau, the stream came out the mouth of a large cavern that water had gouged out over hundreds of years, especially after heavy rain. The cavern extended back further than the power of Nick's flashlight beam. The cavern was at the bottom of a sheer rock face of some thirty-metres high. Nick, noticed some stick like figures drawn upon the cave's two-metre long wall. Nick was not aware he had discovered some ancient aboriginal rock drawings.

Both he, and Tuffy were having such a good time, Nick, had not realised the afternoon light was fast disappearing. As the sun sank behind the tall trees higher on the rim of the old crater, he decided they had better stay in the cavern for the night. Nick, quickly gathered firewood for light, warmth, and to cook whatever his mum had packed for him.

Mary, had packed him a small fry pan, sausages, and pre-boiled potatoes wrapped in silver foil. As Nick cooked, Tuffy, who had laid down on the other side of the fire, suddenly jumped to his feet, his bristles standing up on his back. A low growl emanated out of his mouth as he moved towards the front of the cave.

"Tuffy, what is it?" asked a nervous Nick, as he peered out into the semidarkness.

As his eyes grew accustomed to the darkening sky, he could see the outlines of five or more dogs, all medium to large size, and they seemed to be creeping slowly, but surely towards the cave. The growl that was now coming out of Tuffy, was something Nick, had never heard before, and a cold shiver ran down his back as he realised the pack of dogs were after them.

Tuffy, positioned himself between the pack and Nick, his body like a coiled spring, ready to explode into action. His growling exposed his huge canine teeth, and that growl made Nick's blood run cold a second time. Nick, became very scared, and he had good reason to be scared for this pack was out to kill. Arming himself with a part of a tree branch he had collected for firewood, he stood behind the fire, shaking with fear. Then out of the corner of his eye he saw the outline of a dog in mid-air coming straight for him, teeth flashing in the firelight. Nick, braced himself for the impact, which did not come. Tuffy, had launched himself and caught the dog in mid-air less than a metre in front of Nick. As they crashed to the ground, Tuffy, had the other dog by the throat, and began savaging him. Two other dogs rushed in at Tuffy, he turned to face this new threat as the first dog got to his feet, and looked to join in the fight against Tuffy. Nick, swung the branch as hard as he could at the dog's head, but the dog moved slightly back, and the branch crashed harmlessly onto the floor of the cavern.

Then, all at once, the attack stopped, and they were gone. Nick, shook with fear, and tears ran down his cheeks. But Tuffy, once again moved forward and to the right with that blood-curdling growl. Nick, strained to see through his tear-filled-eyes into the darkness to where Tuffy was looking. As his eyes cleared of tears, he could just make out the outline of a huge dog on top of a boulder to the right of the cavern entrance. The dog was snarling and baring its teeth, and Nick, shuddered with sheer terror. Leaping off the rock onto the ground, and into the light of the campfire, Nick, saw it was a large white and tan coloured dog, and he thought, *this will not end well*. To his surprise, this new dog did not look at him and Tuffy, but out into the darkness where the pack had run off. The wild dog's growl was as frightening as Tuffy's. The dog stood there howling out into the darkness. Nick, noticed that Tuffy's bristles had settled down and his growl had gone, but his eyes were fixed upon this new intruder. Nick, sensed that somehow there was a connection between these two dogs, and that they were not enemies. The two dogs stood there looking at each other. Then the other dog vanished into the darkness of the bush. Nick, hugged Tuffy, with tears streaming down his face, thanking him for his protection.

At home, Nick, never mentioned following the stream, or the incident with the wild dogs. He thought if he told his parents he had disobeyed them, he might not be allowed to go camping again by himself.

CHAPTER 9

BARNABY MAXIMUM SECURITY PRISON GUARD COMPROMISED

Edgar Clement Putman, became governor of Barnaby Maximum Security Prison in 1986. Governor Putman, saw the good in people, and believed in the rehabilitation of hardened criminals. In the four years as governor, there had been fewer incidents within the prison population. This was accredited to Putman's prisoner management program, which he instigated within the first six months of his ten-year appointment.

Each year in the last week of November, Governor Putman, arranged for an entertainment afternoon and evening for the 300-plus prisoners with three performances. The show comprised a theatrical troupe, a comedian, and a band. Governor Putman, encouraged the prisoners to help make the stage props, and stage scenes, and set up the stage, and change the scenes during the shows.

In February 1991, the fifth year of Governor Putman's appointment, Jimmy Tan, was sent to Barnaby for 15 years. Outside the prison, the public remained fearful of Jimmy Tan and his gang, even though he was in prison, which to Jimmy was just a slight interruption to his plans. Through visitors to the prison, and secret coded letters, he continued to run his gang from within the prison walls. And within a month of arriving at Barnaby, Jimmy, started planning his escape. His first order to his gang was for them to get to any prison Guard that they could compromise. They were tasked to work him into a position where the only way out was death, or to take orders from Jimmy without question.

The second order, Jimmy, gave his gang was that he needed a full set of building plans of Barnaby Prison. They had to work through any contacts within the New South Wales Government, Public Works Department, call in any favours owed, or do whatever was necessary to get those plans. The third order, after getting the plans, was to eliminate the person, or persons involved.

Ron Alder, was a prison guard for six years, and before that a member of the Australian Federal Police for five years. He had spent most of his time working in Australian embassies in southeast Asia, he grew to love the people, their customs, and their food. Ron had recently gone through a very bitter divorce and custody case. Trying to recover from the effects of his wife walking out on him, and her winning sole custody of their two children, he took two weeks' annual leave from Barnaby. Driving to Sydney, he headed for China Town to find some solace from the grief of his shattered family life.

He spent most of his two weeks in and around China Town in Sydney, gambling and losing, and making out with Asian women. During his time there, some of Jimmy's men noticed him and sent to him a Chinese beauty, Rosie, to draw him deeper into the sordid side of China Town. Ron, was quickly and easily lead into a web where he got heavily into debt. For the next four days, Ron thought he was in heaven, with a beautiful woman by his side, and an increasing acceptance at illegal gaming houses, with easy access to finance.

When the time came for Ron, to go back to his home in Riverbend, Rosie, pleaded with him to come back as soon as possible. Ron, could hardly believe his luck; a beautiful Asian woman was pleading for him to come back. The sex he had with Rosie, was not like anything he had ever experienced before in his life. Working a ten-day roster, with an extra forty-five minutes each day, meant that at the end of each roster he had five straight days off. This allowed him to spend four days every two weeks, apart from travelling time, with Rosie. He was so infatuated with Rosie, he was blinded to the fact he was being worked over and dragged into a situation where there was only two ways out.

After six months of gambling, he was heavily in debt, and unable to pay his way out. He was confronted by two rough looking Asian men, who spelled out in no uncertain words that their boss wanted his money, as soon as possible. Returning to Rosie's flat, he found the door kicked in and Rosie, looking like she had been ten-rounds with Mohamed Ali. Little did he know, that the injuries to Rosie were the results mainly of good make-up, apart from a real black eye and split lip, that Rosie agreed to and was paid for.

"Ron, you must pay," said Rosie. "These men they will hurt you and me, if you don't, I am very frightened, you must pay them."

"But I haven't got that type of money. My wife took me to the cleaners eight months ago. I don't have the money." He cried, and tears rolled down his cheeks. "Let's just go away; come back to my place, they will never find us there."

"No, we can't do that. They will hurt my old mother, my sister, and brother. No, we must pay them what they want."

"Let's just go to the police," said Ron.

"Oh, no police, they would kill my family. Don't go to the police, they can't help us," sobbed Rosie.

"Maybe I can talk to them and work something out," said a scared Ron.

"Yes, we talk to them, I no want them to hurt my family."

"Could your family help us out, do they have any money?" asked Ron.

"No, they are like peasants, they don't got much money, no money. Oh, what will we do?"

"Rosie, you said we could talk to them. Who, are they? Where are they?"

"We must see Mr Yong, he is very powerful man in China Town," said Rosie.

Mr Yong, was Jimmy's right-hand man, the one who had been playing Ron and drawing him into a web with no way out.

Rosie, took Ron to see Mr Yong who said, "Ah, Mr Ron, you owe me a lot of money, and I heard you can no pay, not good!"

"You will get your money, just don't hurt Rosie or her family, and I will find a way of paying you back."

"You have one month. You make sure you pay me. If you don't . . ." Yong drew his finger across his throat.

"You, will get your money, just don't hurt anyone," spat out Ron.

"I will see you one month from today, with my money and I will hurt no-one."

A very desperate Ron returned to work trying to figure out where he would come up with $26,000 in one month. A month later, Ron returned to see Yong, but with only $11,450.

"Mr Yong, I only have $11,450. You must give me more time to get the rest."

"I will give you two more weeks only, for your health, after that you must have my money."

Ron, went with Rosie, back to her flat and talked to her about how he could raise the money. The next morning Rosie's phone rang. She answered it and was soon in tears and screaming, "Where is he?" she asked the caller. "Prince Alfred Hospital? Is he going to die?" she asked.

Ron was by her side as she hung up the phone. "What is it? What's wrong?"

"My brother is in hospital, I must go to him."

"I will come as well," said Ron.

Arriving at Prince Alfred Hospital, they made their way to the third floor, ward 6b.

They entered the ward, and Rosie screamed as she saw a young Asian man, one of Jimmy's gang with one leg in traction, his head bandaged, and one arm in plaster all from injuries he sustained in a motorbike accident. Rosie, and the young man talked in Chinese and after a couple of minutes Rosie, turned and said to Ron, "Mr Yong's men did this because you did not pay all the money. I told you they will hurt my family."

"But he said he wouldn't hurt anyone," replied Ron, with a scared look upon his face. "I will go back and see him. Rosie, I will make this right, you will see. I will do whatever it takes to make it right."

"So, Mr Ron, you will do anything, what you mean by that?" asked Yong, when Ron turned up to see him.

"Anything you want me to do, I will do it, just don't hurt Rosie, or her family anymore."

"OK, you come here tomorrow, and we will get something for you to do. But, Mr Ron, you no let me down, you make sure you will do anything."

The next day, Ron, turned up with Rosie to see Mr Yong. "Well, here I am. What do you want me to do?"

"You work at prison, don't you?"

"Yes, Barnaby Maximum Security Prison, why?"

"We have a good friend there, and he needs some things given to him."

"What, you want me to smuggle things into a prisoner? That's not on. I won't do that for you or anyone."

"But you said you would do anything."

"Anything but that. If I get caught, I will lose my job and end up in prison myself. No way am I risking that." Said a defiant Ron.

"You saying, you won't do that?" asked Yong.

"That's right, I will do anything but that."

At that moment, Yong, nodded to one of his men who moved quickly to Rosie, grabbed her by her hair and dragged her away, Rosie, acted accordingly and screamed, "Help me, Ron, don't let him hurt me."

A very frightened Ron swung around looking straight at Yong. "Fuck you, you prick, OK, I will do it, just don't hurt Rosie. Let her go."

Rosie was being dragged towards the door, screaming.

Yong said to Ron, "You don't do what you say you will, I will kill her, and all her family."

Ron nodded, and Yong's man let Rosie go.

Getting to her feet, she ran back to Ron and hugged him. "Please, don't let them hurt me or my family. Please, please do what they say."

"Yes, I will do anything, Rosie, I am so sorry," said a crying Ron.

After a couple of minutes, Ron looked again at Yong and said, "OK, I will do what you want, but you must tell me what I am smuggling into the prison."

"No! Mr Ron, you don't need to know, you no asked question, you no look, you just deliver parcels."

"OK," said a defeated Ron.

Come Christmas of '91, Yong, informed Ron that his debt had finally been paid. To keep Ron as their go-between, Yong, told Ron he was now on Jimmy's payroll and would receive $2000 per month. For five months, Ron passed written Chinese messages to and from Jimmy. Among the items smuggled into Jimmy, were cartons of cigarettes, which Jimmy used to gain information and co-operation from other prisoners.

In May of '92, Jimmy heard his gang had the full set of prison building plans, which was to cost $10,000, and the employee who provided the plans had been reported missing to the police. His body was later found in a creek that ran into the Parramatta River at Homebush.

The plans were rolled up and placed into a cardboard cylinder nearly a metre long. This posed a problem for Ron, as there was no way that he could get them into the prison by hand. Yong, told him there was an extra $2000 for him if he could. Ron, decided that as head of the prison workshop he could get the cylinder into the prison in a delivery of timber from Riverbend, as he did the ordering each month, and he was in pretty well with the timber truck delivery driver, Gary, who also liked to bet on the ponies.

Eight days before May's timber delivery, Ron approached Gary at a pub in Riverbend, "Hi mate, how is it going?"

"Not bad, not bad at all. Last Saturday I won $85 on the ponies, which was not bad for 10 minutes of work. How's your betting going?"

"You know, win a bit here, lose a little there. But over-all since Christmas, I am up over $6,000."

"Shit, $6,000, you are having me on, aren't you?"

"No, look, I will show you my racing bank book (a bank account Ron set up to put some of his monthly payment from Jimmy). See, the balance is $6,279.00."

"Fuck me," said Gary. "I wish I had your luck. I could sure do with some extra cash as my girlfriend will have a kid in six weeks."

"That is great news, congratulations," said Ron.

"Yeah, it will be good, but we will really miss Carly's weekly pay until she gets back to work."

"I'm sure you will get through. You never know when some opportunity will pop up. You just have to be ready to grab it with both hands."

"Yeah, yeah, I have heard all that before, but nothing ever pops up. Maybe you could give me some of your tips for next Saturday."

"I haven't looked at them yet," replied Ron.

Eight days later, Gary delivered the May order, unloaded his truck and said to Ron, "Well, Ron old chap, everything has been unloaded, so I'm off, see ya next month." Gary got in his truck and drove out through the two checkpoints.

Five days before the June delivery of timber, Ron, made a point of running into Gary at a pub in Riverbend. "Hey, you still interesting in earning some extra cash? I know how you can make $500, real easy."

"How? Who do I have to kill?" asked Gary.

"No, you don't have to do anything like that, all you need to do is bury this paper cylinder in the middle of our next timber delivery, and don't tamper with it."

"What, take that into the prison?"

"Yeah, it is just a metre-long paper cylinder."

"What's in it, drugs?" enquires Gary.

"No, you know the guard everyone calls old Tom? It is his sixtieth birthday and in the cylinder are blown up photos of when he was a youngster—you know the one's mothers take of their young children running around nude. Also, his wife Judy, has given some other photos and papers, that will cause old Tom, and a couple of other guards, to cop heaps from their fellow guards."

The only part of what Ron told Gary, that wasn't true, was the contents of the cylinder.

"Why don't you just take it in yourself?" asked Gary.

"Everything we carry into the prison is inspected, and there are some that work in that security, and bag search who, between you and me, have too big a mouth and would let it out. So us guards putting on this party want it to remain secret to the last minute. We have all chipped in, and we will give you $500 to do it."

"Gee, I will do it for nothing," said Gary.

"That's what I thought you would say, but your baby is due soon, and Carly won't be working, so this $500 will help, just take it," Ron hands him the money.

The timber parcel was delivered. Ron extracted the cylinder from the middle of the timber and hid it in the electrical parts storeroom adjacent to the wood working block. Ron, arranged for Jimmy to be given the job of stock taking and make an exact inventory list of electrical spare parts. Over the next couple of weeks, Jimmy's trained architectural eye poured over the plans, hoping to find a way out. Unknown to Jimmy, the plans for the front of the prison, the visitor and staff carparks and access roads into and out the prison area were altered after concerns from the inhabitants of Barnaby. They said that the noise of buses and staff vehicles, especially on the change of shifts at 8.30pm and 4.30am, would be disruptive to residents. The residents suggested a different route which was accepted, but the amended plans were overlooked when they were stolen.

Jimmy's, first thoughts were to go down through the drainage system, but as he studied the plans, he realised that would not work. The prison had been built with a water conservation policy, where all the used water, drainage and sewage went through the prison water filtration plant built on five hectares on the northern perimeter of the prison. The whole area was chain wired with razor wire on top. The plant was in operation 24-seven and was constantly under video surveillance, and the floodlights made the night brighter than the day. Another option had to be found.

Looking again at the plans, Jimmy believed he found a blind spot on the western perimeter wall, near where delivery trucks entered the prison. This area was completely fenced off to inmates. In the area between wall towers five and six, Jimmy believed that there was a four-metre spot in the outside wall, that could not be seen from tower five or tower six. This was the only weakness that Jimmy could find in the prison security, but how to make use of it and how to gain access to this area was the problem—a problem Jimmy was intent on solving. Having no more need for the plans, Jimmy stuffed them into the burnable rubbish skip from the wood working block. Burned into his brain was this blind spot, his hope of escape.

Making discrete enquiries, Jimmy found out that the only time prisoners were able to move freely in this area, was on the day of the yearly November show. But only prisoners with a special "trust standing" were allowed access, as it was the easiest and most direct way for moving screens, and stage props, to the hall from the wood working block, where all screens and stage props were made and stored.

Jimmy, also learned that these trust standing prisoners had limited supervision whilst in this area. Les Murphy, a prisoner who worked out in the prison gym with Jimmy, was one such prisoner. Jimmy decided to further the friendship with Les. In November '92, Jimmy became part of the team that set up the stage and changed the scenes during the play, but he hadn't gained a trust standing status. After working on the different sets and scenes for the show, Jimmy's creativity was noticed, and he was asked to take control of the November '93 Show. Jimmy, talked to those in charge, he outlined a proposal where he would design a system of interchangeable and interlocking frames, made with tubular steel that could be used every year. You only had to cover the frames with fabric and paint your scenes on them, thus saving heaps of money and time each year. Edgar C. Putman, took a keen interest in Jimmy's design system of interchangeable frames, but what they all missed, was that with the right combinations, the frames would make a strong ladder that could be used to scale the prison wall and anchor the rope going down the outside of the wall.

Jimmy's proposal was accepted, and the show was scheduled for the last week of November '93. This was his escape date, but he had to gain that all important trust standing. This gave him a little less than 12 months to plan his escape from the escape-proof prison. In Jimmy's estimation, he would need four other prisoners to join him. Les Murphy had kept himself fit, often working out with Jimmy;

he had always spoken the truth, kept his word, and would not let anyone stand over him. Les, was Jimmy's number one choice.

Others Jimmy thought about were, Bob Walker, and Bull Maloney—Bob only because he already had a trust standing rating, even though personally Jimmy had no time for him. He chose Bull for his resourcefulness, and his contacts through the OMG. Once outside, the bikie world could easily hide them and move them around, which would be a great advantage to help them stay free. That Bull, was already a regular trainer in the gym, and often spoke with Jimmy, and Les, meant that any growing association between the three would not draw much attention from the guards. There was one spot open and Jimmy had not decided who that should be, so he left it open for now.

One afternoon, in a casual conversation with Les, Jimmy said, "Les, I'm planning on breaking out of this place, and I would like you to come with me."

Surprised, Les replied, "No thanks, I made one mistake that got me in here. All I want to do is serve my time and get back to my family. But thanks for the offer, at the most I could be out of here in a little over seven years. Maybe sooner with good behaviour, in fact it could be in less than four years."

"That is still a long time. And anything could happen to you or your family."

"No, I have learnt my lesson, and I will serve my time. And I do not want to know anything about your escape that will penalise me anymore."

This wasn't the response Jimmy had hoped for, and so he turned his attention to Bob Walker, a man for whom he had no respect. So, a strange association began between the two. Bob was keen. He wanted to get out and settle a score with Dr Burman, whom he blamed for his incarceration. And there was no future in just serving out his time, because, when he was released in 2008, he would be deported to England to stand trial for another murder committed in 1977.

In the meantime, Jimmy approached Bull, to sound him out. "Aye, Bull, can I talk with you?"

Jimmy was surprised and scared when Bull replied, "You are planning to break-out, and you want my help."

Jimmy, was knocked for six with Bull's reply, and all he could say was, "Who said that?" His mind raced as the only two he had spoken to were Les, and Bob. "Who told you that?" asked Jimmy, trying not to look too bewildered and scared.

"No one," said Bull. "It's just that I noticed you taking an interest in and talking to that prick Walker, so I figured he must have something you want, or he knows something you need to know, something important to you. And some shit has happened between you and Les Murphy, as you aren't as friendly as you were before you took an interest in Walker. What did Les say, or do, that has caused this shift?" Jimmy was still trying to collect his thoughts when Bull said, "I'm right, aren't I? You are planning to escape. If you want my help, you can have it provided that I go as well."

Without answering Bull, Jimmy, turned and walked away looking for Bob. Finding Bob, he confronted him, "Did you fucking well talk about my escape? Did you run off at the mouth? Who have you told?"

When Bob looked into Jimmy's eyes, he knew this was not a man to jerk around. He saw death in those cold brown eyes and a shiver ran down his spine. "No, I haven't said any fucking thing. Shit, I wouldn't do that, you got to believe me."

By the tone of his voice, and stark fear in his eyes, Jimmy knew that Bob had not talked. Jimmy never entertained the thought Les had spoken to anyone about his planned escape. He had known Les for a year, and he was as straight as a gun barrel.

Two days later, while in the gym, Jimmy walked over to Bull and said, "Yes I am, and yes I want you to come."

"Great, you can count on me," said Bull.

Over the next couple of weeks, Jimmy shared with Bull, the blind spot he had found between wall towers five and six, and that the only time each year that prisoners were allowed to be in the area was Show Day, in the last week of November.

"Well," said Bull "that information you have isn't exactly true, I go into that area once a bloody month mowing the fucking lawns, shrub trimming and clean-up detail. Two hours once a month with five prisoners and two screws."

On his next clean-up detail in the restricted area, Bull confirmed that there was a blind spot of about ten feet. "How in the fuck did you know that?" asked Bull.

All Jimmy said was, "I have my sources," and left it there.

Jimmy, talked to Bob Walker about the trust standing name tags, and Bob, told him that the tags were red with a photo ID. And that there was no way of getting any as internal security controlled them. Each person signed their own tag out, and it must be signed back in, so there was no way of getting any to make copies of.

Jimmy, approached Ron Alder, and asked how he could get some blank trust standing tags. Ron, shook his head and said that there was no way.

"What if I said you would get paid $500 for each blank tag you get? I would want maybe five tags, so that could be up to $2,500," said Jimmy.

"Shit," said Ron, "I could sure use the money, but believe me I can't get them, I am not in internal security. I can only go as far as the fucking front desk, and to do that I have to have a bloody good reason to be there. Only internal security guys can get those tags."

Jimmy, wondered how he could overcome this latest setback, and he still needed at least two more people in his escape plans. Using the contraband that Ron smuggled in for him. Jimmy, let it be known two free cartons of smokes were being offered for the name of any prisoner who had a paid screw in internal security.

Three days later, a prisoner gave him the name of the Bettini Twins. "When do I get my smokes?" asked the informant.

"As soon as I can confirm your information, but I am good for it," said Jimmy.

Of the Bettini twins, Jimmy, considered the one with the brains whom you could deal with fairly, was Angelo, but his twin Vince, was a bit of a loose cannon with a cruel, sadistic streak in him.

Out in the exercise area the next day, Jimmy, approached the twins. "Ah, Angelo Bettini, can I have a word with you?"

Angelo, pretended he didn't know who was talking to him; he slowly looked Jimmy up and down, and wondered why he was now talking to him, as they hadn't spoken a word to each other since Jimmy arrived at Barnaby.

"Why should I talk to you?" replied Angelo.

"Yeah, slopehead, why should we talk to you?" interjected a hostile Vince.

Jimmy, glared at Vince, and something in Jimmy's eyes caused Vince to look away.

Angelo said, "Come on, boys, no fighting." Turning to face Jimmy, he asked, "What's your name?"

This put Jimmy off a bit, as he thought everyone in Barnaby knew who he was, ever since he had to defend himself against two very big prisoners, who didn't like Jimmy running a black market in smokes and other contraband. They wanted a 50 percent share for letting him operate. They confronted Jimmy, as he was about to go into the showers. Ox, the larger of the two who was just all muscle, grabbed Jimmy and threw him against the shower wall, and pinned him there with a giant forearm across his chest.

Kelly, the so-called-brains of this dumb and dumber pair, told Jimmy plainly, "If you, you little Chinese shit, sell anything, or trade anything in this prison. you pay me 50 percent. If you don't, we will cut your fucking balls off and stuff them down your throat. You understand, you little prick?"

Feeling trapped, Jimmy nodded, and Ox removed his arm from Jimmy's chest and stood towering over him.

"I have to pay you 50 percent of what I get," repeated Jimmy as he moved to his right and away from the wall.

"That's it, prick," replied Kelly, "if you don't, and we find out about it, you're one dead Asian. You got that now, arsehole?"

Jimmy, was now away from the wall and standing slightly crouched five feet directly in front of Ox, "I will tell you this, you will get fuck-all from me, and if you ever lay your greasy, dirty, hands on me again, I will kill you."

Kelly, and Ox, look at each other, lost for words. Apart from Bull, they were the most feared prisoners in Barnaby, and no-one had ever spoken to them like this.

Kelly, looked at Jimmy and said, "You are a fucking idiot."

At the same time, Ox, moved towards Jimmy, with a deadly grin upon his face. But before he had moved two feet, Jimmy, exploded like a jack-in-a-box, hitting him with a powerful right foot kick to the left side of his head. Ox, reeled to his right as his legs buckled and then collapsed under him, and he was out cold before he hit the floor.

Kelly, moved to his right to get out of the way of the sprawling Ox, and Jimmy, having composed himself, stepped and then leapt towards Kelly, smashing his right elbow into Kelly's face. As he staggered back, Jimmy, hit him with a flying dropkick right in the chest. Kelly, lurched back and fell over the unconscious Ox, hitting his head hard on the concrete floor.

Jimmy, moved over to him, bent down and repeated his warning. "If you, or your mate ever lay a hand on me again, I will kill you. You got that, arsehole?"

Kelly, nodded and lay there as Jimmy went for his shower. Word of Jimmy beating both Kelly and Ox, circulated rapidly among the prisoners, and within 24 hours everyone knew about Jimmy Tan. *So how come Angelo doesn't know who I am?*

"My name is Jimmy Tan, and I have a proposition for you."

"You have a proposition for us? OK, spill it," said Angelo.

"I heard you have a screw on your payroll from internal security. I need to get something from him."

"Now, just say your information is true, what's in it for us?" Asked Angelo.

"I can get money paid into any account you like on the outside or given to anyone you name. I will pay $5000 for what I want," said Jimmy.

"What is it you want?" asked Angelo.

"I need to get five blank trust standing tags."

"What do you want them for? These won't be easy to get. What are you planning?"

"Tell me, can you get them, or are you just jerking me around?"

"I can get them, but I won't unless you tell me what you're got planned."

"You can guarantee delivery?"

"Sure, but I have to know what you want them for."

"I am planning on breaking out of here."

"What makes you think you can do that?" asked Angelo.

As they talked, the hooter went for lunch, so they walked off towards the meal-room. Because there were too many other prisoners within earshot, Jimmy said, "I will get back to you."

The next day Angelo said, "Well, this is what those little cards will cost you. You can stick your $5000 up your arse, I don't need your money. But Vince and I must be in the escape team."

Feeling that he must accept Angelo's offer, Jimmy agreed and said, "Well, it all depends on you getting the five tags; no tags and the deals off."

"And you, you little prick, you betray us, and I will cut your fucking heart out," said Vince.

Jimmy, looked straight into Vince's eyes until Vince looked away. Jimmy thought, *Yes, one day I will have to kill you.*

Three days later, Angelo caught up with Jimmy and showed him six blank-trust- standing-tags.

Jimmy, could hardly believe his eyes, "Aye, that was quick, but how come there are six cards?"

"Apparently, they are packed in packs of six, something about security and not having loose cards lying around. But that shouldn't be a problem, should it? And we are included, right?" Jimmy, kept his word and gave the prisoner who put him onto Angelo, his two cartons of cigarettes.

It's early June of '93, and Jimmy felt things were getting out of hand, and he was losing a bit of control. He thought Angelo would be a good asset on the team on the outside, but Vince was a loaded gun ready to go off at any time, especially if Angelo wasn't present. But those tags were essential, so Jimmy answered, "Yes, you two are included."

In July '93, Jimmy arranged for Ron Alder's home to be robbed of all his electrical entertainment gear, and anything that could connect him with Rosie, Yong, or Jimmy himself. After the robbery, Ron knew that he couldn't bring the police in to investigate the robbery, as he could not explain how he purchased everything on his prison guard wages, as he was sure his betting books would show that he had won a bit of money, but not enough to pay cash for all that was stolen. Since being on Jimmy's payroll, Ron had deposited just under $40,000 in cash into his bank account.

After the robbery, Jimmy made a point of talking to Ron. During the conversation, he asked Ron how things were going, and how Rosie was.

"She is a bit upset," replied Ron. "My place was robbed about a week ago and they cleaned out, my music system, four TVs, and everything electrical. It was worth over $30,000. I'm really pissed off. If I ever get my hands on the pricks that cleaned me out, I will kill the bastards."

"What about the cops? You had it insured, didn't you?"

"No police, I couldn't explain how I paid cash for them, you know, how do I tell them I got the money off you? No, I will just have to start over again."

"Would you like to earn $3,000 in one go?"

"Sure, but what do I have to do?"

"This is very easy for you, I think. You can use the photo ID machine here, the one that produces all photo IDs?"

"Of course, I can."

Just then another guard strolled over. "Aye, what are you two talking about?"

"I've just been asking Jimmy a bit about China. I am thinking of saving and going over there for a look. To go and walk on that Great Wall of China. Jimmy here has walked upon it."

"Is that so, Jimmy?" asked the new guard.

"Yes, many times. But I have to go now, maybe we can talk again, it is good to, how do you say, refresh my memory," said Jimmy as he wandered off.

CHAPTER 10

LES JOINS THE ESCAPE TEAM, RON ALDER'S LAST ACTIONS

Young Morgan turned six years of age in June, and on Gail's, June visit she arranged with Governor Putman for a room to be set aside so that Les, and Gail, could have a small party for Morgan. Les, was thrilled and so excited with the visit and party.

Come July, four days before visitation day, Les, received a phone call from Gail. "Les, it's me Gail, look I won't be able to visit you this month, sorry."

"Why, why can't you?" inquired Les.

"Well, I have a doctor's appointment on the same day."

"Hell, can't you change the appointment? You only get one day a month to visit me, couldn't you have arranged it better?" Replies an agitated Les.

"Les, honey, it was our local doctor, Dr Brown, who arranged the appointment with a specialist. It's the only day he can fit me in."

"A specialist? What type of specialist? What's wrong with you?"

"Honey, I have a lump in my right breast, and Dr Brown thought I should see a specialist as soon as possible, especially with my mom dying with breast cancer. But don't worry, Dr Brown, is just being careful."

"Bloody hell, I don't like the sound of this, let me know after you see the specialist."

After her visit to the specialist Gail, rang Les, "Les, the specialist looked at the results of the mammogram and ultrasound. He said that the lump doesn't look good, and it is most likely cancerous."

"Shit," interrupted Les. "What is he gonna do?"

"I am having a biopsy next Tuesday, and if needed, I will have an operation straight away. But don't worry, the specialist said he should be able to cut it all out as we found it early. And later he will start me on a course of chemotherapy, and that should clear me of cancer." Gail, was struggling to hold back her tears, and afraid to let her fears be known. "Don't worry, Les, I will be all right, I am in good hands. Dr Brown, said this specialist is one of the best in Australia."

"What about Morgan? Who will look after him?"

"Your sister Jane, and her husband Rodney, have volunteered to look after him. Morgan, will love being with his cousin Ben, as Ben is only seven, a year older than Morgan."

Gail, missed the August visitation day because of the side effects of the chemo. Les, worried about Gail, and the thought that like her mother, she might not survive, scared him. Just the thought he might lose the love of his life terrified him. As a result, he joined Jimmy's breakout team.

Jimmy, rightly pointed out to Les, that if they pulled this off and escape, the police would have Gail under surveillance, and the chances of him getting to see Gail were very slim. But Les was not listening, and because of their friendship Jimmy agreed that Les could come.

While working in the woodworking block, Ron approached Jimmy, who asked why Rosie had given him an envelope containing $3000 in cash.

"Remember the blank trust standing tags I wanted?"

"Yes, and I told you I can't get them," said Ron.

Jimmy, reached into his pocket and pulled out six blank tags and replied, "Yes I know that, I already have them, all I want you to do is to put these guys photos on them." He handed Ron a list of six names: Jimmy, Les, Bull, Bob, Angelo and Vince. "Just get these guys on these tags and that three thousand is yours."

The following Monday, in the woodworking block, Ron handed Jimmy the six completed tags.

"Thanks, Ron, I won't forget it."

Ten days later, the second week of August, Governor Edgar C. Putman posted on the prison noticeboard in the woodworking block a notice about the death of Ron Alder, in a single vehicle accident while he was driving back from Sydney. The police had put the cause of the accident down to speed, and drink driving. As Jimmy read the notice, a knowing smile crossed his face.

Jimmy, had been as cunning as the foxes and wild dogs that had been coming in increasing numbers to Hidden Valley. And John Mann's skills with his rifle and skinning knife were being honed as well. The foxes all had their winter coats and good pelts could bring in just on $100 each.

The date of the '93 November Show was set down as Thursday 25 November. With this date fast approaching, Jimmy, revealed to the other five how it would all unfold. All six were now part of the stage-hand-crew for the show.

When the day arrived, Jimmy, Les, and Bob all had trust standing tags legitimately and worked the first two shows, timing trips back to the woodworking block through the fenced off delivery truck entrance. Jimmy set the time to go over the wall on the third of the five-stage scenes changes; this was when the two sections that formed the ladder were all together, and on their way back to the woodworking block. The only loose end to tie up was that the four with legitimate trust tags who had signed them out, would need to surrender them, and sign the return book earlier, so that there were no extra tags to alert the guards that something was wrong. They did this after they helped set up the stage for scene two. Jimmy, handed out the counterfeit tags to the other five escapees that would get them into the escape area.

With the co-operation of four other trust standing prisoners, whose families would receive an envelope containing $5,000 each after the escape, Jimmy was assured that the ladder would be taken back to the woodworking block so it would not arouse the guard's suspicion.

The six would have 6.5 minutes to get up and over the wall around eight-ten p.m. The guards normally did their nightly cell count at eight o'clock, but tonight it would be ten o'clock in the escapees wing. If the dummies in the beds fooled the guards, they would not be discovered missing till six o'clock muster the next morning.

Jimmy, had also arranged for two four-wheeled drive vehicles with dark-tinted windows to be ready on a dirt road off the Crims's Highway one kilometre from the prison.

CHAPTER 11

THE WILD DOG ATTACK

Not long after moving to Hidden Valley, John, borrowed Josh's 303 rifle to do a bit of fox hunting, but the slow projectile speed of the 303 made hitting what he aimed at near impossible. However, he did scare a number of foxes. Later, he borrowed Morris Cooper's standard 22 rifle, and got his fair share of rabbits, but just couldn't get the range on a fox seventy-five metres or more away.

One Sunday, after the church service, John, was speaking to a group of male members, telling them how he really liked going out hunting foxes, but how he was frustrated with the limitations of both the 303, and 22.

Charlie Price, a retired farmer and a member of John's congregation, told him about his 22-250 five shot Winchester. He explained how the 22-250 projectile speed was far greater than the standard 22, and the old 303, and with the greater speed the projectile travelled flatter and true. Once you sighted in the scope for a set distance, it only took a slight adjustment up or down, for distances closer or further away. Charlie, said he had no more use for the rifle and that John could have it for a month's trial, and if happy with it he could purchase it for $200 including the scope.

Before the month was up, John gave Charlie the $200. He had sighted the scope for 200 metres, and this enabled him to hit a fox in the head up to 200 metres away. In the early stages, Josh, took John out spotlighting using his old one-ton flat top. So impressed was Josh about John's shooting, he openly said John was one of the best bush shots he had seen. Josh, also taught John how to skin a fox, and then to dry the pelt.

The coming of Tom and Shirley Green's flock of Jacob Sheep, to Hidden Valley saw the number of foxes in the valley increase, and this suited John and his hunting. And all those living in the Valley gave John permission to shoot on their property.

November '93 was a traumatic time for Tom and Shirley, especially Thursday 11 when out on their usual early morning drive around their property, in their old paddock bashing ute. They headed for the large paddock, joining the national park on the western side of the valley. This paddock held one hundred and twenty-seven, two tooth ewes, and wethers—the result of four years of careful breeding, culling and selecting from their prized Jacob Sheep. As they crested a rise, their eyes beheld a scene of utter carnage, which made Shirley scream. As they entered the paddock, they counted forty-three dead sheep, all ripped to pieces. As they continued to drive, they came across twenty-six that would have to be destroyed because of their injuries. Another twenty-four would need vet treatment for their wounds, and only thirty-four were lucky to escape unscathed from this terrible attack.

Within half an hour, Josh, Sally, John and Mary, had responded to Shirley's distressed phone calls. Mary, and Sally, stayed by Shirley's side, supporting and consoling her; all three were in tears. Josh, Tom, and John put the twenty-six out of their misery, and Josh, walked around looking for signs on the ground as to what had happened.

"Dogs, wild bloody dogs, that's what done this," said Josh. "They live in the national park, and the rangers and authorities do bloody nothing about them, they even deny their existence."

"How many do you think were involved?" asked John.

"Five maybe six, but there was one bloody big bastard going by the paw prints on the ground," replied Josh.

"Josh, what did you just say?" said Shirley, "Only five, maybe six? It looks more like bloody twenty."

"No, Shirl! Five or six, would do this much damage easily."

Tom, went to Shirley, and wrapped his arms around her saying, "I'm so sorry about this, love, I'm so sorry for your pain and distress, but we will get over it, we will get over it with the help of our friends here in the Valley."

Josh, and John, continued to look around.

"There's something funny happened here," said Josh. "Something, or someone has run them off, or called the dogs off. Usually, once they get into the pack-attack frenzy, they do not stop until they cannot run anymore. No, something has interrupted their attack, what, or who I don't know, but Tom and Shirley can thank their lucky stars that they intervened as they still have about half of their flock alive."

"Has this ever happened before?" asked John.

"No, not in the Valley," replied Josh, "but until the Greens came there had never been sheep here. I'm not putting blame on Tom and Shirley. The dogs have been seen before, but cattle are a bit big for dogs and they will fight back as well."

The residents of Hidden Valley rallied to support Shirley, and Tom Green, after the dog attack. Josh, warned them that the dog pack would return and that the residents should do regular patrols.

Josh said, "I will contact the national park and see if they will do some dog baiting in the area."

However, the National Parks and Wildlife rangers refused to accept that there were wild dogs hiding in The National Park.

Sarcastically, Josh said, "Should we start a dog tree, like the one up around Eucumbene? You guys are burying your heads in the sand, if you think there are no wild dogs operating out of National Parks."

"OK, we will send a ranger over in the near future," said the ranger to pacify Josh.

Josh, told the others that, in the near future, to National Parks meant sometime in the future, but not the near future.

The residents commenced a spotlighting patrol twice nightly, the first just after dusk, the second around midnight. On his free days from church work, John, and Tuffy did a quick daylight patrol. For eleven days there were no sightings of the dog pack, then on the afternoon of Monday 22 November '93, John, with his eldest son, Nick, and Tuffy, were up at the back of Josh's land where it bordered the National Park. As they rounded a large outcrop of boulders, Tuffy, suddenly stopped and looked directly into the National Park. When John and Nick reached Tuffy, they saw a large white and tan coloured dog dashing off into the bush some sixty metres inside the National Park. John, had no time to get a shot off, and Tuffy, let out a little bark as the dog vanished from sight in the bush. As they passed Josh's house, they reported to Josh they had seen a large dog running off into the bush.

John, kept up the afternoon patrol for the next three days and on Thursday 25 November, he headed for home early, with the weather closing in and looking very dark and threatening. He was within a kilometre of home when light rain began to fall. It was four-fourty-five.

CHAPTER 12

THE ESCAPE

Over at Barnaby, the second live show had just entered the fifth scene. When that was over, it would be mealtime, and the third and final show would begin at seven o'clock. The sky was dark with a heavy cloud cover, perfect for an escape. After they set up the second scene, Jimmy, Les, and Bob, handed in their tags, saying to the guard they wanted to sit down and enjoy the show.

The guards did not notice an extra three prisoners removing scene two, as all they were checking were IDs. The escape went like clockwork; it took them six minutes and twenty-five seconds for six prisoners to climb the ladder and drop down the outside prison wall by rope. The time was eight-twelve. As arranged, four other prisoners removed the ladder, broke it down and took it back to the woodworking block.

Keeping their eyes on towers five, and six, the six escapees used the landscape bushes as cover as they moved quickly away from the prison down to the edge of the delivery driveway. They came to a T-intersection and Jimmy was a bit confused as the plans he had looked at had no intersection, just a slight bend to the right. As they stood there, they saw headlights approaching from their left. Diving to the wet ground behind some bushes, they watched as the car went out of sight to their right.

Jimmy, went left, the first wrong decision as that took them to the prison car park. They covered 200 metres at a good pace when headlights appeared behind them and they raced to the western side of the road and hid as three more cars and a bus carrying guards for the eight-thirty shift change arrived. When one car returned within minutes, Jimmy, realised they were heading towards the prison car park, and it was not in the place the plans had shown, he questioned himself, *Am I going in the wrong direction? According to the plans we should walk away from the carpark, so are we going in the wrong direction?* He informed the others, and they made their way back pass the T-intersection. It was now eight-thirty-five. As they moved past the intersection, several cars and the bus left the car park and passed them. Through the bushes, the escapees saw that all these vehicles turned left and then disappeared. The six cut through the bush as the vehicle waiting for them was told to move out at nine o'clock, if the escapees hadn't turned up.

The second mistake they made was cutting through the bush, which brought them out seventy metres west of the dirt road, where the two escape vehicles were waiting. As they emerged from the bush and stepped onto a village tar-sealed back road, and not the Crims's Highway, Jimmy said, "We need to find a dirt road off to our right just a bit further along from here."

The sky was dark, and the rain made it hard to see more than twenty to thirty metres in front. They moved as quick as they could west, every step taking them further from the escape vehicles. Twice cars coming from the prison and heading to their homes in the village made them head for cover in the bushes along the road. They finally stumbled upon a dirt fire trail, at the same time, on the other side of the village, 300 metres to their left, on a parallel road, the Crims Highway, two four-wheeled-drive vehicles, with darkened windows headed down the highway away from the prison. Cautiously, the six moved up the dirt road looking for their vehicles, but none were found. When Jimmy, looked at his watch and realised it was nine-ten, he knew his boys had left and they were on their own.

CHAPTER 13

LOST IN THE BUSH

The rain started coming down heavier, and Les, pulled out a cloth bag from under his jacket in which were six large plastic garbage bags with three holes cut in them making a makeshift raincoat for their upper body. They had now been free for an hour and they made a group decision to continue walking the dirt fire trail putting as much distance between them and the prison. They all agreed the rain would wash away their tracks and dogs would not be able to pick up their scent. They didn't know that this trail was leading them deeper into the mountains in an arc, veering to the south. In the dark they walked and stumbled, as they negotiated the rough fire trail which in parts had become slippery with the rain, and both Vince, and Bob, slipped crashing to the ground.

When morning finally came, the heavy cloud cover and continuing rain made it nearly impossible to tell where and when the sun rose; the day just grew lighter. Looking at the vegetation and trees, Les, being a bushie, could tell which direction was north, and he estimated that with the difficulty in walking the fire trail, they had travelled about seven to ten kilometres from the prison. They were now tired, hungry, wet, cold, and angry feelings arose among them, especially with Vince.

The news on the radio Friday morning 26 November, contained details about the escape of six dangerous prisoners from Barnaby Maximum Security Prison, forty kilometres as the crow flies, northwest of Hidden Valley. Police advised the public not to approach any of them.

The escape became a good talking point in Riverbend, and in Hidden Valley. The local radio station, and the local paper The Riverbend Post, approached John in his official capacity as church minister, and asked his thoughts about the escape. John, expressed his fear for the general community with these six fugitives on the loose. But for him personally and the other residents of Hidden Valley, the wild dogs posed a greater threat.

Later that day, the police asked over the radio for the community's help in identifying two four-wheeled-drive vehicles seen driving down Barnaby Drive from the prison not long after nine o'clock last night. They asked the drivers to come forward to help rule out that way of escape, but nothing came of the request. With no sightings and no reported break-ins of properties close by the prison, the police began to lean towards the idea that the two mysterious vehicles had provided them a means of escape. If that was the case, the escapees were well and truly gone from the area, but they would continue searching the area near the prison.

The police were concerned about the mix of the escapees, all considered dangerous, but with no obvious link between them. In fact, the Bettini Twins and Bull would be enemies on the outside. Bob was a loner, Les, was just a good guy, and Jimmy probably considered himself the superior one of the six. The search parties found no clues outside the prison as the rain had washed out all hopes of the dogs finding a scent. With the heavy rain and the low clouds, an aerial search was also impossible, and the bad weather was forecast to last another three days at least.

Around midday, being extremely tired, wet, cold, and hungry, the escapees looked for some shelter from the consistent heavy rain. Les, being the only bushie in the group, suggested they descend into a valley to the fast-flowing mountain stream they could see from the fire trail.

"Why should we do that?" asked Angelo.

"Because, streams like this one with fast-flowing water over many years, gouge out the banks under large outcrops of rock, forming a cave, we find one and we are out of the weather," replied Les.

They quickly descend to the fast-flowing stream and started trudging along it's bank, after a couple of kilometres the weather took a turn for the worst, with lightning, and thunder, cracking almost right on top of them. As the violent storm came closer, they became desperate to find shelter. They come across a rock face and huddled up against it, protected from the wind and rain, but cramped and terribly uncomfortable. As they huddled against the rock face, a flash of lightning struck a tree directly opposite on the other bank, the exploding tree sent sparks and branches flying around.

"Hell," said Bob and Bull in unison. Another said, "Shit."

Then they heard the tree crashing to the ground, another lightning flash illuminated where they were, and both Bull, and Les, noticed the light going through bushes and lighting up a cave just 10 metres away. They moved to the bushes and disappeared, as they pushed their way through. Once through, they stood there waiting for the next lightning flash. When it came, they could hardly believe their eyes. In the split second of light, they thought they saw a cave with bunks set-up inside. They went back through the bushes and called the other four. The cave was dark, so they stood in the opening waiting for another flash. After 20 minutes and numerous flashes, they located a kerosene lantern which Les got working and from its light they saw four camp stretchers, a kerosene-stove, a pot, a frying pan, an old heavy duty camp kettle, and in a large wooden box were cans of food, flour, sugar, tea and coffee, and three more kerosene lanterns. Against the back wall, there were three fly-fishing rods and tackle, and at the front, adjacent to where they first entered the cave, was a large stack of dry firewood, and the remains of a fire in a stone fireplace.

"This must have been a fishermen's camping cave," said Les.

"For us it is the fucking Ritz," said Bob.

It did not take long for Les, to get a good fire going, and for all to warm up, and start drying out. Vince, found two very sharp filleting knives in sheaths, and gave one to Angelo, which meant they were now armed and twice as dangerous. Vince, moved to get more wood from the stack, when suddenly he froze, and his face drained of all blood. Jimmy, noticed this and moved towards the woodpile to see what was wrong. Vince, just stared at the stack, but Jimmy could not see what Vince had seen.

"What is it Vince?" he asked.

Stuttering Vince replied, "Snake."

Jimmy, had just reached out his hand towards the stack, when movement in the stack revealed a large snake. He let out a scream and jumped away. His scream brought Vince out of his trance-like state, and he made a hurried retreat from the stack.

Bob, grabbed a length of wood and moved towards the stack. "I will fix the bastard."

Les, jumped up and said, "Leave it to me, guys." Using a kerosene lantern, he inspected the stack and saw a Red Bellied Black Snake. "Don't worry, guys, it's just a blackie, he won't hurt us."

"I won't give him the fucking chance," said Bob. "The only good snake is a dead one."

Les, stood in front of Bob. "He is just like us getting out of the rain, he won't hurt us if we leave him alone," said Les, as he took the piece of wood out of Bob's hands.

The physical size of both Vince and Bull made them too big for the stretchers, so the other four claimed a stretcher each. After eating some canned food and a damper that Les made from the flour, they decided they should all get some sleep.

Saturday, the rain pelted down, so the six stayed in the cave till Sunday morning, the Red Bellied Black Snake vacated the cave overnight. During the morning, the rain ceased its intensity, which gave Les the chance to go exploring. He found a small creek with good-sized yabbies (a small freshwater crayfish). He caught twenty-two and boiled them up for lunch. Later in the afternoon, Bull, and Bob, returned with Les to the creek with an empty twenty-litre plastic bait bucket, one and a half hours later, and after numerous nips, they had just about filled the bucket with yabbies and went back to the cave to cook them.

CHAPTER 14

RISING RIVER, WILD DOGS TROUBLE HIDDEN VALLEY RESIDENTS

Saturday morning in Hidden Valley and some of the residents inspect the Peaceful River, which had become a torrent, but it hadn't as yet flooded the valley's exit.

"Let's ask Josh what he thinks," suggested Tom.

Walking over to Josh and Sally's house, Morris Cooper asked, "Aye, Josh, do you think it will flood the road, and stop us getting out?"

"Morris, I have lived in this valley for forty-eight-years and I have only seen it flood bad four times. Once, it cut us off from the outside for around six to eight hours, however, the worst flooding isolated us for five and a half days."

Of the four houses in the valley, only the Mann's house is on the better side of the river, they don't have to cross the river to get out of the valley, but if the river floods the crevasse they won't be able to get out, but the river would have to rise at least another metre to trap them.

Josh, said to the Greens, and Coopers, that they should park their cars on the other side of the river from their homes. "You guys can use my house footbridge to cross the river."

Josh's footbridge straddled six huge ironbark posts sunk at different heights. The two outside posts were only 1.5 metres high, the second and fifth were at a height of three metres, and the middle two just on four metres above ground. Each pole had a two-metre cross member (150x100 ml) notched into the top of each pole. The walkway spanning the six poles was made of 75ml square heavy-duty galvanised mesh bent into vee-shaped, with a flat bottom of sixty centimetres, with sides rising a little over a metre high, all welded together. This was the only way to cross the river when it was in flood.

Tom and Shirley Green, on Josh's advice, moved their flocks. The pregnant ewes were moved to a small paddock just at the back of their house. In the paddock was a large partly filled hay barn, this would be an ideal shelter for the ewes. The other sheep, the two-tooth flock they moved to the bush paddock, a partly cleared paddock, but with enough bush to offer some protection to the sheep from heavy rain. The only problem was that this bush paddock bordered the National Park, and the flock may be in danger of another wild dog attack. Josh hoped that the rain would keep the wild dog pack holed up in their own hideout.

Sunday came, and with it the rain eased to just the occasional shower, with the sun trying its best to break through the clouds. The Greens moved their two-tooth sheep to a larger paddock, one in from the National Park.

Coming home from the Sunday morning Church Service, the Manns had a quick lunch and then John, Nick, and Tuffy, went out to patrol the five kilometres of northern farm fences that bordered the National Park. John, thought the dogs may be hungry and will come after the Green's sheep.

It was near five-thirty when the three reached the paddock where the attack took place, and as they passed through the gate Tuffy's hackles rose, and that low growl was back, John, wonder what Tuffy was growling at, when Nick said, "Those dogs are nearby dad."

Looking in the direction that Tuffy had fixed his gaze, John, glimpsed a pack of dogs racing for the cover of the bush and boulders some 250 to 300 metres away. John quickly raised his rifle and squeezed off a shot at the retreating dogs. The bullet hit a brown dog which cartwheeled and crashed dead to the ground, and the others swerved quickly to the side, and then they were gone.

John, and Nick, climbed over the fence, while Tuffy jumped it, and inspected the dead dog. There was no trace of the others anywhere; they had just vanished into the bush. As it was getting late, they headed off to the Greens who had invited the Mann's family to the evening meal. Mary, and the other three children were already at the Green's when the three turned up. Tom, asked John about the gunshot they had heard, but before John could answer, Nick excitedly told them of the incident, "You should have seen it, the dogs were running really fast, and dad took a shot at one and the bullet just about blew the dog's head off, it was a great shot at running dogs."

John, wondered how Nick knew that the dogs were nearby, just with Tuffy's growl. He still didn't know of Nick, and Tuffy's, encounter with the pack, when Nick first heard that low growl in Tuffy. But the conversation moved away from the dogs as Mary, was busy drying Nick's hair, and the chance never came for him to ask Nick, and soon he forgot about it.

CHAPTER 15

SUZUKI ACCIDENT, LES GIVES HIMSELF UP

On Sunday morning, the escapees pack as much food as they could into some fishing backpacks, leave the cave and climbed back up to the fire trail. They continued walking in an easterly direction. Les, was in his element. For him, the bush was alive with wildlife; roos hopped away through the undergrowth, and a deer crossing the trail in front of them was startled and bounded off into the bush. There were king parrots, galahs, sulphur-crested cockatoos, and wombat droppings on the fire trail. Les, thought he heard the unmistakable 'creaky door' screech of the gang-gang cockatoo. And occasionally the raucous laughter of the laughing kookaburra, which seemed to mock them as they walked, not knowing where they were, or where they were headed. Around midmorning, as they rounded a bend on the trail, they came across a huge wedge-tailed eagle feeding on the carcass of a bush wallaby. The escapees stopped in their tracks as the massive bird, standing over a metre tall, used its massive beak to rip flesh from its bones.

"What in the bloody hell is that?" shouted Jimmy.

"That is a wedge-tailed eagle, the biggest bird of flight in Australia. It's beautiful, isn't it?" said Les.

Hearing voices, the eagle looked around at the group and considering them as no threat, continued ripping flesh and eating it. When the six were about twenty metres away, the huge bird spread its wings and took off. Les, watched in awe as this majestic eagle with a wingspan of just under three metres lifted off. As they passed the carcass, Les, looked at it to see how the wallaby had died, and noted a group of parallel mud lines across its back, just up from its tail. He realised a vehicle had killed it. As Les enjoyed the beauty of the bush, he forgot he was an escaped prisoner. He saw different trees from iron bark, to mountain ash, and turpentine. He was struck by the trees' beauty and their height.

The ill feeling between the different escapees that had risen on Friday morning still simmered, especially between Vince and Bob.

"I swear to you, Angelo, I will kill that fucking bastard Bob, he just pisses me off," complained a very agitated Vince.

"Just control yourself till we get out of this fucking bush, as we don't want to split the group up," replied Angelo.

"Aye, Jimmy, do you have any bloody idea where we are?" enquired Bull.

"We have to find a farmhouse, or someone who can give us some bloody directions," said Vince.

Two kilometres from where they saw the wedge-tailed eagle, the fire trail forked. After a group discussion, they turned right. After walking for an hour, the trail started climbing steeply up a bluff and forty minutes later, they came to the end of the fire trail on one of the highest peaks in the area, where a fire observation platform had been erected. Climbing up to the top of the tower, Jimmy, Les, and Angelo, looked for kilometres across rugged bush lands with deep valleys and saw nothing but trees.

Two hours later, they returned to the fork. They were tired, hungry, dirty, and dangerous. Their ill feelings were now just about at boiling point. They moved along the other trail which took them up and over a lower range to that on which the fire tower stood and back down to a river. There they ate some food, rinsed their faces, and had a drink of the cool mountain water. As they crossed a natural ford, they heard a low flying helicopter.

"Quick," yelled Angelo, "into the bush. It might be the fucking cops."

They all make a quick dash of fifteen metres to the cover of the bush. Within seconds, a New South Wales Polair 3 helicopter flew up along the river. This made them nervous as they wrongfully assumed the police knew that they were still in the mountains. The flight was the last of the search team, as the police believed two-vehicles had whisked them away on the night of the escape.

The escapees decided to be more careful, as they wrongly reasoned that if the police were conducting an aerial search, they would also have people on the ground searching.

As they walked, the noise of a vehicle approaching from behind drove them back into the bush. Soon a small Suzuki 4-wheel-drive came past with two occupants, a male and female. They thought it was part of a ground searching party, and more vehicles would follow close behind, but it was just a young couple out doing some bush-bashing.

Fearing other vehicles, the six left the fire trail and went bush. Struggling their way over some very rugged terrain, they traversed a couple of gullies. The deeper and rougher the terrain, the deeper the tension became between them. They made comments like, "fuck this fucking bush, we are lost," "who wants to die in the bloody bush?" and "we were better off in Barnaby than we are in this jungle." Down in a gully, they heard two vehicles approaching.

"They are really looking for us, listen to them."

Later in the afternoon, as they climbed up out of yet another gully, they came across a fire trail. Standing in the middle of the trail, five of the escapees argued about which direction they should be going. Les said nothing until they decided to go left.

"Ah, guys, you can't go that way unless you want to go back to Barnaby," said Les.

The other five turned and looked at him.

"How do you know that?" asked Jimmy.

"It's really simple. We started today walking looking into the sun when the clouds had cleared. If you go your way, you will still be walking into the sun, and now late afternoon. That means we are going back the way we came," explained Les.

"You're right, you're bloody well right," said Bull. "I'm glad someone's got some bloody brains."

They turned right and started walking along the fire trail once more.

"Just keep listening for any voices or car engine noise as those searchers won't be far away," said Angelo.

As they walked, the clouds started coming in low, dark and heavy with rain from the west.

"We had better look for somewhere to sleep. By the look of those clouds, we are in for some more shitty weather. I don't want to be wet tonight," said Bull.

Les, suggested they return into the gully with the second creek they'd crossed, as there was sure to be a cave or rock ledge they could get under.

They were looking for a way down into the gully when they discovered the little Suzuki had run off the road, rolled a couple of times, and was back on its wheels some twenty metres from the fire trail. The young couple were seriously hurt with very faint pulses. The vehicle was too small for all six to get away in if they could start it. And even if they drove off in it, they were bound to run into the search party. In the end, they just walked away.

"We can't just walk away, these two people need help or they will die," argued Les.

The five disagreed with Les, "Fuck you, Les, if we help them, we will be back in Barnaby tonight. No fucking way," said Vince.

"This is so wrong," replied Les. "What if they were your kids, wouldn't you want someone to help them? We can't just walk away, it's murder."

Angelo moved over to Les and threatened him. "Leave them, or you will die here with them. There is no way I will let you help these two, they are just about dead anyway. If the other searchers don't find them, they will be dead by morning. So, move your fucking arse, or get ready to die."

The other five virtually push Les down the gully. He realised he could not fight the group, so he went along with them. Finding the creek again, it wasn't long before they found a huge overhanging rock ledge to provide them with cover from the rain. Les, started gathering some firewood and soon had a fire going, trying to convince the others he had forgotten about the young couple.

"I will look for some yabbies up the creek a bit, anyone want to help?" asked Les, hoping no one would take up his offer.

The only thing the others wanted to do was sit down and eat some food they had taken from the fishermen's cave.

Les, moved upstream, turning rocks over on the edge of the creek as well as some just under the water. Gradually moving up the creek and around a bend where he dropped the yabbies, and the small bucket, and started climbing back up to the road, praying that the young couple were still alive.

Finding the vehicle once more, he checked the two inside. As he touched the young woman, she groaned, "Help me, please help me."

"I will do everything I can for you, but I must get you to a hospital," said Les. He saw the young man had blood coming out of his right ear but could not rouse him. Finding a winch attached to the front bull-bar. He planned to winch the Suzuki back onto the fire trail. First, he had to winch the vehicle five metres to the right and then up the twenty metres to the trail. But there was no handle on the winch. Searching where he can in the vehicle, he finally located the handle under the back-passenger seat. The winching of the vehicle over the rough ground caused the young woman to groan, and Les, kept apologising to her. The rain started falling, wetting the injured couple, so he found a tarp and rope in the back of the Suzuki and covered the young couple.

After an hour, the other five prisoners realised Les had disappeared.

"I bet the prick has gone back to that car," said Vince. "Let's go after him and finish him off."

They started to go back, but only Les knew where they had descended into the gully, and the others had no real idea where the vehicle was. When the rain became heavier, most of them decided it was better to be dry than get soaked searching the bush. However, Vince convinced them to continue the search.

"If he makes it out of here, he will know where to send the police," said Vince.

They moved out in a wide line through the bush. Vince thought he had remembered where the Suzuki was, so he headed back along the creek they had followed, and for a big man he moved quickly.

A little over an hour later, and Les had finally got the Suzuki back onto the fire trail, and now had to move the driver. That is when he discovered that the driver's right leg was broken. Taking all the care he can, he quickly put a splint on the leg and gently lifted the driver into the back seat. The young man groaned and cried out in pain.

"I'm sorry, mate, but I have to move you, or you will die."

Les, jumped into the driver's seat, praying that the vehicle would start. He turned the key, and nothing happened. He checked the lights and horn, but there was nothing. Looking under the bonnet, he saw the lead to the positive battery terminal had come off the pole. Pushing it back on, he used the winch handle to hammer the connector down tight onto the positive pole. Trying the ignition once more, he was delighted to hear the engine splutter a couple of times and then burst into life with a strange knocking noise. He closed the bonnet and then turned the lights on; there was only one low beam but two high beams with the passenger headlight pointing to the tops of the trees.

Then he looked up and saw Vince racing towards him with a knife in his hand, and a murderous look on his face. *Is this how I am going to die?* he wondered. Pushing the accelerator down, the Suzuki started to splutter and move towards Vince, who had moved onto the driver's side of the track, waiting for Les to draw near. The Suzuki was only doing about 25 kph, slow enough for a person to jump in. Vince, stood on a rock to gain a bit of height, and readied himself to launch onto the Suzuki and go for the kill.

Behind him, Les, heard the others shouting out, "Stop." Looking around, he saw the others racing towards him. He knew he had a slim chance of getting past Vince, and if he stopped Vince would kill him. He grabbed the detachable winch handle sitting on the passenger seat and hoped his timing was spot on. As Vince, launched himself at the Suzuki, Les, hurled the handle as fast and straight as he could. He had one chance only, Vince, was mid-air when he saw the handle coming straight for his face. He raised his hand in a protective move, but the handle hits him just above his right eye, splitting his eyebrow and sending blood running down his face. As a result, Vince crashed onto the side of the vehicle and falls heavily to the ground.

Doing his best not to go too fast and bounce the injured couple around, it took Les just on two hours to get out of the National Park and onto a tar-sealed road. Not knowing where he was, he turned right, hoping and praying he had made the right decision. Because of the damage the Suzuki sustained when it rolled, Les found anything over 55/kph made the vehicle shake violently and effected the steering. Forty minutes later, he came to a major crossroad with the sign to Erinville pointing to the left, seventeen kilometres away. Turning left, Les reached the outskirts of Erinville twenty-two-minutes later. A notice board with arrows indicated the information centre, the town centre, police station, and hospital. Five minutes later, he pulled up outside of a small regional hospital. Blasting the horn, he attracted the attention of the nurse at the front counter who came to the door and saw the smashed-up vehicle.

The nurse pressed the emergency button at the door as she rushed out to the vehicle. Within minutes, two other nurses have arrived to help. After checking the two young people, they started to stabilise them while the third rushed back to the front desk to call in a doctor.

Directly opposite the hospital stood the town police station. The commotion from the hospital attracted the attention of a young constable, who crossed the road to see what was going on. When he saw the wet and dirty Les, the officer recognised the prison clothes he was wearing, and he knew Les, was a prison escapee.

Hightailing it back to the station, he rushed to the duty sergeant and blurted out, "Aye, Sarg, one of those escaped prisoners is over at the hospital."

"You're kidding me, aren't you?" the duty sergeant said.

"No! Really, honest to God."

The duty sergeant called the patrol car back from its rounds and told the senior constable to go back to the hospital through the staff carpark and rear door. He was to wait out of sight inside the hospital and only move out when he saw the two officers approaching from the station.

The nurses had stabilised the two injured people just as the doctor's car turned into the driveway. All eyes were on the two injured people, and Les, was concerned about their well-being, so no one noticed three police officers had surrounded him. Les, was arrested, and admitted he was one of the escapees from Barnaby Maximum Security Prison. Les, was placed in one of the two cells, while the sergeant rang his superior officer, who told him to contact the Escapees Task Force hunting the escapees.

On Monday morning 29 November, detectives from the Escapees Task Force arrived to interrogate Les, who was very candid and told the detectives he didn't know the whereabouts of the other five. He told them the reason he left the group was to get the two injured young people to hospital.

"Look, I really don't know where they are except to say that they are in the bush heading in a south-easterly direction from the prison. I don't even know where I am now. Sure, I read the sign that said Erinville, but where is Erinville? I don't have a clue."

One detective asked, "When you made that decision to get those two to a hospital, you must have known that you would probably get caught doing it?"

"Yes, yes, I did, but I couldn't live with myself if I didn't help. What if it was my family hurt? I would want someone to do the same for them. You just can't walk away from people when they need help."

The Escapees Task Force now had concrete evidence of what had happened after the escape. The two mystery vehicles were the intended getaway mode, but the five were actually on foot in the bush. They restarted aerial patrols over the National Park, in an expanding arc from northeast to southeast of Barnaby Prison.

The doctors at the Erinville Hospital, told the task force that Les had saved the lives of those two young people. The young man had a fractured skull, fractured right leg, a broken right shoulder, internal injuries and facial injuries. The young lady had a ruptured spleen, a fractured arm, head and chest injuries, internal injuries and facial injuries.

Les, was put back into the system and returned to Barnaby, where he would be held till his court appearance for escaping lawful custody. At Barnaby, he was placed in an isolation cell with no contact with other prisoners.

The five escapees stayed put on the Monday with storms and heavy rain all around them.

CHAPTER 16

SECOND DOG ATTACK, PEACEFUL RIVER STARTING TO FLOOD

On Monday afternoon in Hidden Valley, John, Nick, and Tuffy went out on the afternoon patrol of the farms, concentrating on the paddocks where the Green's flocks were located.

Approaching the paddock from the south where the two-tooth ewes were being held, a strong wind blew into their faces. They walked up to the top of a rise in the paddock next to the two-tooth paddock, and they saw the flock hard up against the fence as if they had been driven into it. Straightaway, John, thought the dogs had come back. Climbing over the fence, they rounded a small stand of trees. Their hearts sank as they looked over the paddock and saw dead and mauled sheep, and the dog pack once again racing towards the national park and shelter.

How did they know that we were coming? John thought. *We were downwind of them, so something other than us has chased them off. Maybe it is the Greens.*

From where they were, they saw the blood on the sheep that lay there dead or close to death. A couple were trying to get away, but their back legs were broken. John, saw a large white and tan coloured dog near one of the injured ewes. Quickly, he raised his rifle to his shoulder and lined up the wild dog in his scope. As he slowly squeezed the trigger, he noticed there was no blood around the dog's mouth or down the front of his chest, and he hesitated. Nick, feared his dad was about to shoot the dog and pushed him sideways.

"What did you do that for?" asked John.

Tuffy barked, and the dog glanced in their direction. When it saw them, it turned and headed for the scrub and safety of the national park. Nick, explained to his dad how the dog had helped run off the pack during his camping trip.

"Dad, he is a good dog, please don't shoot him."

John, embraced Nick and gave Tuffy a hug. "We had better go and give the bad news to Tom, and Shirley."

Walking towards the Green's home, John tossed things around in his head and called into Josh's house first.

"Aye, Josh, remember when the first dog attack took place, and you were looking at the tracks? Remember, you said something, or someone had run the pack off?"

"Yes, why?"

"Well, there is a big dog who isn't part of the pack, and I had this feeling today that he had chased off the pack just before we arrived. They could not have heard us or smelt us as the wind was in our faces."

Arriving at the Greens, John, delivered the words Tom, and Shirley, had been dreading. Immediately, they all rushed to the two tooths' paddock, and for the next hour they helped the best they could with the injured sheep. Nineteen were so badly mauled they had to destroy them. The residents decided to step up their patrols to morning, afternoon, and evening.

Josh, also told the other residents of Hidden Valley he believed the Peaceful River would flood in the next couple of days, because of the heavy rain in the area, especially in the north.

"If it floods," said Josh, "it will cut us off from the outside with no way in and no way out. And if it floods, I reckon we are in for the mother of all floods. We will be trapped for a week. That's my opinion; you can take it or leave it."

"How quickly does it flood?" asked Anne Cooper.

"You know that big flat rock down by the cattle grate at this end of the gorge going out of the valley?"

"Yes," said Anne and Morris in unison.

"Well, when the water reaches the top of that rock, we have five, maybe ten hours to get out depending on how much more rain we get. So, if anyone needs to leave the valley, they had better make the move sooner rather than later before we are trapped."

At eight-thirty the next morning, Tuesday, Tom Green phoned the National Parks and Wildlife head office in Sydney. He talked to a Robert Coleman, who was in charge of all rangers. After Tom, had finished explaining the recent attack on the Green's sheep, Coleman, told him he had just authorised a dog baiting program for the national park which would happen over the next couple of weeks. He told Tom, to look out for the ranger and his team.

CHAPTER 17

THE ESCAPEES AND THE NATIONAL PARK RANGER

The rain was still falling north of Hidden Valley but, clearing to the west where the five escapees were hiding. There was now a real desperation in them as they had no clue where they were, and they didn't know which direction they should go to find a homestead or town.

They climbed up out of the valley to the ridge opposite, where they had found the crashed Suzuki. Reaching the top, they found another fire trail and followed it. Unbeknown to them, this fire trail headed south west toward Hidden Valley, and a catastrophic meeting with its residents.

Early in the afternoon, the five rounded a sharp right-hand bend and saw a vehicle in the middle of the trail. They prepared to dart into the bushes until Jimmy said, "Aye, where is the driver?"

The others saw that there was no-one in the vehicle, so they quickened their pace towards it, and saw it was a National Parkes and Wildlife vehicle. Just as they reached the front of the vehicle, they heard someone coming out of the bush. The ranger stepped onto the trail and looked up to see Bull, Vince, and Angelo at his vehicle, with Jimmy, and Bob close by. His senses immediately told him he should get out of there fast. He turned and ran into the bush, and he heard the men call out, "Stop, we just want to talk to you."

But something told the ranger if he stopped it wouldn't end well, so he continued to run through the bush. The five gave chase, fanning out. Vince, kept to the trail, while the other four, especially Jimmy, raced behind him to stop the ranger from going down into the valley. The ranger cleared rocks and bushes in his headlong run but, misjudged the height of one rock. His foot clipped it, and he crashed heavily to the ground. Gathering himself, he saw that the only way to go was back up to the road as Jimmy was now below him, and the other three were closing in on him. He didn't see Vince stalking him above on the trail. Vince, saw the ranger heading for some large boulders, so he hid and waited. He heard the crashing footsteps and the ranger's heavy breathing, who was in fear for his life. The ranger scrambled past the boulders and ran right into Vince. He looked up into the fierce eyes of a cold-blooded killer and then down at Vince's hand where there was a filleting knife.

He yelled, "No, don't ki—"

Vince's, knife cut the ranger's plea off mid-sentence, as he plunged the knife into the ranger's stomach and pulled it up.

"Now, run you fucking bastard," said a gleeful Vince.

Bob, and Angelo, arrived first to find the ranger was dead.

"Fuck," said Angelo, "why did you kill him? We wanted to get help to get out of the bloody bush. He can't tell us a fucking thing now."

Jimmy, and Bull, finally caught up and saw the dead ranger.

"Jesus Christ, who did this?" asked Bull.

"Vince," said Bob.

"You ignorant bastard, why did you have to kill him?" Bull, asked and took a step towards Vince.

Vince, realised he was in trouble and raised his right hand holding the knife, but Bull, was very quick for a big man. His left hand grabbed Vince's right wrist as his right fist smashed into Vince's face. Bull, was just about to continue his attack when he felt a knife against his neck.

"Back off, Bull," said Angelo, "I'm not happy either, but he is my brother and I won't let you hurt him."

Bull, slowly turned towards Angelo, weighing his chances of beating him when Jimmy said, "Bull, the guy's dead and there is nothing we can do. Let it go."

"Angelo, if you ever hold a knife against me again, you had better be ready to use it," Bull, warned him.

"I am, and I will, now back off," said a cool calm Angelo.

As Angelo, helped Vince to his feet, Vince said, "I will kill the fucker."

"Calm down. Your time will come, but we just don't want to die out here in the bush first. We have more chance if we stick together and work as a team at the moment," replied Angelo.

The air was tense as they trudged back to the ranger's vehicle.

Jimmy, dropped back to Bull and told him, "Don't turn your back on Vince, he will stab you the first chance he gets. And watch Angelo; he is more deadly than Vince."

In the vehicle, Bob found a National Parks and Wildlife ranger's jacket that fitted him. They all piled into the vehicle with Bob at the wheel, and Vince in the front passenger seat. They drove the same way that they had been walking only because it was away from the prison. But it was as if an unseen force was drawing them in this direction.

Sticking to what looked like the most used fire trail, they drove for hours, twice ending up at dead ends. Late in the afternoon, the ranger's vehicle spluttered to a stop.

"What's wrong now?" asked Angelo.

"Fucking thing is empty, no fuel," replied Bob.

"Fucking hell," mouthed Bull, "and we are still lost in these shithouse mountains."

Where they ran out of fuel was high on a ridge which offered a spectacular panoramic 270-degree view over the surrounding terrain. In the distance to the south, they saw cleared land which was three kilometres west of Hidden Valley.

"That," said Bob, "means, food, shelter, and bloody transport. That is where we have to get to."

Pushing the vehicle off the fire trail, they covered it with branches rather than set it on fire as the smoke would pinpoint their position. Setting their course south with their eyes on a high plateau ten kilometres away as the crow flies, they continued climbing up and down valleys. When it got dark, they sheltered against a sandstone cliff face. Jimmy wandered off to relieve himself. Within minutes, the four heard a scream and the sound of pounding feet as Jimmy came racing back, trying to stop his pants from falling down.

"There is a fucking crocodile that came at me, it nearly got me," he yelled.

Bull said, "There are no bloody crocodiles out in the fucking bush."

"Well, I got some news for you, there is one out there and he is about two and a half metres long," replied a very scared Jimmy as he did up his pants. "The bloody thing made me shit my pants."

Together, they walk back to see if they could find this so-called crocodile. What they found was a perentie goanna which had scurried up a large blue gum tree.

Bull, started laughing, "Look, you silly Asian, have you ever heard of a crocodile climbing a bloody tree? It's just a goanna."

"It looked like a fucking crocodile to me," said a sheepish Jimmy.

Meanwhile, in Hidden Valley, the Cooper's twin daughters Liza, and Jenny, arrived home after finishing their uni commitments in Sydney. They were looking forward to a couple of days on the farm, riding their horses and camping if the weather permitted. On the coming Friday, the family was going to a relative's wedding in Melbourne on the Saturday.

On Wednesday morning, the five escapees woke to light rain. They were cold and hungry. The supplies they had taken from the fishermen's cave and the little they had scrounged from the Suzuki and the ranger's vehicle had all gone. The tension within the group was high.

Vince, continued to fume about Bull, and had told Angelo he would kill Bull once they were out of the bush. Angelo, expressed his concern that a real war could start between them and Bull's bikers, if they found out about it. He was also worried that Bull, and Jimmy, had formed a strong bond, and Jimmy's men could come after them. Bob, also seemed more inclined to stick with the other two, forming a division in which they were outnumbered. Wanting to play it safe, Angelo cautioned Vince about his intentions.

CHAPTER 18

HIDDEN VALLEY

The five escapees were determined to get to the farming land in the distance as quickly as possible. It was mid-afternoon on Wednesday when they reached the high plateau above Hidden Valley. They came across a well-worn animal track that they followed to the south. It was the same track Josh, and Sally, walked back in 1942, when they walked to the edge of the crater that formed Hidden Valley. When the five stood on the edge of the crater, it was a different valley to the one Josh, and Sally, were captivated by all those years ago. On that day they had looked down into a beautiful, heavily bushed valley, with a sparkling stream meandering its entire length.

For most people standing where the five escapees now stood, the valley was still picture perfect with green paddocks, cattle and sheep, out-buildings and four homesteads. But this beauty was lost on these five men. They could not see the beauty; all they saw was food, shelter and transport. It was still a very hard valley to enter from the rim. The five searched for a way down from the ridge to the valley floor. They were determined not to spend another night sleeping out in the bush.

It was around this time, at four-thirty, when Anne Cooper, went on her two-hourly inspection of the flat rock near the cattle grate. This time when she looked, she saw that the water was just fifteen centimetres from the top, a rise of twenty centimetres in two hours. If Josh was right, they had to leave the valley tonight if they wanted to make the wedding on Saturday.

Anne, had feared this as she watched the steady rise of the river that day, and she had already packed the car and suitcases for just such an emergency. On returning to her home at five o'clock, she spoke with Morris, and they agreed that they would leave within the hour. Anne, rang Shirley Green, to tell her their plan to leave early. And she asked Shirley, if she would pop over and feed the house pets. Shirley, wished them God's speed, safe travel, and a great wedding. She told them they would look forward to seeing them back next Tuesday. Anne, informed the other residents of their early departure.

John, Nick, and Tuffy, went on their afternoon patrol and approached the back of the Green's property, the bush paddock where the last attack had taken place just two days ago.

As they entered the paddock, Nick said, "Aye, Dad, there's people up on the ridge."

John looked but couldn't see. "Where, Nick?"

Nick pointed to his right.

Looking intently where Nick was pointing, John said, "Yes, I can see them."

Looking through his rifle scope, he saw three men. Two were going out of sight behind some trees, but the last man, Bob Walker, was wearing a National Parks and Wildlife jacket.

"I don't believe it, it's the ranger. National Parks have kept their word and are out there laying bait for the wild dogs. We must call in and tell the Greens; I bet it will surprise them."

On hearing the news from John, Tom exclaimed, "Boy, that's a quick response, it's nearly too-good-to-be-true."

"Let's not knock them," replied John. "If they are successful in the baiting, you two will sleep a lot easier. Anyway, we had better keep going as the river is rising fast. Come on, Nick, we have to go."

"Let him finish his cake and drink," said Shirley. "Talking about the river rising, the Greens are going any moment now to beat the flood waters, or they will never make their niece's wedding on Saturday."

As the five escapees slowly climbed down from the rim of the crater, a kilometre away from the Cooper's homestead, Anne, rang Shirley, to let her know they were leaving, but the phones were dead. The rising flood waters had entered Telecom's cable boxes and cut off all the phones in the valley. It was six o'clock when the Cooper's vacated their home, got into two vehicles and headed off towards Melbourne. They passed the flat rock, which was now underwater, and the river was rising very fast.

"If we left it any longer, I don't think we would have made it out as that water is rising quick," said Morris.

CHAPTER 19

THE ESCAPEES INVADE THE HOMES AND LIVES OF RESIDENTS

The five escapees were only 200 metres from the Coopers when they saw the family get into vehicles and leave. Not knowing if anyone was left in the house, they used every bit of cover, bushes and farm sheds to get closer. Moving through the open-fronted machinery shed, they passed the Cooper's two kelpies locked in their pens. The dogs looked at them but made no noise. On entering the house through the unlocked back door, Bob, and Vince, located the kitchen and started eating whatever they could find. Jimmy, Bull, and Angelo, quickly made a search of the house to make sure it was empty. Jimmy, found clothes that fit him, and Bull found the .22 rifle and 23 shells.

Jimmy, tried the phone and slammed it down. "Fucking thing is not working."

After eating, the five spread out throughout the house to sleep. Vince took Morris and Anne's double bed, Angelo, and Bull, each took one of the twin's bedrooms, Jimmy, was in the boy's room, and Bob had the lounge. He turned the TV on, the late news we being read, he watched the story about the recapture of Les Murphy, one of the six prison escapees, who had saved the lives of a seriously injured young couple. Bob, decided to wait till morning to inform the others.

John, Nick, and Tuffy, arrived home just on six-fifteen. Mary, had a lovely baked dinner for the family.

At the table, John said to Mary, "The Coopers are leaving for the wedding as soon as they can."

"Yes, I know, in fact they left half an hour ago," replied Mary. "Anne, rang me earlier to say that, and to let us know that they will be in a motel in Parkside, a suburb of Melbourne right on the Bay. They want to do some swimming."

"Oh yeah, we saw the ranger and his crew up on the ridge, I guess they are laying bait for that wild dog pack."

"I'm sure Tom and Shirley will be relieved," replied Mary.

At midday on Thursday, the five searched the out-buildings looking for a vehicle and found the unregistered paddock bashing ute. They listened to the radio and watched the TV to try to find out what the police were doing. The TV news said the police were combing the bush to the north of Barnaby. That information didn't help the five, as they had no idea where they were.

With all the comforts of home, they stayed put and out of sight, hoping the phones would be fixed so they could contact their own people.

Late in the afternoon, Bull suddenly exclaimed, "Shit, here comes a bloody woman."

They quickly got out of sight as Shirley Green moved past the house towards the old fridge next to the kelpies' pen. She made sure that the dogs and horses all had food and water. She filled the cat's dish and had a quick look around outside before she headed off home. The five watched her disappear behind some bushes.

Shirley, checked the river and her driveway, which was a good metre under water. She wondered how long it would be before they could get out.

On Friday morning, the rain continued with the odd thunderstorm. The Mann kids were having a great time not being able to go to school and playing outside in the rain. They ran down to Josh's footbridge and walked over the swollen river. The bridge was the only way the other residents of the valley could reach the Mann's house. They crossed the bridge, saw Sally and Josh, and waved madly to them. They walked over and said hi to Blitz, gave her a pat, then headed off home.

By early afternoon, the rain had stopped, but the heavy cloud cover remained. The five escapees had tried to work out where they were and how they could contact their people. They made plans to invade the other houses in the valley.

Vince asked, "Are we going to leave any witnesses alive?"

Bull, and Jimmy, looked in disbelief at Vince.

Bull remarked, "You fucking hurt anyone else and your brother won't be able to help you. I promise you that, arsehole."

"No, Vince, we need people alive to help us get back to Sydney, if they cause us no problems, we will just tie them up," said Angelo, as he tried to lower the level of hostility between Bull and Vince.

Later in the afternoon, Shirley returned to check and feed the animals, and the five in the house didn't notice her until the kelpies started barking excitedly as she got their food out of the fridge. As they ducked out of sight, they forgot that the back door was slightly ajar. As Shirley moved from the dogs towards the horses, she saw the open door and went to secure it, thinking the wind had blown it open. Reaching the back door, she saw the light on in the kitchen. Walking in past the laundry into the kitchen, she came face to face with Bob Walker, who grabbed her. Shirley started screaming. Bob feared her scream would be heard and punched her in the mouth, telling her to be quiet or she would be hurt worse. The other four rushed into the kitchen and Shirley was filled with terror as she realised, they were the escaped prisoners.

They questioned Shirley, about how to get out of the valley and she told them they would have to wait till the river level dropped, as it was the only way out.

"How many other houses are there?" asked Bull.

She tried not to show how terrified she was, but her quavering voice gave her away. "There . . . there . . . are four houses."

"How many people are there?" enquired Angelo.

"Well, the Coopers who own this house have gone to Melbourne, then there's Tom and me, Josh and Sally, and the Mann family, John and Mary and their four children. John is a minister of religion."

"How do you contact someone outside of this valley?" Jimmy asked.

"With the road flooded, and the phones out, we can't contact anyone," said Shirley as she started to sob.

"Shit, doesn't someone have a way of contacting people?" raged Bull.

"No! Part of the beauty of living out here is the isolation that the valley offers," replied Shirley.

"What about bloody computers?" interjected Vince.

"Yes, we have one and the Manns have one," replied Shirley.

"Great, we will send an email," said a pleased Vince.

The others started to get excited, until Jimmy pointed out that you needed a phone line, and as the phones were out, the computers were as well.

"What about cars?" asked Angelo. "How many are there?"

"I can think of three, but you can't use them because the road is underwater."

"How long before the river drops?" asked Bull.

"It is the first flood we have seen," said Shirley. "But, Josh, the guy who has lived here for fifty years, said it could last for a week or more. Can I ask what you will do with me?"

"If you cause us no fucking trouble, you might be lucky to live," said Vince in a chilling tone.

"Where is your house, how far away is it from here?" asked Angelo.

"Just a ten-minute walk, I don't really know how far it is."

"Do you have a gun at your place?" asked Bull.

"No, we don't like guns."

"Does anyone in this valley have a gun, apart from this one here?" enquired Jimmy.

"I don't know, there isn't a need to own one in the valley," said Shirley, not wanting to give them too much information.

"OK, enough talking, lead us to your house."

As they approached the back of the Green's house, they rounded the machinery shed and walked into Tom, who had just returned from checking the ewes.

Tom, saw the blood on Shirley's face and looked at the five men. "Who in bloody hell did this?"

"Shut up," said Bull, holding Morris's .22 rifle in one hand. "If you want to survive, keep your mouth shut. No questions, no problems, and you may just live to be an old man. But, I am warning you, try anything stupid and these guys will cut your fucking heart out without blinking an eye. You understand?"

The five searched the homestead, the sleepout, and all the sheds for weapons, but only found some boning knives. On searching the sleepout, Jimmy, walked into a room with a huge king-size bed, with a wrought iron bedhead and bed end.

"This is where we will tie these two up; tie their hands to the bedhead and their ankles to the bed end," Jimmy told the others.

The room was originally designed to be a storeroom but had ended up as the parents' bedroom. It had a high window running right across the back wall that dropped seventy-five-centimetres; it was designed to let light in rather than looking out. The door could be padlocked from the outside.

"With that lock on, even if they untied themselves, they wouldn't be able to escape. I cannot see them getting out through that window even if they were not tied," said Jimmy.

Tom and Shirley were tied to the bed. Later, as it got dark, the escapees decided Shirley should cook them dinner. Reluctantly, Shirley agreed, if she and Tom could eat too.

"You don't try anything stupid and you and your old man can eat and survive. But you try doing anything stupid, you're dead. Do you understand what I'm fucking well saying?" asked Angelo.

After they had eaten, Tom and Shirley, were taken back to the room and tied to the bed once more. The door was locked. The five escapees discovered Tom's bar concealed behind a set of four bi-fold louvre doors. Soon Bob, and the Bettini twins, were enjoying a heavy drinking session. Bull, and Jimmy, enjoyed throwing down some two beers each, as they were wary of Vince. They knew that they were not on his Christmas card list. Although, they had never spoken about it, both men inwardly knew that for them to survive, one of them would be forced to kill Vince, and possibly Angelo as well.

Around ten-thirty, Vince, was plastered as he staggered through the house and into the lounge room where Jimmy and Bull were watching the late news.

Seeing Jimmy on the settee, Vince mumbled, "There you are, you fucking little slant-eyed prick. I'm going to show you who's fucking boss around here."

As he moved towards Jimmy, Jimmy stood to face the challenge, but Bull, poked a leg out and Vince crashed face first into the carpeted floor, and promptly fell asleep. On hearing the noise, Angelo, and Bob, rushed into the lounge to see Jimmy standing over the prone Vince. Fearing the worst, Angelo glared at Jimmy, who returned the stare. Both men had death in their eyes.

Bull, stood up, moved towards Angelo and said, "Your brother is okay; he tripped over my feet and fell asleep. Nothing else happened."

Angelo knelt down alongside Vince just as he began to snore.

Bob interjected, "Aye, listen you guys, they're talking about us."

A TV reporter was interviewing the leader of the task force. "Inspector Mark Kidd, do you know where the escapees are now?"

"No, not really," replied the inspector. "It's as if they have vanished into thin air. We just can't pick up on any trail as the weather and all this rain hasn't helped us find them. But I promise you, the police will recapture them."

That night, Jimmy locked the bedroom door and, as an added bit of security, he moved a heavy chest of drawers up against the door.

CHAPTER 20

THE KILLINGS BEGIN

On Saturday morning, the sun shone brightly, but the river was still swollen. The five decided to move onto the next house, Sally and Josh's home. They made use of any form of cover as they crept up to the homestead. They advanced slowly, keeping a keen eye for any sign of life from within the house and out-buildings.

Jimmy, and Bob, moved off to search the big machinery shed and other buildings, leaving the others to check out the house. Josh, never notice two men keeping low and moving towards the sheds, he was too involved in bookwork in his office. Approaching from a westerly direction, the escapees don't see Sally, working in the garden on the eastern side of the house. Keeping Sally, company was her favourite dog, Blitz, a five-year-old Queensland blue heeler. As Vince went through the front gate on the western side, the old spring that automatically closed the gate gave its familiar creaking sound. Sally missed it, but Blitz immediately went to investigate the noise.

JOHN A. W. INMAN

Rounding the corner of the house, Blitz saw the men moving towards the front stairs and approached in an aggressive growling manner. As she moved towards the men, Bull, whose only fear in life was being attacked by a dog, a legacy of a dog attack when he was just nine years old, swung the .22 at the advancing Blitz, and fired. Blitz, let out a horrendous yelp as the bullet ripped through her body. She stumbled and fell, drawing her last breaths.

Sally, heard the shot and hurried around the corner of the house. Josh, also heard and looked out the window. He saw the men and realised the danger, immediately reaching for his 303 rifle he kept loaded on top of the shelves. With the 303 in his hands, he moved quickly through the house towards the front door. Jimmy, and Bob, looked at each other when they heard the 22 and ran towards the house.

When Sally, saw Blitz was dead, she threw her forty-eight-kilogram frame at the men, screaming. Vince, grabbed her and carried her screaming up the five stairs. He kicked open the front door and threw Sally to the floor, like a rag doll. At the same time Vince burst through the front door, Josh, entered the lounge room opposite the front door and saw Vince throw Sally to the floor. Reacting immediately, he raised the 303 to his shoulder and fired directly at Vince who was desperately trying to back out the door. The bullet hit him just under the ribcage on his right side. Staggering and falling backwards, he fell back onto Bull, knocking him off his feet. Both fell to the floor. Jimmy, and Bob, heard the boom of the 303 and hesitated, wondering what in hell was going on.

"Let's not rush into this," Jimmy said to Bob. "We better be careful as it does not sound good."

Angelo, sprang into the room with his filleting knife in his hand. Josh, quickly used the rifle bolt to eject the spent cartridge, reset the bolt and aimed the 303 at Angelo. He said calmly, "Stop where you are, and drop the bloody knife."

Vince, was groaning on the floor, and blood was spreading on his shirt.

"You fucking old bastard, why did you shoot him? I will kill you, you old prick."

Angelo, started to move towards Josh, who pulled the trigger, but the only sound was of the hammer falling on an empty chamber.

Angelo, stepped over Sally, moving closer to Josh who took the rifle by the barrel and held it back over his right shoulder, like holding a baseball bat. As Angelo, moved closer, Josh saw murder in his eyes, and knew he would have to connect with Angelo, if he was to survive. Using all his strength, he swung the rifle in a powerful arc aimed at Angelo's head, but Angelo ducked, and the rifle smashed into the stone wall surrounding the open fire. The force shattered the stock from the barrel, and the firing mechanism. Josh, tried a reverse swing with the barrel, but it passed harmlessly inches in front of Angelo's face. Angelo, was upon him in an instant, sinking the fishing knife up to its hilt, and as he pulled the blade through Josh's mid-section, he coldly looked Josh in the eyes until all signs of life left his body. Sally, on regaining her feet, saw Angelo murdering Josh, and attacked him with all her might. Angelo swung her down to the floor, coldly knifed her in the throat, and let her bleed to death.

Jimmy, and Bob, reached the front door, just as Bull got to his feet. They moved into the room and saw that Vince had been shot, and Josh and Sally were lying dead in large growing pools of blood.

"What in the fuck has happened here?" shouted Jimmy. "What have you done, you stupid idiot?"

From the shooting of Vince, to the murders of Josh and Sally, only 50 seconds had passed. Angelo, was in no mood to answer any questions as he was on his knees by his twin brother, trying to stem the flow of blood.

Bull, inspected the wound and said, "It's a clean shot, it's gone right through hitting no bones. It is not that bad," said Bull. "I've seen worse gunshot wounds that haven't proved fatal."

They moved Vince to a bedroom, and searched the house till they found a first aid box. When they cleaned up the wound, Vince cried, and carried on like a hurt child.

CHAPTER 21

THE MANNS ARE
CONFRONTED BY EVIL

Over at the Mann's house, John and Mary, were finishing a late breakfast on their front patio. The kids and Tuffy, were running around having fun. John heard the two rifle shots and thought it was strange someone was shooting a .22. Morris Cooper, owned the only .22 in the Valley, but he had left for Melbourne before the river flooded. The roar of the 303, not long after the .22, really caused John some concern. *Has the dog pack come in close to Josh's place? Has he borrowed the .22? Something isn't right here,* he thought.

"Sweetie, I'm just going over to Josh's to see what all the shooting is about."

"OK, say hello to Sally for me. Please thank her for the scones she sent over yesterday and take her cake tin back with you."

John, wasn't thinking of anything sinister; he was more curious why the two shots had been fired.

After seeing the carnage in the lounge room, Bob, sat down out on the veranda on the old lounge. He immediately let out a terrified scream, as the sleeping python moved under him. Terrified, he leapt over the railing and fell heavily on the ground near Blitz's body. Jimmy and Bull rushed out and see Bob sprawled on the ground.

"What's your bloody problem, what is the matter with you?" asked Bull.

"I just sat on a bloody big snake on that lounge," replied Bob.

Immediately, Jimmy and Bull move away from the lounge, looking everywhere for the snake, which had slithered off the veranda and gone under the house.

As this happened, John was crossing the footbridge and saw Blitz's body on the front lawn. Three strange men were standing there, all talking very excitedly.

"Aye, guys, there is a fellow coming over the bridge," said Bob in a low voice.

Stopping abruptly in his tracks, John looked closely at the three men. Although they were dirty, he recognised the prison uniforms on two of the men. He had visited Barnaby Prison twice as a fill-in chaplain. John, was instantly aware he was in danger, and that something terrible had taken place at Josh and Sally's home; he turned and ran.

"Stop, or I will shoot your fucking head off," yelled Bull.

John smiled to himself, *You won't hit me with Morris's .22 at this distance unless I am very unlucky.*

Bull fired two quick shots; one hit somewhere on the bridge behind John, and the other was nowhere near him. John ran as fast as he could. He cuts through some bush and a small stand of ironbark trees in a more direct line to home. Bull, Bob, and Jimmy, give chase, but did not know the shortcut John had taken, so they ran along the farm track and gave John extra time.

John raced into the driveway, saw Mary still sitting on the patio, and yelled at her to get the kids into the house immediately.

Responding straight away to the urgency in her husband's voice, Mary, called the children and told them to hurry inside. Melitta and Katie, were only twenty-five metres away and moved quickly into the house. Nick, had been cleaning out Tuffy's run and came running to see what all the excitement was about. John reached the house, rushed into the bedroom, grabbed his 22-250 and quickly filled it with five shells. He raced back out to the front of the house.

"What's going on?" asked a scared and worried Mary.

"I don't really know, but those escapees are here in the Valley, and one shot at me. I think they are coming here. Where's Mitch? Does anyone know where he is?" yelled John.

"Quickly, kids, where is your brother, where is Mitch?" screamed a crying and frightened Mary.

"He said he was going down to the river near the front driveway," answered Nick.

"Mitch, Mitch, come quickly," screamed Mary and John in unison.

Mitch, being a typical eight-year-old, had heard his parents calling him and slowly and reluctantly started heading for home. He no sooner got onto the driveway when he heard the pounding footsteps of the three escapees running up behind him.

John yelled, "Run, Mitch, run as fast as you can."

At the same time, Bull shouted, "Stop, kid, stop where you are."

For what seemed an eternity, Mitch stood frozen to the spot. But the frantic screaming of his mother, Mary, made him start to cry, as he once again started running towards his parents. Tuffy, sensing the danger to Mitch, raced headlong down the driveway to protect him.

Bob started yelling, "Stop, kid, stop where you are, don't bloody well move."

"No, Mitch, please run as fast as you can," screamed a crying Mary.

Bull, seeing Tuffy charging down the driveway, raised the rifle to his shoulder and took aim at Tuffy, but everyone thought he was aiming at Mitch. But the only sound anyone heard was the explosive roar of John's 22-250. The bullet hit Bull in the chest, ripping through his heart and he was dead before he hits the ground. Bob and Jimmy, dived for the cover of nearby bushes.

Mitch, with Tuffy close alongside him, ran to his crying mother, who grabbed him in her arms. She turned and saw her husband still with the rifle against his shoulder with a look of unbelief on his face. Mary shook his arm which jarred him back to reality. John, told everyone to move into the house. As they headed into the house, Bob and Jimmy, ran over to Bull to see how he was.

"Shit, that bastard killed Bull, just like that," said Bob, who picked up the 22 rifle and moved back to the cover of the bushes.

"Jimmy, what are we going to do now?" said a shocked Bob. "Fuck that guy."

"We will make them pay for Bull's death. They are all going to die, that is my promise to Bull," said Jimmy.

Inside the house, John rushed to the toilet and threw up, sick at the thought of taking another human's life. Melitta and Katie, had watched the events unfolding before their eyes and were stunned, frightened, and crying. They did not understand what was happening.

John re-joined the family in the front lounge room. Mary hugged him and kissed him, thanking him for protecting Mitch.

"Does anyone know where those men are?" asked John.

"They are hiding in the bushes down by the driveway entrance," said Melitta.

"Dad, who are those men?" asked Nick. "And did you kill that one? What's it all about?"

"I'm not certain what has happened over at Josh and Sally's home, but I think it is pretty bad. These men are the escapees from Barnaby Prison. You might have seen it on the TV. They are very dangerous, and you all need to be very, very brave and do whatever we tell you."

"Are they going to kill us?" asked Melitta as she watched the drive.

"No, no," said Mary. "Someone will come and help us."

"How, Mum? The river is still flooded. No one can get in or out," stated Nick.

Realising that she needed to be calm for the sake of her children, Mary took a couple of deep breaths and answered, "But those men got here somehow, Nick."

"Maybe the river has gone down, and those men just came in on the road," interjected Melitta as she watched the drive.

"No, the river is still in flood as I had to use Josh's footbridge to cross it," said John.

The three younger children sobbed in fear, John and Mary tried to remain calm and help them. Tuffy, was licking their hands, sensing the tension and fear within the family.

"Nick, you and I will check all the doors and windows. Let's make sure that the security locks are in place. Start from that window and go around the house that way, and I will go this way. Mary, you and the girls keep watch, let me know when you see any of those men, especially if they are coming towards the house."

"OK, honey," said Mary.

CHAPTER 22

DEFENDING THEMSELVES

Lying tied and sore on the bed in the sleepout, Tom and Shirley, heard all the gunshots and wondered how many of their friends had been killed, and if that meant they soon would be killed. They started discussing their life together, apologising for hurts they had caused each other, and confirming their mutual love. When the subject turned to their children and grandchildren, the tears flowed as the growing uneasiness about their chance of survival became too much for them.

John, already knew the phones were out of order, but he picked up the handset anyway, and tried to get a dial tone. The silence confirmed his fears—the phones were dead. He now started to plan how he would protect his family.

Mary asked John, "Do you think we should stay in the house or move out into the bush? Would we be better off escaping into the bush?"

"No, I really think we are safer in the house, as in the bush they could easily ambush us. No, I think the house is the best option."

"Honey," said Mary, "I am really frightened. I just want to cry, but I don't want to scare the children any more than they are at the moment."

John moved to Mary, and they hugged and kissed each other.

"I will do whatever it takes to protect you all," he said. "What we need to do is keep a continual lookout for those escapees. We don't want them to surprise us. Having Tuffy, in the house gives us a great advantage as he will hear anyone coming."

It was just after ten-thirty, when John called his family together. "Listen to me, all of you. We need to keep a constant lookout for those men. We will all take turns of one hour each; one will watch from the lounge room, (the lounge room had a large curved floor to ceiling glass wall that gave them a clear view for approximately 220 degrees) and another from the kitchen," said John.

The blind spot was the western wall of the garage and house which had one large window in John's office. John and Nick, spent an hour emptying a large bookcase of books and moving the bookcase to cover the window, then replacing the books and moving the office desk up against the bookcase.

Talking to Mary, John said, "I don't expect them to try anything till it gets dark, which gives us around five hours; that's if they try anything at all."

For the rest of the day, they don't see any sign of the escapees. The shadows lengthened as the sun retreated to the west, where it would soon disappear behind the crater ridge. In the east, dark clouds were rolling in and more wet weather was on the way.

"We had better work out a routine," said Mary, "as we will need to sleep, eat and still keep watch."

"Right," replied John, "I will have Melitta with me, and you can have Nick, Katie and Mitch, but the moment you see anything you must wake me."

They gathered the children and told them what they planned to do.

Katie asked, "How long will we have to do this?"

"I don't know, maybe these guys will just leave the valley and go away," said John, but inwardly he knew they would not leave until they had taken out revenge for the death of the man outside.

"How many escapees are there, Dad?" asked Nick.

"Well, the news said that six escaped, but they caught one, so that means there are still five."

"Four," said Nick. "That guy in the driveway isn't moving; I think you killed him, Dad."

Nick's comment impacted his father, and he again felt sick in his stomach. Unlike Josh's house with its white picket fence, the Mann's fence started from the front corner of the garage nearest the house and continued right around the house, finishing on the back corner of the garage farthest from the house. The fence consisted of eleven strainer posts and stays, a front, side and rear gate, and metal star posts in between. It had four number eight-gauge plain wires (a top, bottom and two middle wires) over which wire netting had been attached and buried into the ground to stop rabbits and foxes from digging under. On top was a single strand of barbwire. Inside this fence, Mary had her chook run with half a dozen black Australorp hens and a rooster, plus her veggie and flower gardens. At different parts of the fence, Mary planted a number of vines, passionfruit, Chinese gooseberries, a grapevine, and scented jasmine vines. All vines were still in the early growing days and did not offer concealment from those inside the home.

Jimmy and Bob, returned to Josh's house to fill Angelo in on the events at the Mann's house.

"What in the fuck was that shot? It sounded like a bloody cannon," asked Angelo as they entered the house.

Jimmy replied, "By the size of the hole in Bull's back, you would think it came from a cannon."

"Bull's dead?" asked a surprised Angelo.

"Yes. That guy is supposed to be a fucking minister of religion, but he just upped and shot Bull down in cold blood," said Bob. "But we will get them all, even those kids, won't we, Jimmy?"

"You can bet your life on that. But we have to be bloody careful, that was a quick shot that guy got off at Bull, and he hit him right in the heart."

"It was just bloody lucky, a fucking fluke," exclaimed Bob.

"No, I don't think it was. That guy knows how to shoot, and he is fucking good at it. It was no fluke; he hit where he wanted to hit," said Jimmy. "But we will get him, and it will be a very sorry day for him."

"How do you plan to do that?" asked Bob. "That prick's rifle is a lot more powerful than this piss weak .22. He will cut us down before we get close enough to do anything."

"We will wait till dark and with this cloud cover we will get right up to the house without them seeing us. Then, we will get that prick. We will come in from three sides as he can't be watching everywhere," said Jimmy. Turning towards Angelo he asked, "How's Vince?"

"He's sleeping right now, but he is running a fever. He really needs to get to a doctor."

"Can't see that happening for a while," replied Jimmy.

Bob, was sent back to watch the Mann's house just in case the family tried to leave.

Inside the house Mary had finished serving a good dinner to her family in the lounge room. John just picked at his meal. Mary knew he felt terrible, and she encouraged him to eat.

"Aye, everyone," said John. "When it gets dark outside, we won't have any lights on in the house. We will need to round up all our torches so that we can use them. If we keep the house in darkness, they won't know where we are and that might be enough to make them unsure of what they will confront if they try to get in the house."

Melitta, volunteered to fetch and check that all the torches are working. Mary looked in her pantry and found a four-pack of Double D batteries to replenish any batteries the torches needed. In the TV room adjacent to the lounge room, John secured the curtains to the architraves using thumbtacks so no torchlight could be seen from the outside.

Jimmy and Angelo, returned to where Bob was watching the house.

"Have you seen anyone, any movement?" asked Jimmy.

"Just a bit in that front room with the rounded windows," replied Bob.

"Well, let us see if they are watching," said a grinning Jimmy, as he moved out onto the gravel driveway and dragged his feet.

Instantly, Tuffy began to bark. What a human ear can hear at one hundred metres, a German Shepherd hears clearly 500 metres away.

"Bloody dog. I did not expect that reaction. We will have to kill that fucking dog," a surprised Jimmy exclaimed, as the three moved quickly to the cover of the bush.

When Tuffy started barking, John looked down the driveway and saw the three men scurrying for the bushes. He smiled.

Patting Tuffy he said, "Good boy, Tuffy, thank God, we have you. Mary, I am going for a walk around the house to see if there are any blind spots and what we can do about them."

"Be careful. Remember they have rifles," replied a worried Mary.

About thirty-five metres south of the driveway entrance, John, checked he's assumption of a blind spot existing on the south-western wall of the garage, but a person would have to cover approximately 100 metres of open ground to get there. This wall of the garage had two large windows with heavy gauge weld mesh covering them, which prevented anyone breaking in. On returning to the house, John told Mary of his concern with the garage wall.

"I'm going into the garage to let them know that we may watch through the windows. I will also throw some hessian bags across the windows and let them see Nick, and myself moving around, hopefully this may prevent them from trying to creep up that way."

While in the garage, John filled the 13 KVA Honda Generator with fuel. They had used it while building the house, and then connected it to the house as a back-up electricity supply.

"Why are you filling that, Dad?" asked Nick.

"Just in case we need it." He pushed the start button and instantly the generator burst into life. "That is great," said John.

As daylight quickly faded due to the dark and heavy clouds coming in from the east, John, explained to the children that if they had lights on inside the house, it would be easier for those outside to see inside. Taking the three torches and some thin cardboard, John made tubes to put over them and limit the spread of light. John, turned on one torch and pointed the beam down to just in front of his feet, to demonstrate to the children how they could use the torches to move around inside the house, without the escapees seeing them.

Melita asked for the second time the same question that she and Nick had been talking about, "Dad, are we going to die?"

The question stunned Mary and John, and they looked at their children with their mouths agape.

"No!" said Mary, as she started to cry.

Trying to be positive, calm and assertive, John held back his tears and said, "Kids, we are in a dangerous situation, but Mum, Tuffy, and I won't let anything happen to you, believe me." Hugging their children, John said, "Now, you must all be very brave. Mummy and I, need your help to watch for those men, especially when it gets dark."

"Will they get into the house when the night comes?" asked Katie.

"No," replied John. "Remember when the other families came to our house for a BBQ, or games night? Remember, turning on those floodlights on the four corners of the house, and the two on the garage? Remember how we saw those rabbits, and that fox way down near the river? Those bad men out there are in for a surprise if they try to creep up in the dark."

"Spot on," said a smiling Nick, as he clapped his hands.

"The other good thing about those outside lights being on, and the house in darkness," said John, "is that we will be able to see them, but they won't be able to see us in the house."

CHAPTER 23

ATTACKS ON THE MANN S HOME BEGIN

Outside, darkness was rapidly shrouding the valley. The escapees decided it was time to make their assault on the house and its occupants. Inside the house, John and Mary had been sitting inside, watching the driveway intently. They had noticed no movement.

Tuffy, lay next to John, but suddenly, got to his feet and his bristles stood up on his back as he looked out the window, growling that same blood curling growl Nick heard months ago in the cavern.

"Quick, Nick, turn on those outside lights, all three switches," said John.

Instantly, the dark night was turned into bright daylight as the six double floodlights lit up an area 100 metres right around the house and buildings. Thirty metres north of the driveway entrance, Jimmy and Bob, who had decided to approach the house across the front paddock instead of walking up the driveway and alerting Tuffy, were frozen in their tracks as the lights caught them out. In a panic, they both turned. Jimmy turned to his left, and Bob to his right, and they crashed into each other. Jimmy was knocked sideways, and Bob fell headlong to the ground. Swearing and cursing, they scrambled back to the cover of the bush. Inside the house, the family broke into laughter as they saw the collision, and mad dash for the bush.

"Fucking hell, this is all we need," said Bob. "It's like the Sydney Cricket Ground with those bloody lights."

"Yeah, this guy is starting to really piss me off," said an irate Jimmy.

"Bob, keep watch while I talk to Angelo."

Jimmy was on his way back to Josh's house and was just about to cross the footbridge when he heard three shots from Bob's .22. He hurried back as fast as he could in the gloom.

"What's all the fucking shooting about?" asked Jimmy.

"Just shooting those shithouse lights out," replied a very angry Bob.

"Right, how many have you hit?"

"None yet, but I am getting the fucking range and getting bloody close."

"You bloody idiot, Bob, you are wasting our bullets," snarled Jimmy. "We only had twenty-three shells. Bull, used one shooting that dog, and two when he shot at that bloody minister guy on the bridge. Now you have wasted another fucking eight, nine, ten. How many fucking bullets have you got left?"

Putting his hand into the pocket of the National Parks and Wildlife jacket, Bob counted. "I got nine shells left."

"Don't go wasting any more on those lights, only use them to kill that prick there in that house," yelled Jimmy.

"Well, then, what in the fucking hell are we going to do about those lights?" said a chastened Bob.

"I don't know right now, but I will think of something," replied Jimmy.

On hearing the first shot, John and Mary moved the children into John's office. In the office, they heard most of the bullets whacking into the brick wall of the garage with a deep thud.

"I guess they're shooting at the lights, but if that's Morris's .22 they are using they will be lucky to get anywhere near the lights," said John.

In the morning, light misty rain was falling over the valley and the escapees had decided to cut off the electricity supply to the Mann's house. Keeping to the bush, Angelo and Jimmy, followed the power lines from Josh's place towards the Mann's home. They noted that the second last power pole in the valley had the Mann's electrical transformer attached to it.

"Good," said Angelo, "we can cut the power off to that prick's house. All we need to do is pull down those wires."

Searching through Josh's sheds, they found several ropes, but no-one could throw one end of the rope over the high electricity lines. Bob went back to the shed and found Josh's eight-foot beach-fishing rod. Locating the fishing tackle, he took out a couple of heavy sinkers and picked up a spool of light nylon rope. Starting up the little Massey Ferguson TEA 20 tractor, he headed back to where Angelo and Jimmy were still trying to get the rope across the wires.

Smiling at their failure, Bob said, "Step aside, ladies, and watch a master at work."

Attaching a heavy sinker to the end of the line, Bob, cast the sinker up and over the wires, but he stopped the spool too early and the sinker snapped the line and disappeared into the bush. Choosing another heavier sinker, he cut the fishing line two metres from the rod, tied the sinker onto the line and then tied the light nylon rope to the fishing line right behind the sinker. They stretched out the nylon rope on the ground and then tied the loose end to the tractor. Clearing a five-metre circle on the ground starting near the tractor, they rewound the rope into a large circle within the cleared area.

"Hope you know what you are doing and not just wasting our time," said Angelo.

"As I said, stand and watch a master at work," replied Bob, as he cast again over the wires. This time the heavy sinker flew over the wires, taking the nylon rope with it.

"You are a fucking genius," said Angelo, as he patted Bob on the back.

Tying the nylon rope to the heavier rope, they pulled it up and over the wires. After retrieving the heavier nylon rope, Bob made a slipknot around the rope going up to the wires. He then tied the rope to the tractor and started backing away from the electricity lines and the slip knot moved up along itself until the loop it had formed gets smaller and smaller, drawing the two electricity lines closer together. Angelo and Jimmy, were still standing under the wires, looking up excitedly, when the tightening loop forced the two electricity wires to touch and caused a massive bang and a shower of sparks. This frightened the life out of both men. Bob, on the tractor, burst out in laughter, but continued to reverse the tractor away from the wires. The sparking stopped as the wires were pulled down from the transformer on the pole.

"Mum," yelled Mitch, "the TV's just gone off."

Mary thought, *That's odd, the microwave has also stopped.* She tried the light switch, but nothing happening. "Honey," she said, "something has happened to the electricity. There are no lights, and no power."

Quickly looking around at the clocks and other electrical appliances, John realised the escapees had somehow disconnected their electricity.

"Don't worry, what they don't know is that we have a generator. But we won't start using that until it gets dark. That means no TV and for meals I will bring in the camp gas cooker from the garage."

In the garage, John checked his fuel supply for the generator and estimated the fuel would not last two nights, with the generator running constantly from seven p.m. to six a.m. *Sunday night around midnight we will have to leave the house. Maybe that will be time enough for outside help to come. When I don't turn up for Sunday morning's service, someone will try contacting us and help will be on its way.*

On returning to the house, John told Mary about the fuel situation, and that they needed to make plans to get away from the house, but he didn't want to do this while there was bad weather.

"Mary, this is the situation as I see it. Six prisoners escaped, one was recaptured, and I shot one. That leaves four more we possibly have to deal with, so the odds aren't good."

"But surely help will come soon," replied an anxious Mary.

"I wouldn't want to bet our lives on that. No one knows what's gone on in the valley, and we can't contact anyone. No! I'm afraid no one is coming to help us. It is all up to us."

"What do you mean, it is all up to us?"

"If those guys hang around, it means that they are after us. If that is the case, it is us against them. We will need to neutralise some if not all of them by whatever means we can. If we have to leave the house, we don't want four of them chasing us, so we have to even things up a bit."

John, had already internally worked through the issue of killing another human being. When he shot Bull, it was more a reflex action. But to deliberately set out to injure, or kill another human being was something he has been struggling with since. He knew that it was a case of him, or them, and not only him but his entire family. The thought of his family being terrorised, hurt, and maybe murdered, gave him a steely resolve to do whatever had to be done.

CHAPTER 24

PLAN TO EVEN
THE ODDS

In the house, John and Mary noticed, that there was only one person keeping watch on the house, and that person was in the bushes down near the driveway entrance. John, shared with Mary his plan that could put Mary's and Tuffy's lives in danger.

If Mary, dressed in John's clothes, and wore his Akubra hat, from a distance the escapees might think it was John, and they might expose themselves, giving John a clear shot with his rifle.

Mary, agreed only after John said that Morris Cooper's .22 had no scope. It only had the barrel sights to use and all the time that John had used it when he first came to the Valley, it never proved true and the greater the distance the worse it was.

They waited till they were as certain as they could be that only one escapee was watching, and Mary, accompanied by Tuffy, went out the back door carrying an axe and heading in a southerly direction parallel with the fence that ran to the driveway.

"Honey, if any shooting starts, hit the ground and stay down."

"You can count on me doing that," replied an anxious Mary.

Mary practiced walking with a longer stride like John's. Tuffy, seemed concerned and ran around Mary, trying to stop her from leaving the safety of the house.

Down at the driveway entrance, Bob saw Mary, mistook her for John, and just as John had hoped, moved across the driveway but then dropped out of sight.

Oh, no! John thought, as he realised Bob had ducked into the old stone quarry. But, he immediately remembered that with all the rain, the quarry would have flooded, so Bob could not disappear into it, he will have to stay near the fence.

John was positioned at the back door, when movement down next to the fence alongside of the quarry caught his eye. Using his scope, he saw that Bob had only moved twenty-five metres along the fence line, up the top of the quarry, and was kneeling by a large ironbark fence post amongst bushes. However, the only clear sight John had of him was part of his left knee and lower leg. John saw the barrel of the .22 rifle pointing in the direction of Mary and Tuffy. Using the brickwork around the back door as support, John hastily raised his rifle and aimed at Bob's leg below the knee.

God, help me to shoot straight. He held his breath and squeezed the trigger, and the two rifles blasted simultaneously. Bob, screamed out in pain, and looking through the scope John saw that he had hit Bob's leg below the knee.

Yelling out her name, he raced out through the back gate and across the paddock towards where Tuffy, was standing over a prone Mary. John feared the worst as he raced towards her. Reaching her, he gently turned her on her back and saw the blood over her face. His heart sank inside of him, and the tears started to flow freely.

"No, no, no, why, God? Why have you allowed this to happen?" he implored.

Amid his worst fears, he failed to see Mary slowly opening her eyes until she said, "I'm alright, love, I just smacked my head on a rock when I dived to the ground. I must have knocked myself out."

John hugged her, until Mary, startled John by yelling, "Look." She pointed in the direction of the house, and Tuffy immediately raced back towards it.

Turning back towards the house, John, saw Jimmy, and Angelo, racing towards the house. Angelo, was a couple of metres in front of Jimmy and moving quickly. Picking up his rifle, John aimed at Angelo and fired. The bullet whistled past Angelo's chest and exploded one of the two-inch by two-inch garden stakes supporting one of Mary's trees she had planted along the driveway. As the stake exploded and fell to the ground, the tree tilted at a 30-degree angle to the ground. Angelo, abruptly stopped, and swung around and raced back towards the driveway entrance and bush cover. Jimmy was in hot pursuit.

John, realised Angelo and Jimmy's intentions were to get control of the house and kids. He was angry at himself for what they could have done and started running towards them, stopping and firing off another two rounds. Suddenly, he was aware that Bob, despite his wound, was now firing the .22 at him. Running in a zigzag manner, he made it back to the safety of the house into which Mary, and Tuffy, had just disappeared. As he reached the back door, a shot from the 22 blasted through the laundry window two metres away.

Katie, came running into the kitchen from the lounge room, saw the blood all over her mother's face, and fainted with shock. John, closed the back door and looked out to see if Bob was visible, before he turned to see Mary bending over Katie.

"What's wrong, has she been shot?" he asked anxiously.

"No, honey, she just fainted when she saw my bloody face. It's all getting too much; Katie is stressed out, as we all are."

John moved into the lounge room where Nick had been watching down the driveway.

"Aye, Dad," said Nick. "When I saw those guys running towards the house I started to send Katie, Melita and Mitch out the back door, but then I heard your rifle and although you missed that first guy, it scared the daylight out of him when that stake was blown apart right next to him. The look on his face was so funny, I couldn't stop laughing."

"You did well, Nick. Where are they now, do you know?"

"Yeah, they just went down into the quarry."

"Keep watching and call me if you see them."

"Sure, Dad."

Ten minutes later, Nick called John to the lounge room. John moved to the window and saw Jimmy, and Angelo, carrying Bob across the driveway to the cover of the bush.

Out of sight of the house, Jimmy and Angelo, go back to get some painkillers from the house Vince was in, and bandages to dress Bob's wound. They also carried back a chaise lounge to put Bob on, somewhere out of sight behind the bushes.

CHAPTER 25

THE PROPOSAL PUT TO JOHN IS REJECTED

At five-ten on Saturday, Angelo's booming voice draws the attention of the Mann's.

"You in the house, you, the minister, can you hear me?"

John walked out the front door and towards the garage with rifle in hand. "What do you want?" he asked.

"If you hand over your rifle, we will let you and your family walk away, and no harm will come to you."

"Why should I trust you after what you have been trying to do? Why don't you just walk out of the valley? I have no intention to give you my rifle."

"OK," said Angelo. "It's your funeral, what with no electricity and in a dark house, you won't know what fucking window or door we will be coming through."

Walking back into the house, John thought, *I'm not much different to those guys. Earlier, I planned and shot one guy and tried to shoot another two. Given the right circumstances, anyone can become a killer.*

CHAPTER 26

THE WAITING CONTINUES

Mary and Katie, prepared a salad with cold meat for the family's dinner at seven-forty-five. As the light faded, John went to the garage through the back door and turned on the Honda Generator. *Hopefully, they will not be able to hear this down at the driveway entrance. Boy, are they in for a surprise.*

The family took up positions at different windows after dinner and stared out into the growing darkness, hoping to see anyone creeping up towards the house. As a bit of extra precaution, John reluctantly, let Tuffy out into the fenced yard that ran most of the way around the house. He knew Tuffy would growl and bark at the approach of any person, just as he always had done even with the other residents of Hidden Valley.

The tension in the house was rising, and the kids were scared. Mary and John tried not to let their children know how scared and worried they were. No one could see anything outside, and the escapees saw no one inside the house. It was nearly nine o'clock when Tuffy started growling and barking near the back door. John yelled to Nick to hit the light switches, and instantly the area right around the house was once more lit up like the Sydney Cricket Ground. From the shattered window of the laundry, John saw Angelo with the .22 rifle twenty-five metres away from the back corner of the garage. Angelo, spied Tuffy outside and quickly raised the .22 to his shoulder. He fired a shot at Tuffy and the shot ricocheted off the steel frame of the back gate, a foot away from Tuffy who was now really releasing that same blood curdling growl he did when he or members of his family were in danger.

From the laundry window, the corner of the garage was concealing most of Angelo, and Jimmy was completely out of sight. John could see Angelo's forearm and only inches of his body, so the .22 rifle was his best hope. Angelo, was steadying himself for another shot at Tuffy when John fired and his bullet smashed into the stock of the .22, splintering it and burying some splinters into Angelo's face. The force of the bullet hitting the rifle and flung it out of Angelo's hands onto the open grass, as he screamed and reached for his face.

"Fucking hell, that arsehole shot me," screamed Angelo, as he and Jimmy raced for the safety of the bush.

Using a gas lantern that they had brought from Josh's shed, Jimmy inspected Angelo's face, which had blood running in rivulets down his face.

"You are pretty lucky none of those splinters went into your eye," said Jimmy.

"That prick will pay. All he is, is a bloody country minister. I will cut his fucking heart out. Who in the fuck does he think he is?"

Jimmy spent five minutes removing the splinters from Angelo's face. "How in the fuck did they get electricity?" enquired Jimmy.

"Shit, I don't know, I thought we cut their fucking power off," said Angelo.

"I bet they've got a bloody generator," said Bob.

"That might have been the noise we heard when we got close to the garage," replied Jimmy.

"Maybe it's time for us to get the fuck out of here while we still can," said Bob.

"No! No! No!" screamed Angelo. "This fuck-arse will not do this to me and live to talk about it. I want to see him and his fucking family dead before I leave this place. I want him to witness his family being killed and the last thing he will ever fucking hear is my laughter as I slit his fucking throat."

"Yes, and I want him for killing Bull," said Jimmy. "But he is pretty good with that bloody rifle, so we will have to out-think him. After all, killing is what we do best, not him."

Back in the house, Katie reported that the men had run back to the bush. John could see the .22 still lying in the paddock.

"I'm going out to get that rifle, it is one big problem gone."

As he went out the back, he gave Tuffy a huge hug and then walked over and picked up the .22, which, despite the shattered stock, could still be fired. Going into the garage to top up the generator, John used his metalwork vice to smash the trigger assembly with the help of his 'gentle persuader,' an eight-pound sledgehammer and threw it into the rubbish bin.

CHAPTER 27

A WEAKNESS IN THE HOME'S DEFENCE IS FOUND

At one-thirty a.m., Mary went out to where John was sound asleep on the lounge, and gently shook him awake saying, "Honey, you told us to let you know when the lights started flickering, well, they just started a couple of minutes ago."

Trying to wake up and understand exactly what Mary was saying, he was soon fully aware of the situation and quickly moved towards the door that led to the garage. All the lights flickered a couple more times and just as John was about to enter the garage, the generator stopped, and everything was in total darkness.

Turning and hurrying as fast as he can back to the house, John yelled, "Quickly, someone bring me a torch. I can't see. Quick."

Mitch, was the quickest to respond as he had been holding a torch all the time. Returning to the garage, he partly filled the generator, pumped the fuel through, hit the electric start button, and the generator spluttered a couple of times, then lights came back on. John, filled the generator to the top and took stock of the fuel and realised that there was not enough fuel for another full night. *We will have to leave the house tomorrow night.*

Back down the driveway, Angelo and Jimmy, were wondering why the lights had gone off.

"It's simple," said Bob, "the generator ran out of fuel and he had to refill it."

"That's his weakness; when we see those lights flickering, we can make our move and get this arsehole," said Angelo.

"It won't be tonight," replied Bob. "I reckon that the generator's fuel tank will last till morning. But we will get that prick tomorrow night. When we see those lights flicker, we need to be up alongside that garage pronto."

Taking turns to watch for any movement, the family got through the night with no more drama. On Sunday morning, John mentally counted his opposition; he had only ever seen four escapees. *Has a second one split from this group, or is it I just haven't seen him? Is he going to be their secret weapon? I must treat it as if I'm still up against three able-bodied and very dangerous men. But as far as I can guess, they haven't anymore firearms apart from Josh's old 303.*

In all the commotion, no-one had noticed that the river's level was slowly falling. Another 36 hours and the valley would once more be open to the outside world. There were still clouds, but the blue was starting to claim back the skies.

John, was exhausted and sat down for breakfast. Within minutes he was asleep at the table. Mary, woke him and sent him to bed, telling him they would call him if they saw anything.

CHAPTER 28

LES MURPHY APPEARS IN COURT

The police had received a report of a missing National Parks and Wildlife ranger, and National Parks had set up a search party comprising six four-wheel-drive vehicles who would check the last area the ranger was known to be. The police helicopter Polair 3 searching for the escapees was told to keep a lookout for the ranger's vehicle. At the same time, Les Murphy appeared in court charged with escaping from lawful custody.

At his sentencing, the parents of the two young people from the Suzuki four-wheel-drive accident make a special appeal to the sentencing judge.

"Your Honour, may I address the court? My name is Michael Smart QC, and I have been engaged to speak for the families of the two injured teenagers hurt in that bush accident."

"Go ahead, Mr Smart."

"Your Honour, if it wasn't for Les Murphy giving up his freedom, these two young people would have surely died a slow and agonising death in the bush, because of the injuries sustained when their vehicle crashed and overturned. That is the opinion of the medical doctors who treated them. These doctors are all experts in their particular fields, and here are their written testimonies. Your Honour, they are present if you want to question them," as he points to the doctors.

Continuing he said, "Your Honour, the two young people had told no one where they were going that fateful day, and the likelihood of them being found and rescued was extremely remote to say the least. But Les Murphy, saw them and was so concerned about their welfare, he knew he had to do something to save them and get them to a hospital as fast as he could. He also knew his recapture was inevitable if he took these two hurt young people to hospital. When the police approached him, he did not resist and the arresting officer report states Les' only concern was for the injured couple. Yes, he escaped from custody, and that is a crime, but if he hadn't escaped these two families would be mourning either the death of a son or daughter, a brother or a sister. I ask you, Your Honour, to take into consideration these facts when handing down your sentence. Thank you for listening."

"Thank you, Mr Smart," said the sentencing judge. "However, Mr Murphy had escaped from lawful custody and I am bound by the laws of this state to enforce a custodial sentence. Mr Murphy, would you please stand? Mr Murphy, you have pleaded guilty to the charge of escaping from lawful custody, from Barnaby Maximum Security Prison on 25 November 1993, therefore I am sentencing you to three years' imprisonment for escaping."

Les's head dropped, and he thought, *Three years? That means 10 more years before I am free.* Les was devastated.

After a pause to let his words impact Les, the judge continued. "Mr Murphy, due to the exceptional circumstances in this case and the fact you gave up your unlawful freedom to save the lives of two strangers, my judgement is that the three years will be served concurrent with your existing term of imprisonment. But let me warn you, if you are ever brought before this court again, you will receive no more favourable considerations. Go and serve your time, and when you lawfully gain your freedom, cherish it and those who have stood by you, namely your wife, Gail, and young son, Morgan."

Gail was sitting behind Les in tears. She hadn't seen Les for a couple of months and blamed herself and her battle with cancer as the reason Les escaped. She had lost all her body hair through the chemotherapy and she was wearing a wig. Just before Les was led away, Gail leant forward and hugged him.

"Les, I love you with all my heart, and so does Morgan. We will wait for you to come home."

"And I love the both of you and I am so sorry for the extra hurt I have brought you."

The court officer moved in. "Come on, Mr Murphy, we must go now."

"Les, I will visit you on the next visiting day, so be strong. I love you."

Les nodded to her and then turned as they led him away.

CHAPTER 29

DET. LUKE CROSS
AND DNA

While waiting in the court's holding cells, Les received a visit from Det. Luke Cross.

"Hi, Les, how are you doing?"

"Not too bad right now. I am very lucky I will not serve any extra time. I intend to keep my nose out of any trouble, do the time and walk out of here a free man. I only hope that Gail will wait for me."

"She'll wait, I'm sure of that," said Det. Cross. "Les, remember when Gail was raped, we found a pubic hair? Well, I filed that away and just yesterday I sent it off to the National Institute of Forensic Science in Canberra who will extract DNA from it. Since the rape, there have been big steps forward in this new science of DNA testing. I think we might be one step closer to proving the Roe brothers raped Gail."

"That will be good, if they can. How good is this DNA stuff?"

"Well, some say it has been too long for an accurate reading of DNA from a hair, but others say that is from a head hair, whereas pubic hair is different. The guys in the lab want to try it, so let's see what they come up with."

"Will this prove it was the Roes that raped Gail?"

"I'm hoping it will tighten the noose a bit more on Allan Roe, but somehow I have to lawfully get a DNA sample from him so a comparison can be made."

Les's ride back to the prison arrived to transport him.

As he was being led away to the prison van Det. Cross said, "I will keep you informed."

Les nodded and said, "Thanks."

CHAPTER 30

LEAVING THE HOUSE

At three-thirty on Sunday afternoon in Hidden Valley, John and Mary packed a couple of backpacks with easy-to-prepare food, warm clothes, and rain jackets. They had decided to leave the relative safety of their house tonight. John asked Nick about the cavern he found when he camped out.

"Nick, can you lead us to that cavern?"

"Sure can, Dad," said Nick, excited to think he could help save his family.

Outside the weather, which had been showing signs of breaking up with patches of blue sky, now looked ominous with dark clouds to the north and the distant sound of rolling thunder. The river was slowly but surely falling.

Angelo and Jimmy armed Bob with a machete and moved him a tad closer to the driveway and with very little cover from the bush. Bob, had a high fever and wasn't really aware of what was going on, and slipping in and out of consciousness. Jimmy and

Angelo kept to the bush so they were not seen circling the house looking for any blind spots from where they could approach the house. They notice that on the other side of the driveway alongside the quarry where Bob had been shot, there was a definite blind spot where they couldn't see any of the house's windows.

"Shit," said Angelo. "We should have fucking noticed that before. If we can't see any of the bloody house's windows, they sure as hell can't see us."

Their plan was to turn the gas lanterns on after dark so those in the house could see it. Hopefully, they would think they were all still down at the driveway entrance. Around midnight, Jimmy would walk through the bush, just out of reach of the light from the house floodlights, to the opposite end of the house. Angelo would go along the top of the quarry and approach the house in the blind spot. When the generator started to splutter, and the lights flickered, both Jimmy and Angelo would get ready to make their dash to the house immediately after the lights went out. Last night the lights flickered for around two-and-a-half minutes before they went out, and it took another two minutes before the generator came back online. That window of approximately five minutes would give them the opportunity to get into the house from different directions. Tonight, sometime between midnight and one-thirty, their window of opportunity would come, and they planned to make the most of it.

In the sleepout, Tom and Shirley were getting desperate. Not only were they hungry and sore, but both had soiled themselves. They had no idea what was going on outside, and who was alive or dead among their friends. Shirley, was low at the point of breaking and held little hope of surviving this ordeal. Tom, tried to be encouraging and optimistic about their survival, and that somehow this nightmare would cease.

In Josh's house, Vince's fever had ceased, but the wound looked like it had an infection. Angelo was desperate to get Vince help, and to get out of the Valley.

"Jimmy," said Angelo, "this bloody place is more of a fucking prison than Barnaby ever was."

Jimmy gazed up at the thickening dark clouds and responded, "Yeah, this fucking weather is giving me the shits too."

At eleven-fifty, Angelo said, "It's time to get into position; keep to the bush, we don't want that prick seeing ya."

Jimmy gave Angelo a look that said, *you think I'm just a dumb Asian, you fucking Italian arsehole.*

The rain had been holding off, but the wind had increased, and a big thunderstorm was heading straight for Hidden Valley from the north. The accompanying lightning seemed to increase in its intensity. As he trudged through the bush just beyond the reach of the floodlights' beam, Jimmy came to a large rock outcrop that he and Angelo had climbed over when they looked for the blind spots to the house. Jimmy started climbing over the outcrop once more and while he was on top, a blinding flash of lightning hits somewhere north of him and silhouetted him on top of the rock. Immediately he dropped down flat on top of the rock. *Shit, did they see me?*

As he climbed down the other side, the floodlights flickered before they were in position. Jimmy was only halfway to where he was supposed to make his assault on the house. Angelo, had been talking to Bob whenever Bob was lucid. Taken by surprise, Angelo raced from the driveway to the blindside of the garage and hoped he would not be seen.

John, had prearranged with Mary that when the lights started flickering, she and the children would quickly put on their wet weather gear and move to the eastern end of the house. When the generator stopped, and the lights went out, they and Tuffy were to move as quickly as they could in the dark to the bush area to the east, the same spot that Jimmy was to make his assault from. Earlier, when John had filled the generator, he'd realised the lights would start flickering a good hour earlier than the night before.

When the lights started flickering, John and his family had to be ready to run for their lives.

As Jimmy was not in position, he launched his assault from where he was across the open front paddock and up the slope to the house. When the lights went out, both Jimmy and Angelo hesitated, not sure if it was just a longer period between the flickering of the lights, or more permanent. John, Mary, and the children moved out of the house and immediately ran for the cover of the bush. They were halfway to the bush when lightning lit up the whole valley. Jimmy stopped in his tracks as he saw the family attempting their getaway and moved back into the bush. Angelo started his run for the safety of the garage wall after the lights went out. Reaching the wall, he stopped to get his breath back and wondered how long it would be before the lights came back on.

As the family made the cover of the bush, John asked, "Is everyone all right?"

"Mitch ran into Melita and knocked her over and she has hurt her shoulder," said Mary.

"Daddy, I didn't cry much, but it is really sore," said Melita.

John gave her a kiss, "You are a very brave girl, sweetheart," he said to her. "I think we have about twenty minutes before they find the house empty, so we better move away from here."

Jimmy saw the family reach the supposed safety of the bush 150 metres away. *You bloody idiot, you have really screwed up now. You just made your biggest mistake and you are mine. We will now meet on my terms, and your rifle will be no good. It will be hand to hand combat and soon you will be as dead as Bull.* He moved as silently as he could towards that part of the bush where he saw the family disappear. He realised that he now had the upper hand with the added advantage of surprise.

CHAPTER 31

FACE TO FACE
WITH JIMMY

As the family and Jimmy moved closer to each other, they came to a small gully which was once the original river bed where the Peaceful River had flowed for many years, maybe hundreds of years ago, but the river had since moved some twenty-fire metres to the north.

Jimmy heard the family moving through the bush and a lightning flash helped him see them enter what usually was a dry riverbed, but now had ten centimetres of water flowing fast through it. He took up position up on the edge of the gully by a huge turpentine tree.

As the family walked along the riverbed, Nick grabbed his father's arm. "Dad."

John stopped and turned to Nick, "What is it, Nick?"

213

"Dad, we can't get to the cavern unless we cross the river, I forgot it's on the other side."

"That is no good for us," said Mary. "We can't cross that flooded river as it's too dangerous, especially at night, and this rain will only swell the river more."

"Okay," replied John. "But we will still head towards the back of the property, we will get to the farm track this side of the river and put as much distance as we can between us and our home."

Suddenly, Katie screamed as she looked past her father. Swinging around, John saw Jimmy less than ten metres away and heading straight for him.

"Aye, prick, we finally meet, now I will kill you," said Jimmy.

John tried to swing his rifle up, but Jimmy was far too quick for him and with an effortless movement he kicked the rifle right out of John's hands. Surprised and stunned at Jimmy's speed, and shocked that he had lost his rifle, John failed to respond to Jimmy's speed, and Jimmy placed a high kick to John's head, cracking his jaw bone and sending him cart-wheeling to the ground. With bells ringing in his ears, he was near to blacking out.

Jimmy didn't know that kicking John was the biggest mistake he had ever made. As he set himself to attack John again, fifty-two kilograms of snarling muscle hit him in the dark and steel jaws clamped down with 238psi upon his arm. Jimmy was knocked sideways and hit the ground, screaming.

Mary ran to John, and helped him get back to his feet, but his head was still ringing, and his legs buckled beneath him. Jimmy was still on the ground, screaming in pain as Tuffy's vice like jaws made his arm numb. Jimmy started kicking at Tuffy, and his third kick glanced off his arm and caught the top of Tuffy's nostrils, which caused him to let go of Jimmy's arm. Springing immediately to his feet, Jimmy's intention was to kick Tuffy again, but as quick as Jimmy was, Tuffy beat him and again had Jimmy's arm in his jaws. Standing this time, Jimmy tried everything—kicking and punching—to get rid of Tuffy until he heard and felt his arm break in Tuffy's jaws. Without warning, the wild dog flung himself onto Jimmy from up on the bank.

"It's the wild dog," yelled Nick.

Jimmy's right arm was now useless as Tuffy maintained his grip and the wild dog gripped his right calf. Face down in the water, Jimmy spluttered and screamed for help.

Mitch was the first to turn on a torch they took from the house.

"Quick, Mitch, bring that to me," said Mary at the same time Katie turned on the other torch. Mary shone the torch onto Jimmy and the dogs.

The fog started to clear from John's head. "Does anyone know where my rifle is?" he asked.

Nick stepped forward. "Here it is, Dad."

"Thanks, son, shine both those torches on that guy."

John told Tuffy to back off, and immediately he let go of Jimmy's arm, and the wild dog let go of Jimmy's leg and moved away. When John walked over to Jimmy, he started to get up, but the growl from Tuffy told him he had better stay where he was. The wild dog disappeared into the darkness once more. Jimmy complained that his right arm was broken. Disregarding his screams, John dragged him over to a black wattle tree.

"Mary, did you pack any rope?" asked John.

"No, sorry I didn't think of that," she said.

"That's alright, I didn't either."

"Dad, there is a small roll of nylon rope in the side pocket of my backpack. I always take it when I go camping," said Nick.

"How many other escapees are here? How many more do we have to deal with?" John asked Jimmy.

"Fuck you, you prick," replied Jimmy, as he started screaming.

John quickly gagged Jimmy, as he suspected his screaming would alert the other escapees. Jimmy struggled, so John called Tuffy, who stood in front of Jimmy and snarled, centimetres from his face. At this, all resistance drained out of Jimmy as he eyeballed

JOHN A. W. INMAN

Tuffy's huge canine teeth. As John pulled Jimmy's arms behind the tree to tie them, Jimmy threw his head back in agony and passed out from the pain of his broken arm. John tied Jimmy's legs, and then the family walked away from him.

CHAPTER 32

THE HOME IS BREACHED

Meanwhile, Angelo armed with the fish filleting knife, had made his way into the house through the laundry door. Inside it was pitch black, and he slowly moved out of the laundry listening for any movement, any sobbing, or heavy breathing but heard nothing apart from the beating of his own heart. As he neared the front room, a flash of lightning lit up the lounge room for a split second and Angelo saw that it was empty. *Fuck it's dark, I surely hope Jimmy's in here. Where in the shit are you people?* It was a full ten minutes before he had covered the whole house and realised the house was empty.

"Jimmy, Jimmy, where in the fuck are you?"

The silence was deafening. Finding his way out the front of the house, he wondered where everyone had gone. *This doesn't look good.*

As the family walked out of the dry riverbed they walked up a slight rise as yet another lightning flash lit up the valley and Katie let out a cry of "oh, no!"

"What is it, Katie?" asked Mary.

"One of those men was standing on our front veranda."

"It's a good thing we left when we did," replied John. "So, what does that mean? Two have been shot, we have that guy tied up back there, and at least one is in our house. That's four of the five. Maybe the fifth man didn't come to the Valley, and maybe there are only four. Sweetie, I'm going over to Josh's house to see if I can help them. Keep Tuffy, with you and go down to where that old corrugated tin pump shed is, it will keep you all dry."

"Dad, that wild dog is nearby," said Nick, "I think he is here to help."

"That's good, now lead your mum to that pump shed."

CHAPTER 33

JOHN FINDS JOSH AND SALLY

John made good time down along the river, a walk he had done plenty of times, and he noticed for the first time the river levels had dropped. *Keep going down*, he said to himself. Reaching Josh's footbridge, John saw the railing of the vehicle bridge just sticking out of the water and knew that if the current rain quickly passed, they might get out of the valley sometime tomorrow. He crossed the footbridge as swiftly as he could without making any sound and ducked behind some bushes to get a look into the house. In the lounge room, a table lamp was switched on, lighting the bottom half of the room. After a couple of minutes, he crept up to the front steps and silently ascended them, stepped to the side of the doorway and peered in. On the floor he saw the bodies of Josh and Sally lying in huge pools of dried black blood. The stench of death filled his nostrils, and he nearly threw up.

With a rifle ready, he moved into the room and froze when he heard a terrible noise. He pinpointed it as coming out of Sally and Josh's bedroom, so John entered the room and in the semi-light saw a moaning and very sick Vince. *So, here is the missing fifth man. Josh must have shot him; that explains the 303 shot we heard.*

Angelo was still at the Mann's house and concerned when Jimmy disappeared and the family had escaped. Something told him he must get back to Vince, so he ran towards the only light he could see—the light from the gas lantern with Bob at the driveway entrance. He stumbled and fell twice over Mary's stone garden edges. Reaching Bob, he grabbed the machete and ran back along the road towards the bridge and Josh's house.

John was leaving the house and as he came to the open front door he paused and glimpsed something coming straight at him—a machete Angelo was swinging from the left side of the door. Instinctively, John raised his arm holding his rifle, and the machete struck the barrel just high of the wooden stock. The force of impact slammed the barrel straight back into John's face, hitting him on the left of his nose and splitting open his left eyebrow. Blood rushed down his face as he slumped stunned to the floor. Angelo stepped squarely into the doorway and using two hands raised the machete behind his head as if he would split John's head open like a watermelon. As he swung, the machete bit deep into the door transom and timber weatherboards across the top of the doorway. Angelo tried to rip the machete out, but it was embedded too deep.

Letting go of the machete, Angelo pulled out the fish filleting knife as John staggered back away from the doorway. Angelo charged at John in a blind, murderous rage. As the filleting knife came straight at John, he swung his right arm at the last second, which still tightly gripped his rifle. It deflected Angelo's charge, who tripped over Sally's dead body. Regaining his balance, Angelo swung the filleting knife in a big arc, which John did his best to avoid. However, the razor-sharp blade cut deep across his chest just above his nipples as he fell backward to the floor with his rifle in both hands. Angelo stepped over Sally's body, ready to dive onto John and sink his knife into him when John pulled the trigger and the bullet hit Angelo halfway between his right nipple and his sternum. Angelo staggered around, feeling his chest. He looked at the blood on his hand and fell backward over Sally's body. Getting to his feet, John moved to Angelo and kicked the knife out of his hand. He knelt to check him. He was breathing, but John knew he was not going anywhere and would probably die from his wound.

CHAPTER 34

IT'S OVER

Leaving Josh's house, John made his way to the old tin pump shed and his family. He passed Bob on the way, who was petrified to see John. Here was this minister whose face was battered and bloodied, and his shirt. He still had that rifle in his hand and was coming straight at him.

John stopped in front of Bob and said, "It's all over, mate, two of you are dead and three are wounded but alive and will face a court sometime soon. We will get the police and ambulance as soon as possible." With that, he walked away towards his family.

Relocating his family who were shocked at the appearance of their husband and father, Mary grabbed him and asked, "What happened?"

"It's OK, it's finished. It's all over and we are no longer in any danger."

They hugged and kissed each other. When they stopped, Mary stepped back to let the children hug their dad and as Melita reached up she screamed.

"Daddy, your chest is bleeding."

"Quick where's the torch?" asked Mary.

As she looked at John's chest, Mary and the children were horrified to see the ugly slash across his chest.

"We will have to do something about that," said Mary.

"Not right now," replied John. "We should first see if we can find Tom and Shirley."

"What about Josh and Sally?" enquired Mary.

"Sweetie, they are both dead."

Hearing this terrible news was too much for Mary, and she collapsed to the ground, crying. "No, no, no! Not Josh and Sally, they would never hurt anyone. Why has this happened?"

The children were bewildered, frightened and crying. As they realised, it was finally over and that they were all safe, the relief was so overwhelming that John broke down and cried. Tuffy, observed his distressed family and tried to comfort them by nuzzling his face into their faces and licking them.

After a while, John pulled himself together and said, "Come on, we have to find Tom and Shirley."

Not wanting his family to see Josh and Sally's home, a house of death, John led his family back to their home. They all got in the family wagon along with a couple of old blankets and a large beach umbrella. As they drove out of their driveway, John stopped and he and Nick took the blankets and put them over Bob Walker, and set up the umbrella to give him more cover from the rain. Bob was running a high fever and in tremendous pain but still noticed what John and Nick are doing. When Nick held water to his lips, it was too much for Bob.

"Why are you helping me? Don't you want to kill me? We were going to kill your whole family, so why are you helping me? Don't you hate me?" Bob asked.

Nick replied, "We believe in God, his love, and forgiveness. He loves you as well. You should seek his forgiveness for what you have done."

Driving down to the Green's river crossing, both John and Mary agreed that the water hadn't fallen enough for their vehicle to cross, so they drove back to Josh's footbridge. As they crossed the bridge and saw Josh and Sally's house, Mary and Katie began to cry and John led them away towards Tom and Shirley's home.

CHAPTER 35

SEARCHING FOR
THE GREENS

On entering the Green's home, Mary was taken back by the smell.

"Poor Shirley," she said, "her home never ever looked like this.'

They searched the house and found no trace of the Greens, so John suggested Mary bath the kids, and look for any food they can eat, while he searched the sheds. He found nothing in the sheds, and the sleepout was padlocked. *Where in the valley are you, Tom?* he wondered.

Returning to the house, John said, "I've checked the two farm sheds and the garage, but I couldn't find any trace of them."

"Did you check the sleepout?" Mary asked.

"No, but there's no need to as it's padlocked, and you can't get in."

"Padlocked? That's strange; Shirley told me they leave it open in case any of their children, and grandchildren come down, and they are not around."

Mary went into the kitchen where Shirley had a key-rack on the wall next to the refrigerator and found the bunch of keys marked, padlocks. Taking the keys, they raced out to the sleepout and the second key they tried popped the lock. They entered the first two rooms and turned on the light switch, but the rooms were empty. The third room was locked from the outside with a sliding barrel bolt lock. Sliding the bolt, John opened the door and walked in to turn on the light. As he did, Shirley let out a scream of terror at the sudden appearance of a blood-covered man.

Mary pushed passed John and said, "It's OK, Shirley, it's only us, Mary and John."

"Shit, what happened to you, John?" asked Tom.

"It's a long story: I will fill you in later, but right now we need to release you two."

After they released their arms and legs. Tom and Shirley found that some of their muscles were not working too good after being tied up and stretched for over three days, from Friday evening until the early hours of Monday morning.

Shirley and Mary, embraced each other with tears running down their faces, while John rubbed Tom's shoulders to get the stiffness out of them.

"What about Josh and Sally?" Tom asked.

"They're both dead," replied John.

They all burst out crying.

After a while, a very angry Tom asked, "What about those bastards, where are they? Have they left the valley?"

"No, they are still here. I think two are dead, two are wounded, and the other is tied up around a tree," replied John in a matter-of-fact manner.

"How did that happen?" inquired Tom.

"As I said before, it's a long story," replied John. "Come, let's go to your house and we can all get cleaned up. The kids have already had a bath at your expense, Tom."

"Has anyone contacted the police?" asked Shirley.

"No, we can't," said Mary. "All the phones are out, and the river is still too high to get out."

"Well, who beat those bastards? Who killed and wounded them?" ask Tom.

"We'll talk about that later," said John.

"John did it," replied Mary. "He saved our family, and he has been wounded, so we better do something for his wounds."

On returning to the house, Mary checked the lounge room where she left the children watching TV. They were now all asleep, so she turned off the TV, switched off the lights, and pulled the door nearly shut.

Mary cleaned up John, the best she could. She was worried about the slash across his chest and his opened eyebrow. "Honey, this chest wound doesn't look good."

"It's a nasty cut," interjected Shirley.

"Yes, it is nasty, and you need some stitches," said Mary.

Mary, washed the wounds with Dettol and water, bandaged right around John's chest, and Shirley gave him some tablets for the pain. It was now two-twenty and Tom asked John to come with him while they checked the river level.

"It's still going down, so maybe later in the morning we will get out of the valley," remarked Tom.

"John, will you come with me to Josh's house? I need to see it."

"It's not good, in fact it is pretty horrendous, but if you want to go, I will go with you."

"Yes, I want you to come. Josh and I had become pretty close, as had Sally and Shirley with their wool spinning and knitting."

On entering the house, Tom ducked around the machete still stuck in the door transom and stopped dead in his tracks when the smell from the carnage inside hits his nostrils. He saw Josh and

Sally, lying there and was almost sick, so he backed out onto the veranda.

"It's worse than horrendous," said Tom, as he took in a couple of deep breaths, steadied himself and re-entered the house. He knelt down next to Josh and said goodbye to his friend. Tom looked at Angelo who had stopped breathing. In the bedroom, Vince was still moaning. "Shit, John, did you do all this damage to these guys?"

"No, I think Josh shot the one in the bed. But that one," he said, pointing to Angelo, "I shot him after he slashed me with his knife."

Tom sensed that John didn't want to talk about the events and said, "I guess the police won't want everyone walking over the crime scene and there is nothing we can do here. We better go back to the girls."

Tom and Shirley, didn't want to spend the night alone, so Mary and John agreed to stay the rest of the night, especially as the children were all asleep. The relief of not being in any danger enabled everyone but John to sleep. He tossed and turned as he retraced the events of the last three days. The pain from his injuries and the fact he had killed two fellow humans made it impossible for him to sleep.

CHAPTER 36

THE AUTHORITIES COME TO HIDDEN VALLEY

Mitch woke at ten-twenty and looked around for breakfast. Within a short time, the whole family, along with Tom and Shirley, were sitting around having breakfast.

After eating, Tom, John, and Nick walked down to the river. To their jubilation, the river was now passable. Tom, and Nick, went to get help. They drove seven kilometres towards Riverbend before they came to the Hill's Farm. When they knocked, Jean Hill answered the door.

"Hullo, how can I help you?" she asked.

"Good morning," replied Tom. "I'm Tom Green, from Hidden Valley and I need to phone the police and tell them those prison escapees are in Hidden Valley."

"By all means come in, the phone is over there," said Jean as she pointed to the oak sideboard.

In a little over half an hour, the first police vehicle entered Hidden Valley, within twenty minutes another four police vehicles, and three ambulances had arrived. Detective Dave Pickett, the senior officer, made the crime scenes secure and let the ambulance officers attend to any injured. But waited until Inspector Mark Kidd, the head of the Escapee Task Force arrived, and to assist him and the task force anyway he can.

John, Nick, and Tuffy took Det. Pickett and the ambulance officers to Josh's house. John, told Nick, to stay at the front gate and led the others up the stairs to the doorway as a large snake slithered off the lounge, off the veranda, disappearing under the house. Dodging around the machete, they entered the house of death.

"There may be one guy alive in that bedroom over there," said John, as he pointed to Josh and Sally's bedroom. "He was shot and wasn't too good yesterday; the other three here in the house are all dead."

"Thanks," replied Det. Pickett, and turning to the ambulance officers he said, "You guys see if the fellow is still alive but try not to disturb anything if you can."

The two ambos went into Vince, who was now in a critical condition. The other four ambos, Dec. Pickett, and three uniformed police officers followed John to Bob, who was also in a serious condition. As they moved in Jimmy's direction, the sound of a helicopter caught their attention and they saw a Pol-Air helicopter descending into the Valley.

"It must be Inspector Mark Kidd, the Escapee Task Force leader," said Det. Pickett, who sent a uniformed officer back to get Inspector Kidd as they moved to where Jimmy was tied to a tree.

Releasing Jimmy, the ambulance officers confirmed Jimmy had a serious broken arm. There were some bite marks on one of his legs from the wild dog. The ambulance officers put Jimmy onto their stretcher while a uniformed officer handcuffed his good arm to the stretcher. As this happened, Inspector Kidd, arrived and introduced himself to everyone except Jimmy.

To John he said, "The uniformed officer said you are responsible for the capture of these men."

Before John could reply, Jimmy looked at him and said, "Aye, you fucking prick, you and your whole family are dead, I promise you."

"Get him out of here," said Inspector Kidd.

Pulling John aside, Inspector Kidd said to John, "Don't listen to that crap, he is just pissed off for being caught." However, the inspector knew John and his family would be in grave danger thanks to Jimmy's underworld connections, but he did not want to spook John at this stage.

As they walked out of the dry riverbed, Tuffy, barked and looked at the bushes fifteen metres away. Through the bushes they saw the wild dog looking at them. Nick, ran towards him with Tuffy.

John yelled out, "Nick, stop."

But Nick, did not want to hear his father, and ran up to the bush as the wild dog backed away. Nick, stopped and stretched out his hand towards the dog who slowly moved forward and smelled Nick's hand, as Tuffy started smelling him. Nick, pushed through the bushes and started patting the dog, whose tail was madly wagging with excitement. The dog stood on his hind legs and reached up to lick Nick's face. Nick, hugged the dog and called out to his dad.

"Can we keep him? Please, Dad."

"Sure, son," replied John, as he looked at Inspector Kidd and lifted his hands in a resigned gesture and said, "it's a long story."

The two dogs and Nick went racing across the front paddock, leaping and jumping and having fun. John, smiled as he looked upon the three of them and thought, *How resilient children are. Last night they might have died, but now half a day later life is full of fun and laughter.*

After looking intently at the tan dog, Inspector Kidd asked John, "What's with this dog?"

"He's been running wild in the national park, why do you ask?"

"My wife and I breed working dogs and sometimes I get to go to shows and working dog trials. I think that dog is a Pyrenees sheep dog."

"A what?"

"A Pyrenees sheep dog. In their homeland they virtually live with the flock of sheep, protecting them from wild dogs and wolves."

"Really," said John, "that makes sense of some things, but that's another story."

The rest of the day passed with Tom, and Shirley, telling their story. A doctor stitched John's eyebrow and cleaned and put in 18 stitches across John's chest, putting him on a course of anti-biotics, starting with an injection into his vein.

Inspector Kidd listened to the Mann family's story. John, broke down in tears as he realised how close he and his family came to death.

"This must have been a terrible and terrifying ordeal for all of you, and I am so sorry about the death of your friends, Josh and Sally Latham. There are counsellors available for you to talk to. They are trained personnel who will help you get back to normal and maybe be able to stop the nightmares from coming or from being destructive. They also help police officers who suffer traumatic experiences. They have helped me over the years, I urge you to let them help you," said an empathetic Inspector Kidd.

"I have to inform you all that there will be a coronial inquiry into the deaths of Josh and Sally Latham, as well as the deaths of the escapees James Maloney aka Bull and Angelo Bettini. You will all be required to give statements and testify," said Inspector Kidd.

By this time, reporters from newspapers, magazines, and different TV stations arrived looking for a story. Inspector Kidd met them to give a brief report.

At two-forty, two cars drive into Hidden Valley bringing the Cooper family home from a wedding in Melbourne. They were shocked to find their home was part of a crime scene. Their friends Josh and Sally dead, and they listen as Tom, Shirley, Mary and the children tell the devastating story of the last week, and John's heroic actions that brought the events to an end.

Later that Tuesday, word filtered through that the missing National Parks and Wildlife Ranger's vehicle had been found, but there was no sign of Ranger Jim Clarke. A police forensic team was called in to inspect the vehicle, and it was not long before they established the escapees had used the vehicle.

Inspector Kidd, had already noted that Bob was wearing a National Parks and Wildlife Rangers jacket, and he made a note to talk to him as soon as the doctors gave the go ahead. For the next couple of days, Inspector Kidd and his team continued their investigation along with the forensic team, trying to fit together the timeline of the events in the valley.

On Thursday morning, Inspector Kidd, and Detective Tim Newton, questioned Bob in the hospital at Barnaby Maximum Security Prison about the ranger's jacket he had been wearing. Bob spilled the beans immediately, telling them about what Vince had done.

"That Italian fat prick killed the ranger with a knife, and we left him up in the fucking bush. I got no idea whereas it all looks the same to me."

"That ranger," said an angry Inspector Kidd, "was Pete McDonald. He was a dedicated family man with a wife and three kids under twelve, and you bastards took him away from them."

It would be another seven weeks before the ranger's body was found and returned to his grieving family for burial.

CHAPTER 37

THE NIGHTMARE CONTINUES

On Thursday afternoon, Inspector Kidd, asked John to walk him once more over the route the family took when they left the house. When they were away from the others, Inspector Kidd said, "John, I need to talk to you about the threats Jimmy Tan made against you and your family."

"That was just talk," replied John, "wasn't it?"

"Those threats are real and the lives of you and your family are in real danger. If you stay here in the valley, you will be killed. There is no way that we can protect you if you stay here."

"But won't it all die down in a couple of months?" asked a frustrated John.

"Look, John, Jimmy Tan's people and the Bettini Twins people, as well as Bull's biker friends, will come after you. Maybe not this month, or next month, but you will have a price on your head, and they will kill you if you stay here. That is the way these guys operate; they are into revenge in a big way."

John, was shocked to his core. "But we have done nothing wrong, we only defended ourselves."

"That doesn't matter to these people; they will want their revenge as that's their culture. And if you stay here in the valley, you will be killed at some point. I know it sounds unfair, and it is, but that is the way it is. And with all those media people out here doing stories on you, this place won't be safe. Every man and his dog will know where this place is and what happened here."

"So, what are we to do? Just pack our bags and go as if we are going on holidays?" asked a visibly upset John.

"No way, these guys will easily track you down if you just move. No, you must disappear. I am sure you're heard the term 'Federal Witness Protection Program?' You would have seen it, or something like it in some movie, or read about in some novel, surely? John and Mary Manns and their children will have to disappear and then resurface with a new identity in a different location."

"What am I going to tell my family after all they've been through? 'Aye, guys the nightmare isn't over, our lives are still in danger, and we now have to disappear, and then resurface as another family, somewhere else in the world. And we have to cut off all contact with family and friends.' Is that what I have to say?"

"Yes, that is exactly what you have to tell them," said Inspector Kidd. "And we will have people from the Federal Government, and the Australian Federal Police to work you through this. For now, though, for the next week it will be safe here in the valley as there will be a strong police presence, but after that we will have to move you to what we call a safe house."

Two days later, a representative of the Federal Government and the Chief Inspector of the AFP, Peter Brewer, visited the Manns. After listening to the family, they talked about their options.

"Because we believe that your lives are still in danger, we are going to move you out of the valley to a Safe House, but the dogs can't come," said the Chief Inspector Brewer.

The family was angry as the grief cycle took its course. After the initial shock and numbness of the events, they felt angry and stressed.

"If we can't have the dogs with us, then we are not leaving the valley," said Mary, crying.

"That's right, we aren't going no-where without our dogs," interjected Nick as tears started to swell in his eyes. "They just can't take them from us, can they, Dad?"

Before John could answer Chief Inspector Brewer said, "We are not taking them off you for good, it will be only for about three months unless the inquiries and trial go longer."

"Why?" asked Mary. "Why do you have to separate us?"

"When we move you, we will need to cover your trail and someone will notice a family travelling with two large dogs and may speak to the wrong people. Word will get back to those who want to do you harm."

"When will we move?" asked John.

"Within days, three at the most," said Chief Inspector Brewer. "You will be only able to take one small suitcase each, and—"

"What!" interjected Mary, "one small suitcase? That is impossible. What about all our furniture, the children's toys, all our photos? That is impossible. It can't be done."

"Mary," said Chief Inspector Brewer, "it is necessary as moving all your furniture and everything else would require a large truck which would be easily tracked. The government will pay for your relocation, and everything you need. I suggest you decide as a family what to take: photos and documents should be a priority."

Over the next couple of days, John, spoke to Nick about the white and tan dog, that Nick had named Hero.

"Nick, we need to talk about Hero."

"What do you mean, we have to talk about him?"

"I think his place is here in the valley, running and looking after Tom and Shirley's sheep. That is what he has been doing all along, protecting the sheep."

"Yeah, but I love him and want him with me."

"I know that Nick, I know you love him, but think about it. He really belongs here. I know it is a very hard decision."

"Do I have to make my choice now?"

"No, think about it, talk to the others, but let me know tomorrow afternoon."

John, gave Nick a big hug. "I love you, Nick."

"And I love you too."

Nick, went for a walk with Hero. An hour later they arrived at the Green's home.

"Hi, Tom, hi, Shirley," said Nick, "I was wondering if Hero and I could go for a walk amongst your sheep."

"Sure, Nick," said Tom, as John had already spoken to the Greens about Hero, but said it was Nick's decision alone. "You know where they are. While you are there, would you leave the gate open to the big dam paddock? I will run them in there later."

"Sure, will do, and thanks," replied Nick.

Arriving at the paddock, Nick climbed over the fence while Hero easily jumped it. As Nick, walked to the gate leading to the big dam paddock, Hero headed off towards the sheep. Reaching the gate, Nick opened it, and then climbed and sat on it watching Hero. Hero moved in and out of the sheep; some were still skittish after two wild dog attacks, but after a while they all settled down and Hero, laid down among them watching. An hour later Nick climbed down off the gate, walked over to Hero to give him a big hug, and said goodbye. Then he stood and walked away as the tears flowed freely down his cheeks.

Reaching the Green's home, he knocked, and Shirley invited him in. She looks around and said, "Where is Hero?"

"He is still with the sheep. I think he wants to stay there."

"Oh," said Shirley. "What does that mean?"

"I was wondering if you would like him to protect your sheep? He will do a great job. That is what he has been doing all along. He has been trying to protect them from the wild dogs. He loves the sheep and I know that he will be happy here, that's if you let him?"

"How do you feel about this, Nick?"

"It is really hard, and it hurts inside really bad." His tears flowed again. "But he really wants to stay here, and it's up to you and Tom. He is a very good dog, he won't be any trouble."

Shirley put her arm around Nick as she said, "Nick, Tom and I, would love to have Hero, and we will love him and look after him as well as he looks after our sheep.

And please tell your mum and dad that the Rangers from the National Parks are right now laying baits for the wild dogs, with that, and Hero protecting our sheep, we think the wild dogs' problem has gone for good.

CHAPTER 38

THE MANNS ARE RELOCATED

Eight weeks after being moved from Hidden Valley, and one week before the coronial inquiry, the Mann's home and out-buildings were flattened to the ground by a massive blast. The authorities know this was a warning to all, mainly John Mann before he gave evidence. Police intelligence learned that a $500,000 price had been put on the lives of the Manns family.

In May 1994, a trial found Vince Bettini guilty of the murder of the National Parks and Wildlife officer, and they were all convicted as being involved in the murders of Josh and Sally Latham. Vince was sentenced to an additional twenty-five years' imprisonment, Bob and Jimmy were given an extra fifteen years with the time to start after they had served out their original sentences. Bob, on release would be deported back to England to face court again for a kidnap and murder back in London, August 1977. Jimmy, would be deported back to China. The three are moved to the Maximum-Security Prison in Goulburn, NSW.

The Manns were relocated to New Zealand with new identities, and Tuffy joined them in July 1994.

On Saturday night, August 6, 1995, masked men invaded the homes of the Coopers and Greens, demanding to know the whereabouts of the Mann family. But no-one knew where they had been relocated. Desperate to learn their location, the invaders became frustrated, and the violence escalated. After two hours, the ordeal ended, and the masked men left. The police were once more called to Hidden Valley. The Coopers, and Tom and Shirley were taken to hospital. At the hospital, the Cooper's second youngest child David collapsed. Tests revealed David had sustained serious and possibly permanent brain damage.

This incident was broadcast on television stations throughout Australia and New Zealand. In their new home on two hectares in Mamaku, thirty-seven kilometres outside of Rotorua and four kilometres off the main Rotorua to Hamilton Highway, the Manns watched the report on TV in disbelief.

John and Mary, were so upset over what had happened in Hidden Valley, especially the brain damage sustained by young David Cooper. John blamed himself for fleeing Hidden Valley without considering the ongoing safety and welfare of the other residents.

Monday morning at eleven-thirty New Zealand time, nine-thirty Australian Eastern Standard Time, John rang the AFP Headquarters in the ACT on Inspector Brewer's direct and secure line.

"Peter, it's John Warner, we just watched a very disturbing news item on the tv about the attack on the Greens and Coopers, we feel it is all our fault. Is there any chance that we can talk to them?"

"I am very sorry, John, but that cannot happen, I am responsible for yours and your family's safety. I have been in contact with them and I plan to visit them. John, all those who live in Hidden Valley, not one of them blames you for what happened there. The Greens have always said that you saved them. I have also spoken to the neurosurgeon who operated on David Cooper, he said that he is nearly 100 percent certain that David will make a full recovery within a year. So, stop blaming yourself."

"Thanks Peter, give them our love and assure them of our prayers. We miss all of them," replied John.

The attack on the Greens and Coopers homes was a planned move by the Bettini Gang in their drive to discover the whereabouts of the Mann family. Lucy Nicoletti, an accounts assistance with the AFP in Canberra, through another trusted worker within the AFP Headquarters in Canberra, was introduced to Leo Mazzarol, a family member. Leo told Lucy, that he can fix her up with a car with an unbeatable price. If she could get the record of all the incoming and outgoing calls for a certain number within the AFP, it would only be for one-month. If she could manage that, then the loan on her car would be completely paid out. Lucy, being young and somewhat naïve, considered the request easy and could not see it affecting anyone.

On the same Monday, Lucy takes a personal call from Leo Mazzarol, "Hi Lucy, to have your car paid off within months I need the phone records of the number I gave you, for the first half of this month. You still have the number, don't you," asked Leo.

"Yes," replied Lucy, "and I will fax it to you as soon as I have it, I am sure your friend will be surprised when you contact him after such a long time."

"If I find what I want, you will have paid the loan back, just go back to work and act as if nothing has happened."

August 17, Lucy faxed the documents to Leo, who immediately handed them over to the Bettini Crime Family. The details of this new lead was passed to Jimmy Tan's men, and the Apache OMG. Now the three gangs started using their contacts to track down a person who rang the AFP. After a week the three Gangs searching isolate six calls to Inspector Brewer's private line from outside of Australia around the end of August. Three from South East Asia who are checked out by Jimmy Tan's Gangs contacts in China. All three prove to be of no interest to them.

The other three are from New Zealand which both the Apaches and Bettini Gangs investigate through their contacts in New Zealand. Locating the premises of the phones involved, two are Australian Government offices. The third in a small country town is checked on Saturday September 9, by a parcel delivery van pulling up at a front gate and is immediately confronted by a German Shepherd. The lady of the house response to the dog's barking, investigates and talks to the delivery guy. She quickly sees that there is no house number on the parcel, but the right street, and tells the driver she doesn't recognises the name on the parcel. But maybe my kids may know them. She calls out to her children who quickly come to the gate, one daughter says that she knows the family and directs the driver to the only two-story house further along the street.

The message back to Robert (King) Maxwell, identification correct, and address is given, the Manns have been found.

CHAPTER 39

DET. CROSS GETS
HIS MAN

In September 1994, Detective Cross and Det. Ambrose contacted Allan Roe and asked him to come into the Tamworth Police Station to help tie up some loose ends regarding his brother John's death at Billy's Hole.

At the interview, Det. Cross told Allan they were reviewing the events of Monday evening, 17 September 1988, at Billy's Hole where Les Murphy killed John Roe.

"He's back in prison, isn't he?" asked Allan.

"Who are you talking about?" asked Det. Cross.

"That bastard who killed John, he escaped, remember?"

"Les Murphy, yes he is still in prison for killing John."

"Good, that's where the prick belongs."

"Allan," said Det. Cross, "I would like you to read a couple of articles about how DNA has helped convict felons in America, England, in the ACT, and in Victoria."

"Do you have the time to help us?" asked Det. Ambrose.

"Sure, anything to help the police."

"Allan, we will leave you to read these articles. And we will come back in approximately fifteen minutes. Would you like a coffee and a couple of biscuits while you read?" said Det. Ambrose.

"Sure, I will have anything that's free—black and two sugars."

"We really appreciate you helping us out here, Allan."

> Police in the United Kingdom first used DNA profiling in 1985. In 1987, profiling helped to clear a young teenager who was the prime suspect in a double rape murder case. Police collected blood samples from 5000 men, and from that they identified Colin Pitchford as the rapist-murderer. He was convicted on that evidence and sent to Prison.

> In Canberra, Desmond Applebee was the first person in Australia convicted using DNA testing, which had been extracted from blood and semen on a rape victim's clothes and was a perfect match to Applebee's DNA. In Victoria, police confronted George Kaufman with DNA evidence, and he confessed to the rape of sixteen women over a four-year period in the south-eastern suburbs of Melbourne.

The detectives observed Allan through the two-way mirror as he read the articles very carefully. After twenty minutes, they returned to the interview room.

"Allan," said Det. Ambrose, "we will need to record this interview as it is part of a police investigation, is that alright with you?"

"Sure, I will do anything I can to help."

"Allan, I must tell you your rights. You do not have to answer any question or questions. You have the right to remain silent. Do you understand your right to silence?"

"Yes, I got nothing to hide. As I said, I'm here to help you."

"Allan, when Gail Pritchard was raped the forensic team found a pubic hair that didn't belong to Les Murphy, it belonged to one of the rapists. I filed it away, knowing one day the time would come when DNA testing was used as evidence to obtain a conviction in courts in NSW, and the other states and territories within Australia. I knew that I would be able to find and convict the rapists with that evidence. That day has come. We now have the DNA of one of the rapist who raped Gail Pritchard, and we will shortly have them convicted and sent to prison."

As Det. Cross finished talking, he placed in front of Allan the report from the National Institute of Forensic Science that on the front page read, 'DNA Testing of pubic hair in Gail Pritchard rape case. DNA extracted for evidence.'

Det. Cross, gamble that Allan wouldn't want to read the report. Allan sat there staring at the report, but made no move to touch it, or read it.

"We know who the rapist is, and now his DNA will get him convicted and sent to prison. What do you think of that?"

"I don't know, I really don't know," replied a very shaken Allan Roe.

"Well, why do you think we asked you to come here today?"

"I don't know, I really don't know," replied Allan and as an afterthought he said, "I'm here to help you in an investigation, aren't I?"

"Well, Allan, what did you think of those articles we gave you to read?"

"Not much."

"We asked you here for a specific reason," said Det. Ambrose.

"What specific reason is that?" asked Allan.

"Well, you think about it, Allan. You read those articles about men who thought they beat the system, but their DNA nailed them. So why do you think you are here?"

"I don't know."

"Come on, Allan, you know darn well why we asked you to come, don't you?"

"I guess you want to arrest me?"

"Why would we do that, Allan? Why do you think we want to arrest you? What have you done?"

"Because we raped Gail Pritchard."

"Is that so?" said Det. Cross. "Who is the we? Was it you and your brother John who raped Gail Pritchard?"

"Yes, we did it; I didn't want to, but John made me." Replied a very nervous Allan.

Allan Roe confessed to raping eight women; seven with his brother John and one a year after John's death. Det. Cross, then asked about the events at Billy's Hole on that fateful Monday evening.

"Allan, the night John was killed, did you attack and rape someone north of Glen Innes earlier in the evening?"

"Yes, she was an attractive dark-haired girl, and we told her that if she said anything we would have her killed. I guess she was so frightened that she didn't report us."

"Allan Roe, I am arresting you for the rape of Gail Pritchard in 1986."

With Allan Roe's confession of being a serial rapist and his recanting of his version of events at Billy's Hole, Det. Cross had enough evidence to get Les Murphy's case re-examined. Allan, had told them how Les had identified himself that night, and how John had bragged about raping Gail Pritchard, and how he would first kill Les, and then rape and murder Gail. As a result, Les's murder conviction was overturned and redetermined as self-defence.

Les, was released from prison early in October 1994 and went home to Gail, the love of his life, and to start a new relationship with his son, Morgan. Gail was now in remission from her breast cancer.

CHAPTER 40

THE MANN FAMILY ARE FOUND

Twelve months later, in the late evening hours of Saturday October 28, 1995, on New Zealand's North Island just outside of Rotorua, the residents of Mamaku were sleeping peacefully when three masked men burst into the farmhouse in the small timber mill town. They were armed with sawn-off shotguns and in less than forty-seconds had slaughtered everyone inside the house.

The murders was big news, and it wasn't long before it was reported all over New Zealand, and the East Coast of Australia.

Chief Inspector Peter Brewer received a call at his home at one-thirty the next morning. "Hello, Inspector Brewer, my name is Detective Sam Emery of Rotorua Police. I am sorry to be ringing you at this time."

"Good morning to you, detective, I guess this is urgent, what can I do for you?"

Det. Emery, was wary at first, not wanting to give out too much information. He asked Chief Inspector Brewer, "What is your relationship with the Warner family from Mamaku, formerly known as the Mann family?"

"Why are you asking? Has something happened?"

"Please, inspector, just answer the question."

Inspector Brewer quickly summarised the Mann's story. "I set up their new IDs and got them out of Australia."

"Inspector Brewer, I have some terrible news for you. The family was murdered last night."

"What! The entire family?" asked a very shaken Chief Inspector Brewer, as he sank down into his chair.

"No, not all. Young Nick, wasn't at home as apparently he and his dog went to visit a young lady down South Road, a fair walk from his home. He was lucky he wasn't at home. He was the one who phoned us after coming home and finding his family dead. He told me about you and who was after them."

"Does anyone else know that Nick is still alive?" Inspector Brewer asked.

"No, only myself and my partner."

"Well, keep it that way. Do us a big favour and do not tell anyone else about Nick. Report that all six were killed. I will have it fixed with your people in the Government."

The AFP arranged with the New Zealand authorities for six coffins to be flown back to Sydney for burial. Inspector Brewer also arranged for an AFP Officer and a Psychologist to help 16-year-old Nick through the effects of the trauma he has been through, then to bring him back to Australia in one month's time. Feeling responsible for Nick's safety, Inspector Brewer arranged for him to stay with his sister Karen, a practicing clinical psychologist ministering to soldiers suffering from mental issue as a result of combat. Brewer's brother-in-law Colonel Michael Lockwood of the Australian Army was based in Perth. The AFP approved this move as being in the best interests of young Nick.

The day after the funeral in Sydney, Inspector Brewer, was told an AFP accounts assistant named Lucy Nicoletti was found drowned in her home pool. She was trapped by her hair in the pool filter system in the bottom of the pool. Authorities ruled it a tragic accident, saying she fell into the pool after a heavy bout of drinking. There were no suspicious circumstances.

The NSW police after the investigation into the Hidden Valley episode informed Inspector Brewer of Josh and Sally Latham last will dated October 1, 1993. And as it would impact on the Mann's family they thought he should know. None of the residents of Hidden Valley knew anything about this will which said; ----- so if they passed away their farm was to be sold to a family who would fit into and enrich the valley residents' lives. The money from the sale would be set aside for any major projects within the Valley that the residents all agreed on.

Inspector Peter Brewer, spoke to the Greens and Coopers about the Mann's property, which had been destroyed in an explosion. He said he had been in touch with the relatives of both Mary and John, about what to do with the property. He did not lie, as he had spoken to Nick about Hidden Valley. Nick, said that he would like the other residents to use the land and just pay the council rates each year. He planned to return to Hidden Valley after he had fulfilled his promise to his dead family. Brewer thought that this would be a financial benefit to Nick in later years.

Nick and Tuffy, were united at the home of Colonel Michael Lockwood at the Australian Army Base in Perth. Where Karen would be helping with his grief as she watched for any signs in Nick's behaviour that pointed to a possible continuing trauma, but instead she saw Nick, was a well-balanced young man who was grieving the loss of his family in a healthy manner.

While on the base, Nick took a great interest in the German Shepherds the army trained, and always took Tuffy with him. One day, one of the trainers who had noticed Nick's interest, approached him saying, "That is a mighty fine dog you have there, and he looks completely under control even while off lead. Did you train him?"

"Yes, and no, it was my dad mainly," said Nick proudly. "I think he is at least as good as your best dog."

"That is a great wrap. Can he track a person, detect a bomb and stop an attack?" asked the trainer in a friendly manner.

"I don't know about tracking a person, or detecting a bomb, but I know for sure he would defend me with his life," replied Nick.

"So, he has been trained as a protection dog?" asked the trainer.

"No, but he has done it in the past," said Nick.

"Sorry, young fellow, my name is Simon, Captain Simon Carter. May I ask what your name is?" inquired Simon.

"Sure, it is Nick, and this is Tuffy," answered Nick.

"He is truly a magnificent dog. Can I pat him?" asked Captain Carter.

"Sure," answered Nick.

Simon patted Tuffy. He loved what he saw. "You are sure he will defend you?"

"Absolutely certain; would you like to test him out?" asked Nick.

"Yes, I would very much like to test him out, but you will have to put him back on the lead," said Captain Carter.

"That is OK," said Nick.

Capt. Carter, told Nick to wait there for five minutes when he would return. True to his word, he returned and took Nick and Tuffy to the other side of the kennels to a large paddock with lots of bushes. A track wound its way around and through the bushes. "Nick," said Capt. Carter, "there are other trainers hiding amongst the bushes. I want you to walk around the track with Tuffy on lead. Wait till I signal you from on top of that tower in the middle of the paddock, then walk slowly around the track. If another trainer tells you to do something, it will be what I am telling him in his ear-piece, OK?"

Nick, nodded and as Simon moved off to the tower, Nick said to Tuffy, "Aye, Tuffy, I have just bragged about how good you are, so let's show them."

Tuffy and Nick began their slow walk. They were 30 meters into the bush when a heavily padded trainer came rushing at them. Immediately, Tuffy moved to intercept this intruder, grabbed the padded arm and pulled the trainer to the ground.

"Call off your dog," yelled the trainer.

"OK, Tuffy let him go," Nick said.

Tuffy, instantly released his grip on the man's arm, but he never took his eye off the trainer. The same thing happened with the other three trainers; not one got close enough to touch Nick.

Nick and Tuffy, moved back to where Captain Carter had left them. The captain approached them with a smile on his face. "That was fantastic," he said.

Suddenly, Tuffy moved past Nick, and made the same blood curdling growl Nick first heard in the cavern. Turning to where Tuffy was looking, Nick saw another army soldier walking straight towards them. The growling got louder as the soldier came closer. Tuffy, positioned himself between Nick and this soldier. Capt. Carter watched all this happening and waved to the soldier, who promptly changed direction and walked away. Tuffy's hackles settled down, but he never took his eyes off the other soldier until he walked around the corner of a building.

"Wow," said Simon, "you were telling the truth. That soldier was the second last trainer who attacked you on the track. We didn't know if Tuffy was only interested in the padded arm, but he knew that guy even though he wasn't padded up. You are sure he wasn't trained as a protection dog?"

Nick face beamed with the biggest smile and shook his head.

"Nick, I have an offer to put to you, would you like to hear it?" asked Captain Carter.

"An offer? What do you mean? Yes, tell me about it, please," said Nick.

"Can we use Tuffy in our breeding program for army dogs? I don't think you went far enough in your praise of Tuffy. I have been involved with Shepherds for seventeen years and I have only seen two other dogs as good as Tuffy."

"That would be sensational, but what about me?" asked Nick.

Unknown to Nick, Captain Carter had already inquired about Nick and Tuffy, and knew they were living with Colonel Lockwood and his family. He had already spoken with Karen Lockwood but didn't know she was helping him. She had told the Captain the idea was brilliant and that he should put it to Nick.

Nick was permitted to work around the kennels, helping to socialise puppies, and learn how to train dogs. This he continued to do until he entered the army after finishing his HSC.

In 2005, Nick left the army to join the AFP and fulfil the promise he made to his dead family to bring all those involved in their murders to justice.

That story will be told in the second novel in 2020/2021.

THE END

AUTHOR'S NOTE

The genesis of this fictional story was the author's imagination and personal experiences. The names of friends' past, and present were constantly introduced, but their portrayed characters are fabrications. Little research went into the writing of this fictional novel. Procedures of law enforcement agencies and courts are solely my creation to fit my story rather than being an accurate account of legal processes.

Printed in the United States
By Bookmasters